Brett Easton Ellis is the author of *Less Than Zero, Rules of Attraction* and *American Psycho*, all available in Picador. He was born in 1964 and raised in Los Angeles. He is a graduate of Bennington College and lives in New York City.

Bret Easton Ellis

The Rules of Attraction

PICADOR

published by Pan Books

First published in USA 1987 by Simon & Schuster, Inc.
This Picador edition published 1988 by Pan Books Ltd,
Cavaye Place, London SW10 9PG

9 8 7 6

© Bret Easton Ellis 1987

ISBN 0 330 30186 1

Printed and bound in Great Britain by
Richard Clay Ltd, Bungay, Suffolk

For

Phil

Holmes

The facts even when beaded on a chain, still did not have real order. Events did not flow. The facts were separate and haphazard and random even as they happened, episodic, broken, no smooth transitions, no sense of events unfolding from prior events—

Tim O'Brien
Going After Cacciato

FALL
1985

and it's a story that might bore you but you don't have to listen, she told me, because she always knew it was going to be like that, and it was, she thinks, her first year, or, actually weekend, really a Friday, in September, at Camden, and this was three or four years ago, and she got so drunk that she ended up in bed, lost her virginity (late, she was eighteen) in Lorna Slavin's room, because she was a Freshman and had a roommate and Lorna was, she remembers, a Senior or a Junior and usually sometimes at her boyfriend's place off-campus, to who she thought was a Sophomore Ceramics major but who was actually either some guy from N.Y.U., a film student, and up in New Hampshire just for The Dressed To Get Screwed party, or a townie. She actually had her eye on someone else that night: Daniel Miller, a Senior, a Drama major, only a little gay, with blond hair, a great body and these amazing gray eyes, but he was seeing this beautiful French girl from Ohio, and he eventually got mono and went to Europe and never finished his Senior year. So this guy (she doesn't even remember his name now—Rudolph? Bobo?) from N.Y.U. and her were talking under, she remembers this, a big poster of Reagan that someone had drawn a moustache and sunglasses on, and he was talking about all these movies, and she kept telling him that she'd seen all these movies even though she hadn't, and she kept agreeing with him, with his likes, with his dislikes, all the time thinking that he might not be a Daniel Miller (this guy had spiky blueblack hair, paisley tie, and, unfortunately, the beginnings of a goatee) but was still cute enough, and she was sure she was mispronouncing all these filmmakers' names, remembering the wrong actors, naming the wrong cinematographers, but she wanted him and she could see that he was looking over at Kathy Kotcheff, and she was looking back at him and she was getting incredibly smashed and kept nodding and he went over to the keg to get them some more beer and Kathy Kotcheff, who was wearing a black bra and black panties complete with garter belt, started talking to him and she was getting desperate. She was going to go over and drop some names, mention Salle or Longo, but felt it would be too pretentious, so she walked up behind him and simply whispered that she had some pot in her room, even though she didn't but hoped that Lorna did and so he smiled and said that seemed like a good idea. On the way up the stairs she bummed a cigarette that she was never going to smoke from someone and they went to Lorna's room. He closed the door and locked it. She turned the light on. He turned it off. She thinks she said she didn't have any pot. He said that was okay and brought out a silver flask that he'd filled with the grain alcohol punch before it had run out downstairs and she was already so drunk on that plus beer that she drank more of it anyway and before she knew it they were on Lorna's bed making out and she was too drunk to be nervous. Dire Straits or maybe it was Talking Heads were playing downstairs and she was blind drunk and even though she knew this was like sheer madness she couldn't stop it or do anything else. She passed out and when she came to, she tried to take off her bra but was still too drunk and he had already started fucking her but he didn't know she was a virgin and it hurt (not that badly, only a little bit of a sharp pain, but not as bad as she had been taught to expect, but not exactly pleasant either) and that's when she heard another voice in the room, moaning, and she remembers the weight on the bed shifting and realizing that this person on top of her was not the N.Y.U. film student guy but someone else. It was pitch dark in the room and she could feel two pairs of knees on either side of her and she didn't even want to know what was going on above her. All she knew, all that seemed certain, was that she felt nauseous and her head kept banging against the wall. The door she thought he locked flew open and shadows came in saying that they had to put the keg somewhere and the keg was rolled in, knocking against the bed and the door closed. And she was thinking that this wouldn't have happened with Daniel Miller, that he would have taken her gently in his big strong Drama major arms and undressed her quietly, expertly, taken the bra off with grace and ease, kissed her deeply, tenderly, and it probably wouldn't have hurt, but she wasn't with Daniel Miller. She was there with some guy from New York whose name she didn't know and God only knows who else, and the two bodies above her continued moving and then she was on top and even though she was too drunk to stay on top, there was another person holding her up, propping her up, while another touched her breasts through the bra and kept fucking her and she could hear the couple next door arguing loudly and then she passed out again, then woke up when one of the guys hit his head against the wall, slipping off the bed taking her with him and both of them hitting their heads against the keg. She heard one of the guys throwing up in what she hoped was Lorna's wastebasket. She passed out again and when she woke up, maybe thirty seconds later, maybe a half-hour, still being fucked, still moaning in pain (they probably thought she was turned on, which was definitely not the case) she heard someone knocking on the door. She said, "Answer it, answer it," or at least that's what she thinks she said. They were still on the floor when she passed out again. . . . She woke up the next morning, early, on the bed for some reason, and the room was cold and reeked of vomit, the half-empty keg leaking onto the floor. Her head was throbbing, due partly to the hangover and partly because it had been banged against the wall for she didn't even know how long. The film student from N.Y.U. was lying next to her on Lorna's bed, which during the night had been relocated to the center of the room, and he looked a lot shorter and with longer hair than she remembered, his spiked cut wilted now. And in the light coming through the window she saw the other guy lying next to the film student—she wasn't a virgin, she thought to herself—the boy lying next to the N.Y.U. guy opened his eyes and he still was drunk and she'd never seen him before. He was probably a townie. She had actually gone to bed with a *townie*. I'm not a virgin anymore, she thought again. The townie winked at her, didn't bother to introduce himself, and then told her this joke he had heard last night about this elephant who was wandering through the jungle and who stepped on a thorn and it hurt a lot and the elephant was having trouble pulling it out so the elephant asked a rat who was passing by to "Please pull the thorn out from my foot" and the rat made a request: "Only if you let me fuck you." Without hesitation the elephant said okay and the rat quickly pulled the thorn from the elephant's foot and then scrambled up behind the elephant and began fucking. A hunter passed by and shot the elephant, who then started to moan in pain. The rat, oblivious to the elephant's wounds, said, "Suffer baby, suffer," and kept on fucking. The townie started laughing and it was a joke she wished she would forget, but it has stayed with her ever since. It was beginning to dawn on her then that she didn't know which one she had (technically) lost her virginity to (though odds were good that it was the film student from N.Y.U. and not the townie), even though that seemed to be beside the point for some reason on this post-virginal morning. She was vaguely aware that she was bleeding, but only a little. The guy from N.Y.U. burped in his sleep. There was vomit (whose?) all over Lorna's trashcan. The townie was still laughing, doubled up naked with laughter. Her bra was still on. And she said to no one, though she had wanted to say it to Daniel Miller, "I always knew it would be like this."

SEAN The party is starting to end. I get to Windham House right when the last keg is being tapped. The deal in town went okay and I have some cash so I buy some weed from this Freshman who lives in the cardroom in Booth and get high before coming to Thirsty Thursday. There's a Quarters game going on in the living room and Tony is filling a pitcher with beer.

I ask him, "What's going on?"

"Hey Sean. Lost my I.D. Pub's out," he says. "Brigid's got the hots for that guy from L.A. Wanna join in?"

"It's okay," I say. "Where's the cups?"

"Over there," he says and goes back to the table.

I get some beer and notice that this hot-looking Freshman girl with short blond hair, great body, that I fucked a couple of weeks ago, is standing near the fireplace. I'm about to go over and talk to her, but Mitchell Allen's already lighting her cigarette and I don't want to deal with it. So I stand against the wall, listen to REM, finish the beer, get more, keep my eye on the Freshman girl. Then some other girl, Deidre I think her name is, black spiked hair that already looks dated and trendy, black lipstick, black fingernail polish, black kneesocks, black shoes, nice tits, okay body, Senior, comes over and she's wearing a black halter top even though it's like forty below in the room and she's drunk and coughing like she has T.B., swigging Scotch. I've seen her stealing Dante in the bookstore. "Have we met?" she asks. If she's joking, it's just too dumb.

"No," I say. "Hi."

"What's your name?" she asks, trying to keep her balance.

"It's Peter," I tell her.

"Oh, really?" she asks, looking confused. "Peter? Peter? That's not your name."

"Yeah it is." I've still got my eye on the hot Freshman but she won't look over here. Mitchell hands her another beer. It's too late. I look back at Dede Dedire whatever her name is.

"Aren't you a Senior?" she asks me.

"No," I tell her. "Freshman."

"Really?" All of a sudden she starts coughing, then sips her Scotch, actually downs it, and says, her voice rasped-out, "I thought you were older."

"A Freshman," I tell her, drain my cup. "Peter. Peter the Freshman."

Mitchell whispers something in her ear. She laughs, and turns away. He keeps whispering. She doesn't move. That's it. She wants to leave with him.

"Like, I could've sworn your name was Brian," Deedum says.

I consider the options. I can leave right now, go back to my room, play the guitar, go to sleep. Or, I could play Quarters with Tony and Brigid and that dumb guy from L.A. Or, I can take this girl off-campus to The Carousel for a drink, leave her there. Or, I can take her back to my room, hope the Frog is gone, get stoned and fuck her. But I don't really want to do that. I'm not into her all that much, but the hot-looking Freshman has already left with Mitchell and I don't have any classes tomorrow and it's late and it looks like the keg's running out. And she looks at me and asks, "What's going on?" and I'm thinking Why Not?

So I end up going home with her—she's dumpy but horny, from L.A., her father's in the music industry but she doesn't know who Lou Reed is. We go to her room. Her roommate's home but asleep.

"Ignore her," she says, turning on the light. "She's insane. It's okay."

I'm taking off my clothes when the roommate wakes up and starts freaking out at the sight of me naked. I get under D's blankets, but the roommate starts crying and gets out of bed and D keeps screaming at her, "You're insane, go to sleep, you're insane," and roommate leaves, slamming the door, sobbing. We start making out but she forgets her diaphragm so she tries to put it in, squeezing the foam all over her hand but not getting any into it and she's too drunk to know where to put it. I try to fuck her anyway but she keeps moaning "Peter, Peter" so I stop. I'm thinking about throwing up but do some bonghits instead, then flee. Deal with it. Rock'n'roll.

PAUL We were already smashed when we got to Thirsty Thursday and the night was still young and the light-haired Swedish girl from Connecticut, very tall and boyish, came on to me, and I let her. Drunk, but still knowing perfectly well what I was getting myself into, I let her. I had been trying to talk to Mitchell but he was much more interested in this supremely ugly slutty Sophomore named Candice. Candy, for short. I was semi-appalled but what could I do? I started talking to Katrina and she looked very charming in her black Salvation Army raincoat, and the sailor's cap with the one tuft of blond hair peeking out, her eyes wide and blue even in the darkness of the living room at Windham House.

Anyway, we were drunk and Mitch was still talking to Candie and there was this girl at the party I really did not want to see and I was sufficiently drunk now to leave with Katrina. I suppose I could have stayed, waited it out with Mitch, or come on to that boy from L.A., who, despite being too sunburned, was well-muscled (red-muscled?) and seemed withdrawn enough to try anything. But he was still wearing his sunglasses and playing Quarters and anyway, rumor had it he was sleeping with Brigid McCauley (a "total tuna" according to Vanden Smith), so when Katrina asked me, "What's going on?" I lit a cigarette and said, "Let's go." We were even more drunk by now since we had downed a bottle of good red wine we had found in the kitchen, and when we came out into the crisp October air, it hit us both with a bit of a shock, but it didn't sober us up and we both kept laughing. And then she kissed me and said, "Let's go back to my room and take a shower."

We were still walking across Commons lawn when she said this, her mittened hands in her black overcoat, laughing, twirling around, kicking up leaves, the music still coming from Windham House. I wanted to delay this moment, so I suggested that we look around for something to eat. We stopped walking and stood there, and though she sounded more than a little disappointed, she agreed, and we went from house to house, sneakily raiding the refrigerators, even though all we came up with was some frozen Pepperidge Farm Milanos, a half-empty bag of Bar-B-Que potato chips and a Heineken Dark.

Anyway, we ended up in her room, really drunk, making out. She stopped for a minute and made her way to the bathroom down the hall. I turned on a light and looked around the room, inspecting her roommate's empty bed and the poster of a unicorn on the wall; copies of *Town and Country* and *The Weekly World News* ("I Had Bigfoot's Baby," "Scientists Say U.F.O.'s cause AIDS") were scattered around a giant stuffed teddybear that sat in the corner and I was thinking to myself that this girl was *too* young. She came back in and lit a joint and turned off the light. On the verge of passing out she asked me, "We're not going to have sex, are we?"

Paul Young was on her stereo and I was leaning over her, smiling and said, "No, I guess not." I was thinking about the girl I left in September.

"Why not?" she asked, and she really didn't look all that beautiful anymore, lying there in the semi-darkness of her room, the only real light the glow from the tip of the joint she held.

"I don't know," I said, and then mock seriously, "I'm involved," even though I wasn't, "And you are drunk," though that really didn't have anything to do with it either.

"I really like you," she said before she passed out.

"I really like you," I said, though I barely knew her.

I finished the joint and the Heineken. Then I put a blanket over her and stood there, hands in my overcoat pockets. I considered taking the blanket off. I took the blanket off. Then lifted her arm and looked at her breasts, touched them. Maybe I'll ravish her, I pondered. But it was getting close to four and I had a class in six hours, though the prospect of going seemed fairly remote. On the way out I stole her copy of *One Hundred Years of Solitude* and turned her stereo off and left, pleased and maybe a little embarrassed. I was a Senior. She was a nice girl. She ended up telling everyone I couldn't get it up, anyway.

LAUREN Went to Thirsty Thursday at Windham. Thing I had sort of started I didn't like and I was thinking about Victor and getting lonely. Judy came by the studio already drunk and tried to console me. We got high and I just got lonelier thinking about Victor. Then it's late and we're at the party and notalot is going on: keg in the corner, REM or I think it's REM, beautiful, slow-witted Dance majors writhing about shamelessly. Judy says "Let's leave" and I agree. We don't. We get some beer which is warm and flat but drink it. Judy goes off with some guy from Fels even though I know she has a crush on that guy from Los Angeles who's playing Quarters with Tony, who I like and who I slept with my second term here, and that girl Bernette who I guess is seeing the guy from L.A. or maybe she's seeing Tony, and there's nothing going on and I think about leaving, but the idea of going back to the studio. . . .

Someone comes in I don't want to see so I start talking to this Freshman sort-of-yuppie guy. "Brewski for Youski?" he asks. I look over at Tony, wonder if he's interested. He looks over at me, lifting the pitcher and raises his eyebrows from across the living room and I can't tell if it's an invitation to play Quarters or to get laid. But how do I get away from this guy? But there's someone here I don't want to see and if I go over there I'll have to pass him. So I keep talking to this square. This guy who after every bit of innocuous info he hands me says in a tone that he thinks sounds subversively hip, "Hey, Laura," and I keep telling him "Look my name's not Laura, got it?" and he keeps calling me Laura, so finally I'm about to tell him off when suddenly I realize I don't know *his* name. He tells me. It's what? Steve? He, Steve, doesn't like that I'm smoking. The typical drunk (not too drunk) nervous Freshman. Who is Steve looking at? Not the guy from L.A. but at Bernette who wouldn't go to bed with this guy Steve Square Freshman anyway, but well, maybe she would. Can't stop thinking about Victor. But Victor's in Europe. Brewski for Youski? Jesus. The Freshman tells me I haven't touched my beer. I touch it, running my fingers across the plastic rim of the cup. "Oh that's not what I mean," he says good-naturedly. "*Drink* it," he urges. Stereotype with a Haircut. Why does he even care? Does he actually think I'll go to bed with him? Why won't that person leave? Is Tony even looking over here? Someone from the Quarters game yells for Sean Yes I Am a Scumbag Bateman. Judy pushes past me rolling her eyes up. I ask the guy Steve what's going on. He wants to smoke some pot with me but if I don't want pot he has some good speed. Help. I want to know why I sent Victor four postcards and haven't gotten anything back. But I don't want to think about it and very instantly I am leaving with the Freshman. Because . . . the beer has run out. He asks if we could go to my room. Roommate, I lie. We're leaving now. And I had promised myself that I would be faithful to Victor and Victor had promised me that he, too, would be faithful. Since I was under, am under, the impression that we're in love. But I had already sort of broken that vow in September, which was a complete and utter mistake and now what am I doing?

In the hallway of Franklin House. Ripped poster of *A Clockwork Orange* on his door? No, the next room. The Ronnie Reagan calendar on the door. Is that a joke? In the Freshman's room now. What's his name? Sam? Steve? It's so . . . neat! Tennis racket on the wall. Shelf full of Robert Ludlum books. Who is this guy? Probably drives a Jeep, wears penny loafers, his girlfriend in high school wore his letter sweater. He checks his hair out in the mirror and tells me his roommate's in Vermont tonight. Why don't I tell him that my boyfriend, the person I love, the person who loves me, the person I miss, the person who misses me, is in Europe and that I should not under any circumstances be doing this. He has a refrigerator and pulls out an ice-cold Beck's. Slick. I take a sip. He takes a sip. He pulls off his L.L. Bean sweater and his T-shirt. His body's okay. Nice legs. Probably plays tennis a lot. I almost knock over a stack of economics books that are on his desk. I didn't even know they offer that here.

"You don't have any herpes or anything, do you?" he asks while we undress.

I sigh and say, "No, I don't." Wish I was drunk.

He tells me he heard that maybe I did.

I don't want to know who he heard that from. Wish I was very drunk.

It feels good but I'm not turned on. I just think about Victor and lay there.

Victor.

VICTOR Took a charter flight on a DC-10 to London, landed at Gatwick, took a bus to the center, called a friend from school who was selling hash, but she wasn't in. So I wandered around until it started to rain, then took a subway back to the friend's house and hung out there for four or five days. Saw the changing of the guards at Buckingham Palace. Ate a grapefruit next to the Thames River, which reminded me a lot of the cover of that Pink Floyd album. Wrote my mom a postcard I never sent. Looked for some heroin but couldn't find any. Bought some speed from an Italian guy I bumped into at a record store in Liverpool. Smoked a lot of hash that had too much tobacco in it. Even though they all spoke the same language I did, they were all assholes. It rained a lot, it was expensive, so I split for Amsterdam. Someone playing saxophone at Central Station which was kind of pretty. Stayed with some friends in someone's basement. Smoked a lot of hash in Amsterdam too, but lost most of my stash in some museum. The museums were cool, I guess. Lots of Van Goghs and the Vermeers were intense. Wandered around, bought a lot of pastries, a lot of red herring. The Dutch all know English so I didn't have to speak any Dutch, which was a relief. Wanted to rent a car but couldn't. The people I was staying with had bikes though, so I went biking one day and I saw a lot of cows and geese and canals. I pulled off to the side of the road, got stoned and fell asleep, woke up, wrote a little, took some acid, made a few drawings, and then it started raining, so I biked to Danoever, to a youth hostel where there were some cool German guys who spoke a little English, and then I went back to Amsterdam and spent the night with this really stupid German girl. Next day I took the train to Kroeller in Arnhem where there were tons of cool Van Goghs. Hung out in the sculpture garden and I tried to get high there but didn't have any matches and couldn't find one. Got a ride to Cologne and stayed at a youth hostel in Bonn which was *the* worst youth hostel where there were a lot of really screwed-up kids, and it was too far away from the main part of town so we couldn't do anything. Had a beer then headed South through Munich, Austria, and Italy. Got a ride to Switzerland, said fuck it why not. Ended up spending the night at a bus stop. Wandered around Switzerland but the weather was bad and it was too expensive and I wasn't into the situation so I took a train and then started hitching. The mountains were huge and really intense and the dams were surreal. Found a youth hostel and then headed south with a couple in their early thirties who had stayed at the hostel and they gave me a ride. I spent two days in Switzerland. Then I took a bus from Switzerland to Italy, then hitchhiked to get to this town where there was this girl from school who had graduated and who I was sort of in love with but I had lost her phone number and wasn't even that sure if she was in Italy. So I wandered around and met this totally cool guy named Nicola who had greased-back hair and wore Wayfarer sunglasses and who loved Springsteen and kept asking me if I'd ever seen him in concert. It was then that I felt like an idiot for being an American but only for a little while since I finally got a ride from some French guy in a white Fiat who played Michael Jackson really loud and air-jammed. Then I was in some town called Brandis or Blandy or Brotto. Kids eating ice cream, all the movie theaters playing Bruce Lee movies, all the girls thought I was Rob Lowe or something. Still was looking for that girl, Jaime. Bumped into someone from Camden on the Italy Program and this person told me that Jaime was in New York not Italy. Florence was beautiful but too full of tourists. I was speeding heavily and I spent three days without sleep wandering around. Went to this tiny town, Siena. Smoked hash on the steps of this church, the Doumo. Met a cool German guy in this old castle. Then I went to Milano where I hung out with these guys in some house. Slept in a big double bed with one of them who kept playing The Smiths and wanting me to jerk him off which I really wasn't into, but I had no place to go. Rome was big and hot and dirty. Saw a lot of art. Spent the night with some guy who took me out to dinner and I had a long shower at his house and I guess it was worth it. He took me to a bridge where, like, Hector fought off the Trojans or something. I was in Rome for three days. Then I went to Greece and it took me a day to get to where the ferry leaves. Ferry took me to Corfu. Rented a moped on Corfu. Lost the moped. Got on another ferry and headed for Patras and then Athens. Called a friend in New York who told me Jaime wasn't in New York but in Berlin and she gave me the phone number and address. Then I went to the islands, went to Naxos, got into town really early. Used a bathroom and some guy wanted ten drachmas but I only had German deutsche mark on me and I didn't have anything else, so I gave him my Swatch instead. Bought some bread, milk, and a map and I started walking. Saw a lot of donkeys. By nighttime I had walked halfway across town. Hit an archeological site and lost the trail I was following. I just got stoned and watched the sunset. It was nice, so I headed for the water and bumped into some guy who dropped out of Camden. Asked him where Jaime might be. He told me either Skidmore or Athens but not Berlin. Then I went to Crete, fucked some girl there. Then I went to San Torini, which was beautiful but too full of tourists. Took a bus to the South coast, went to Malta and it made me sick. Started hitchhiking. Then I went back to Crete and spent a day at this beach full of Germans and went swimming. Then I walked some more. That's all I did in Crete, was walk. I didn't know where I was. Everywhere was full of tourists. So I went to this nude beach. Hung out, got naked, ate yogurt and swam with these two Yugoslavian guys who complained about inflation and wanted to make me a Socialist. I bought a mask and snorkled and we caught octopus, live, and beat them to death on the beaches and ate them. I met some guy from Canada, who had stolen a car and done some time in prison, and we hung out and talked about the state of the world, drank beer, caught some more octopus, took acid. This went on for three days. My ass and dick got sunburned. One of the Yugoslavian guys taught me how to sing "Born in the U.S.A." in Yugoslavian and we sang it together a lot. There was nothing else to do, since we had killed all the octopus, and I had learned how to sing every Springsteen song in Yugoslavian, so I said goodbye and left the nude beach. I hitchhiked some more, saw a hell of a lot of donkeys, found a Donald Duck comic in Greek lying in someone's backyard. In Greece, while hitching, some truck carrying watermelons picked me up and this old geezer molested me, then I was attacked by dogs. I still didn't know where Jaime was. Ended up in Berlin but that person gave me the wrong address. Stayed at another youth hostel. Liked the Bauhaus architecture which I hate in America but here looked good. Hitchhiked some more, went to a lot of bars, met a lot of punk rockers, played a lot of checkers, shot some pool, smoked hash. Couldn't get a flight out of Berlin so I went back to Amsterdam and got mugged in the red light district by two small black guys.

PAUL   The last time I saw Mitchell before school started was in September. As usual, we were laying on my bed and it was early, perhaps twelve. I reached over him and lit a cigarette. The people next door were fighting. There was too much traffic on Jane Street, it was either that or something else that was making Mitchell so tense, clutching his wine glass. So much attention paid, so much detail studied, worked over so hard that he loses it all. What was I doing there, I kept wondering. My father worked with his father in Chicago and though their relationship depended more on what was happening over on Wall Street and what table the other could command at Le Français or The Ritz-Carlton, it still gave us the opportunity to meet each other. In New York we would meet at the apartment I lived in last summer. We could never meet at his place because of "roommate trouble," he would gravely tell me. We would meet usually at night, usually after a movie or some bad off-off-off-Broadway play one of Mitchell's endless supply of N.Y.U. Drama friends landed a part in, usually drunk or high, which seemed Mitchell's constant state those last months, when I was breaking it off with someone else. Mitchell knew and didn't care. Usually wild bouts of sex, clothed, early drink at Boy Bar, don't ask.

Up on 92nd we sat at a cafe and cursed a waitress. Then taking a cab downtown we got into an argument with our driver and he made us get out. Twenty-ninth Street, hassled by prostitutes, Mitchell kind of enjoying it, or maybe pretending to. He looked kind of desperate those months. I always thought it would pass, but I was getting to the point where I knew it never would. Just a big night on the West Side and he'll be out of it. Then something ridiculous like eggs benedict at three in the morning at P.J. Clarke's. . . . Three in the morning. P.J. Clarke's. He complains the eggs are too runny. I pick at a cheeseburger I ordered but don't want, not really. I'm amazed that there are three or four out-of-town businessmen still at the bar. Mitchell sort of finishes his eggs, then looks at me. I look at him, then light his cigarette. I touch his knee, thigh, with my hand.

"Just don't," he says. I look away, embarrassed. Then he says softly, "Just not here."

"Let's go back home," I say.

"Whose?" he says.

"I don't care. Let's go to my place. Your place? I don't know. I don't feel like spending money on a cab."

It's now getting depressing and late. Neither of us moves. I light another cigarette, then put it out. Mitchell keeps touching his chin lightly, like there's something wrong with it. He runs his finger through the dimple.

"Do you want to get stoned?" he asks.

"Mitch," I sigh.

"Hmmm?" he asks, leaning forward.

"It's four in the morning," I say.

"Uh-huh," he says, confused, still leaning.

"We're at P.J.'s," I remind him.

"That's right," he says.

"You want to get . . . stoned?" I ask.

"Well," he stammers, "I guess."

"Why don't we . . ." I stop, look over at the businessmen, and look away, but not at Mitchell.

"Why don't we . . ."

He keeps staring, waiting. This is stupid.

I don't say anything.

"Why don't we . . . why don't we what?" he asks, grinning, leaning closer, lips curling, whites of teeth, that ugly dimple.

"There's a rumor going around that you're retarded," I tell him.

In a cab heading toward my apartment, late, almost five, and I can't even remember what we did tonight. I pay the driver and give him too big a tip. Mitchell holds the elevator door open, impatient. We get to my apartment and he takes off his clothes and gets stoned in the bathroom and then we watch TV, some HBO, for a little while . . . and then we went to sleep as soon as the sun started rising, and I remembered a party we were at back in school when Mitchell drunk and angry tried to set fire to Booth House in the early morning. . . . We look straight at each other right now, both breathing evenly. It's morning now and we're not sleeping and everything is pure and bright and clear and I fall asleep. . . . When I woke up, later that afternoon, Mitchell was gone, left for New Hampshire. But the ashtray by the bed was full. It was empty before. Had he watched me sleep during that time? Had he?

SEAN   "It was the Kennedys, man . . ." Marc's telling me while he's shooting up in his room in Noyes. "The Kennedys, man, screwed it . . . up. . . . Actually it was J . . . F . . . K . . . John F. Kennedy did it. . . . He screwed it up . . . all up, you see. . . ." He licks his lips now, continues, "There was this . . . our mothers were pregnant with us when we . . . I mean, he . . . was blown away in '64 and that whole incident . . . screwedthings-up. . . ." He stops, then goes on. ". . . in a really heavy duty way . . ." Special emphasis on "heavy" and "duty." "And . . . in turn . . . you see, it jolted us in a really heavy duty way when we . . . were . . . in . . ." He stops again, looks at his arm and then at me. "Whatchma-callit . . ." Looks back at his arm and then at me, then at the arm again, concentrating as he pulls the needle out, then at me, still confused. "Their . . . um, primordial wombs, and, so, that is why we are . . . me, you, the narc across the hall, the sister in Booth, all the way we are. . . . Do you . . . understand? . . . Is this clear?" He squints up at me. "Jesus . . . think if you had a brother who was born in '69 or something . . . They'd be . . . fucking bonkers. . . ."

He's saying this all real slowly (a lot of it I can't even listen to) as he puts the eyedropper next to his new computer that's humming, his friend Resin, who's visiting from Ann Arbor, leaning up against the table, sitting on the floor, humming with it. Marc sits back, smiling. I thought Kennedy bit it a couple of years earlier but wasn't sure and I don't correct him. I'm kind of wired but still could use some sleep, since it's late, sometime around four, but I like the familiarity of Marc's room, the details I'm used to, the ripped Bob Dylan poster for *Don't Look Back*, the stills from *Easy Rider*, "Born To Be Wild" always coming from the stereo (or Hendrix or Eric Burdon and The Animals or Iron Butterfly or Zep), the empty pizza boxes on the floor, the copy of an old Pablo Neruda book on top of the pizza boxes, the constant smell of incense, the yoga manuals, the band upstairs that's always rehearsing old Spencer Davis songs all night (they suck). But Marc's leaving soon, any day now, can't stand the scene, Ann Arbor is where it's at, Resin told him.

After I fucked Didi I came back to my room, where Susan was, alone, crying. I guess the Frog was in New York. I couldn't deal with her so I told her to get out, then I drove to the Burger King in town and ate it on the way to Roxanne's and had to deal with her new boyfriend, this big mean townie pusher named Rupert. That whole scene was a total joke. She was so stoned she actually lent me forty bucks and told me that The Carousel (where Rupert also bartends) is closing down due to shitty business, and that depressed me. I picked up the stuff from Rupert, who was cleaning his gun case, so coked up he actually smiled and let me do a line, and brought it back to campus. The drive was a cold, long drag, my bike almost kicking out near the college gates, and barely making it through the two-mile stretch of College Drive. I was too stoned and the Burger King food was making me sick and those two miles past the gate on that road at 3AM in the morning was creepy. I smoked some more pot in Marc's room and now he's finishing up. It's no big deal. I've seen it all before.

Marc lights a menthol cigarette, and says, "I'm telling you, Sam, it was the Kennedys!" His arm's bent up, resting on his shoulder, folded. He licks his lips. "This stuff . . ."

"I hear you brother," I sigh, rubbing my eyes.

"This stuff is . . ."

"Is?"

"Is good."

Marc was doing his thesis on The Grateful Dead. At first he had been trying to space the shots out so he wouldn't get hooked, but it was sort of too late for that. I'd been scoring for him since September, and he had been slacking off on his payments. He had kept telling me that after "the Garcia interview" he would have some cash. But Garcia hadn't been to New Hampshire in a long time and I was losing my patience.

"Marc, you owe me five hundred bucks," I tell him. "I want it before you leave."

"God, we use to have . . . wild times at this place. . . ." (This is the part where I always start getting up.) "It's so . . . different now . . ." (Blah Blah) "Those times are gone . . . those places are gone . . ." he says.

I stare at a piece of broken mirror next to the computer and the eyedropper and now Marc's talking about chucking it all and heading for Europe. I look down at him, his breath reeks, he hasn't showered in days, his hair is greasy and pulled back in a ponytail, stained dirty tie-dyed shirt. ". . . When I was in Europe, man . . ." He picks his nose.

"I gotta go to class tomorrow," I tell him. "What about the cash?"

"Europe . . . What? Class? Who teaches that?" he asks.

"David Lee Roth. Listen, can I get the cash or what?"

"I dig it, I can dig it, sshhh, you'll wake up Resin," he whispers.

"I don't care. Resin has a Porsche. Resin can pay me," I tell him.

"Resin's broke," he says. "I'm good for it, I'm good for it."

"Marc, you owe me five hundred bucks. Five hundred," I tell the pathetic junkie.

"Resin thinks Indira Gandhi lives in Welling House," Marc smiles. "Says he followed her from the dining hall to Welling." He pauses. "Can you dig . . . that?"

He gets up, barely makes it to the bed and falls on it, rolling his sleeves down. He looks around the room, smoking the filter now. "Um," he says, head rolling back.

"You've got money, come on," I say. "Can't you lend me a couple bucks?"

He looks around the room, flips open an empty pizza box, then squints at me. "No."

"I'm a Financial Aid student man, I need some money," I plead. "Just five bucks."

He closes his eyes and laughs. "I'm good for it," is all he says.

Resin wakes up and starts talking to the ashtray. Marc warns me that I'm fucking up his karma. I leave. Junkies are pathetic enough but rich junkies are even worse. Even worse than girls.

PAUL My damn radio went off accidentally at seven o'clock this morning and I couldn't get back to sleep, so I stumbled out of bed, immediately lit a cigarette and closed the windows since it was freezing in the room. Even though I could barely open my eyes (if I did I was positive my skull would split open) I could see that I was still wearing my tie, my underwear, and my socks. I couldn't figure out why I was only wearing these three articles of clothing so I stood for a long time staring into the mirror trying to remember last night, but couldn't. I stumbled into the bathroom and took a shower, grateful that there was some warm water left. I dressed hurriedly and braced myself for breakfast.

Actually it was quite nice out. It was that time of October just when the trees were about to lose their fall foliage and the morning was cold and crisp and the air smelled clean and the sun, obscured by graying clouds, wasn't too high yet. I was still feeling awful though, and the five Anacin I popped weren't anywhere near doing their job. Bleary-eyed, I almost put a twenty in the change machine. I passed the post office but there was nothing in my box since it was too early for mail. I got cigarettes and went up to the dining hall.

There was no one in line. That cute blond-haired Freshman boy was behind the counter not saying a word, only wearing the biggest pair of black sunglasses I've ever seen, serving the wettest looking scrambled eggs and these little brown toothpicks which I suspected were sausages. The thought of eating nauseated me to no end and I looked at the boy who just stood there, holding a spatula. My initial horniness gave way to irritation and I muttered, "You're so pretentious," cigarette still in mouth, and got a cup of coffee.

The main dining room was the only one open so I went in and sat down with Raymond, Donald, and Harry, this little Freshman who Donald and Raymond befriended, a cute boy who was concerned with typical Freshman questions, like Is there life after Wham!? They had been up all night doing crystal meth, and they had invited me, but I had followed . . . Mitchell, who was sitting at another table across the dining hall, to that stupid party instead. I tried not to look over at him and that awful fucked-out slut he was sitting with, but I couldn't help it and I cursed myself for not jerking off when I woke up this morning. The three fags were huddled around a sheet of paper composing a student blacklist and even though their mouths were moving a mile a minute, they noticed me, nodded, and I sat down.

"Students who go to London and come back with accents," Raymond said, writing furiously.

"Can I bum a cig?" Donald asked me absently.

"Can you?" I asked back. The coffee tasted atrocious. Mitchell, that bastard.

"Oh, do be real, Paul," he muttered as I handed him one.

"Why don't you just *buy* some?" I asked as politely as someone who's hungover and at breakfast possibly could.

"Anybody who rides a motorcycle, and all Deadheads," Harry said.

"And anyone who comes to breakfast who hasn't stayed up all night," Donald shot a glance over at me.

I made a face at him and crossed my legs.

"Those two dykes who live in McCullough," Raymond said, writing.

"How about *all* of McCullough?" suggested Donald.

"Even better." Raymond scribbled something down.

"What about that slut with Mitchell?" I offered.

"Now, now, Paul. Calm down," Raymond said, sarcastically.

Donald laughed and wrote her name down anyway.

"What about that mean fat trendy girl?" Harry asked.

"She lives in McCullough. She's taken care of."

I couldn't stand this twisted faggy banter so early in the morning and I was going to get up and get more coffee but I was too tired to even do that and I sat back and didn't look at Mitchell and soon all the voices became indistinguishable from one another, including mine.

"Anyone with beards or facial hair of any kind."

"Oh that's good."

"How about that boy from L.A.?"

"But not really."

"You're right, but put him down anyway."

"Anyone who goes for seconds at the salad bar."

"Are you auditioning for that Shepard thing, Paul?"

"What? What are you talking about?"

"That part. The Shepard play. Auditions today."

"Anybody who waits to get braces after high school."

"No, I'm not."

"People who consider themselves born again."

"That rules out the entire administration."

"*Quelle horreur!*"

"Rich people with cheap stereos."

"Boys who can't hold their liquor."

"What about boys who *can* hold their liquor?"

"True, true."

"Put down girls who can't."

"I'll just put down Lightweights."

"What about David Van Pelt?"

"Why?"

"Why not?"

"Well, I slept with him."

"You didn't go to bed with David Van Pelt."

"Yes I did."

"How?"

"He's a Lightweight. I told him I like his sculptures."

"But they're *awful!*"

"I *know* that."

"He's got a *harelip*."

"I know that also. I think it's . . . sexy."

"You would."

"Anybody with a harelip. Put that down."

"What about The Handsome Dunce?"

I vaguely wanted to know who The Handsome Dunce was for some reason but couldn't bring myself to muster the interest to ask. I felt like shit. I don't know these people, I was thinking. I hated being a Drama major. I started to sweat. I pushed the coffee away and reached for a cigarette. I had switched majors so many times now that I didn't even care. Drama major was simply the last roll of the dice. David Van Pelt was disgusting, or at least I used to think so. But now, this morning, his name had an erotic tinge to it, and I whispered the name to myself, but Mitchell's came instead.

Then suddenly they all cackled, still huddled around the paper, reminding me of the three witches from *Macbeth* except infinitely better looking and wearing Giorgio Armani. "How about anybody whose parents are still married?" They laughed and congratulated each other and wrote it down, satisfied.

"Excuse me," I interrupted. "But my parents are still married."

They all looked up, their smiles fading quickly to deep concern. "What did you say?" one of them asked.

I cleared my throat, paused dramatically and said, "My parents aren't divorced."

There was a long silence and then they all screamed, a mixture of disappointment and disbelief and they threw their heads on the table, howling.

"No way!" Raymond said, amazed, alarmed, looking up as if I had just admitted a devastating secret.

Donald was gaping. "You are kidding, Paul." He looked horrified and actually backed away as if I were a leper.

Harry was too stunned to speak.

"I'm not kidding, Donald," I said. "My parents are too boring to get a divorce."

I liked the fact that my parents were still married. Whether the marriage was any good was anyone's guess, but just the fact that most, or all, of my friends' parents were either divorced or separated, and my parents weren't, made me feel safe rather than feeling like a casualty. It almost made up for Mitchell and I was pleased with this notoriety. I relished it and I stared back at the three of them, feeling slightly better.

They were still staring, dumbfounded.

"Go back to your stupid list," I said, sipping my coffee, waving them away. "Stop staring at me."

They slowly looked back at the list and got back into it after that short, stunned silence, but they resumed their game with less enthusiasm than before.

"How about people with tapestries in their rooms?" Harry suggested.

"We already have that," Raymond sighed.

"Is there any more speed left?" Harry sighed.

"No," Donald sighed also.

"How about anyone who writes poetry about Womanhood?"

"Bolsheviks from Canada?"

"Anyone who smokes clove cigarettes?"

"Speaking of cigarettes, Paul, can I bum another one?" Donald asked.

Mitchell reached across the table and touched her hand. She laughed.

I looked back at Donald, incredulous. "No. You cannot," I said, my hysteria building. "Absolutely not. That infuriates me. You are always 'bumming' cigarettes and I won't stand for it anymore."

"Come on," Donald said as if I was only joking. "I'll buy some later. I'm broke."

"No! It also infuriates me that your father owns something like half of Gulf and Western and you always pretend to be broke," I said, glaring.

"Is it such a big crisis?" he asked.

"Yeah, Paul, stop having a *grand mal*," Raymond said.

"Why are you in such a bad mood?" Harry asked.

"I know why," Raymond said slyly.

"Wedding bells?" Donald giggled, looking over at Mitchell's table.

"It *is* such a crisis." I was adamant, ignoring them. I'm going to kill that slut.

"Just give me one. Don't be bitchy."

"Okay, I'll give you one if you tell me what won best costume design at the Tonys last year."

There was a silence that followed that I found humiliating. I sighed and looked down. The three of them didn't say anything until Donald finally spoke up.

"That is the most meaningless question I have ever heard."

I looked over at Mitchell again, then slid the cigarettes across the table. "Just take them. I'm getting more coffee." I got up and headed out of the dining hall. But then I had to stop and duck into the salad bar room because there was the Swedish girl I was with last night, showing her I.D. to the food service checker. I waited there until she walked into the serving area. Then I ran quickly downstairs and headed for class. I thought about trying out for that Shepard play, but then thought why bother, when I'm already stuck in one: my life.

I sat at a desk not listening to the drone of the professor, glancing over at Mitchell, who looked happy (yeah, he got laid last night) and who was taking notes. He looked around the room, disgusted, at the people smoking (he quit when he came back—how irritating). They probably looked like machines to him, I imagined. Like chimneys, spurts of smoke rising from that hole in their heads. He looked at the ugly girl in the red dress trying to look cool. I looked at the graffiti on the desk: "You Lose." "There Is No Gravity. The Earth Sucks." "The Brady Bunch Slept Here." "What Ever Happened to Hippie Love?" "Love Stinks." "Most Cab Drivers Have Liberal Arts Degrees." And I sat there feeling like the hapless lover. But then I remembered, of course, that now I'm only hapless.

LAUREN Wake up. Hair needs to be washed. I don't want to miss lunch. I go to Commons. I look disgusting. No mail today. No mail today from Victor. Just a reminder that the AA meeting is going to be in Stokes instead of Bingham next Saturday. *Dawn of the Dead* tonight in Tishman. I have four overdue art books from the library. Bump into weird-looking girl with pink party dress on and glasses who looks like a victim of shock treatment searching for someone's box. Another minor irritation. Walk upstairs. Forgot my I.D. They let me in anyway. Cute guy wearing Wayfarer sunglasses serves cheeseburgers. Ask for a plate of fries. Start to flirt. Ask him how his flute tutorial's going. Realize I look disgusting and turn away. Get a Diet Coke. Sit down. Roxanne's here for some reason sitting with Judy. Judy's picking at tofu lettuce celery rice French fry salad. I break the silence: "I'm sick of this place. Everyone reeks of cigarettes, is pretentious, and has terrible posture. I'm getting out before the Freshmen take over." I forgot ketchup. I push the plate of fries away. Light a cigarette. Neither one of them smile. O . . . K . . . I pick at a spot of dried blue paint on my pant leg. "So . . . what's wrong?" I look around and spot Square out of the corner of my eye at the beverage center. Turn back to Judy. "Where's Sara?"

"Sara's pregnant," Judy says.

"Oh shit, you're kidding," I say, pulling the chair up. "Tell me about it."

"What's to tell?" Judy asks. "Roxanne's been talking to her all morning."

"I gave her some Darvon," Roxanne rolls her eyes up. Chain-smoking. "Told her to go to Psychological Counseling."

"Oh shit, no," I say. "What's she doing about it? I mean, when?"

"She's having it done next week," Roxanne says. "Wednesday."

I put the cigarette out. Pick at the fries. Borrow Judy's

ketchup. "Then she's going to Spain, I guess," Roxanne says, rolling her eyes up again.

"Spain? Why?"

"Because she's crazy," Judy says, getting up. "Does anyone want anything?"

Victor. "No," I say, still looking at Roxanne. She leaves.

"She was really upset, Lauren," Roxanne's bored, plays with her scarf, eats fries.

"I can imagine. I have to talk with her," I say. "This is terrible."

"Terrible? The *worst*," Roxanne says.

"The worst," I agree.

"I hate it when this happens," she says. "I hate it."

We finish the fries, which are pretty good today. "It's awful, I know," I nod.

"Awful," she says. More agreement. "I'm beginning to think romance is a foreign concept."

Ralph Larson. Philosophy teacher walks by with tray looking for a place to sit followed by my printmaking teacher. He looks at Roxanne and says, "Hey baby," and winks. Roxanne smiles big—"Hi, Ralph"—and she's looking now at me, eyes saucers, still smiling big. I notice she's gained weight. She grabs my wrist. "He's so handsome, Lauren," she breathes, pants, at me.

"Never invite a teacher to your room," I tell her.

"He can come by anytime," she says, still squeezing.

"Let go," I'm telling her. "Roxanne, he's married."

"I don't care, so what?" She rolls her eyes up. "Everyone knows he slept with Brigid McCauley."

"He'll never leave his wife for you. It would screw up his tenure review."

I laugh. She doesn't. And I slept with that guy Tim who got Sara pregnant and what if it was me who was getting an abortion next Wednesday? What if . . . Ketchup on the plate, smeared, make unavoidable connection. I wouldn't let it happen. Judy comes back. Next table: sad-looking boy is making a sandwich and wrapping it in a napkin for

41

hippie girlfriend who isn't on the food plan. Then it's the Square walking toward the table. Whirl around and tell Judy to tell me a joke, anything.

"What? Huh?" she says.

"Talk to me, pretend you're talking to me. Tell me a joke. Hurry. Anything."

"Why? What's going on?"

"Just do it! There's someone I don't want to talk to." Point with my eyes.

"Oh yeah," she starts, we've played this before, warming up, "that's why, it all, you know, happened. . . ."

"That's why?" I shrug. "But I thought, you know that, it happened . . ."

"Yeah, that's why . . . uh, see, do . . ." she says.

"Oh, ha ha ha ha ha . . ." I laugh. It sounds fake. I feel ugly.

"Hi, Lauren," Voice Behind Me says. Stop laughing, casually look up and he's wearing shorts. It's October and the boy is wearing shorts and has a *New York Times* business section under one arm. "Is there room here?" Gestures at our table where he's about to put his tray down. Roxanne nods.

"No!" I look around. "I mean . . . no. We're expecting someone. Sorry."

"Okay." He stands there, smiling.

Leave, leave, leave. Use ESP . . . anything.

"Sorry," I say again.

"Can we talk later?" he asks me. Leave. L-E-A-V-E. "I'll be in the computer room."

"Sure."

He says "Bye" and walks aways.

I look for another cigarette and feel a little shitty, but why? What does he expect? I think about Victor, then look up, and ask for a match and say "Don't—"

"Who's he?" they both ask.

"—ask. No one," I say. "Give me a match."

"You . . . didn't," Judy says, cocking her head.

"I . . . did," I mimic the head movement. "Oh boy."

"He's a Freshman. Congratulations. Your first?"

"I didn't say I was interested, dahling."

"He's got such a nice ass," Roxanne says.

"I'm sure Rupert would love to hear you say that," I tell her.

"I have a feeling now that Rupert would agree with me," Roxanne says sadly.

And that's a weird thing to say and I wonder what she means. It reminds me of something I don't want to be reminded of. I tell Roxanne to give me a call and tell Judy that I'll be in my studio. Go back to my room and decide to skip video class and take a bath instead. Clean the tub out first. Dorm's quiet. Everyone at classes or maybe still sleeping. Great, hot water. Bring a pad and some charcoal and my box and put some Rickie Lee Jones on. Smoke a joint and lay there. Tried calling Victor last night when I came back from Steve's room, crying, couldn't stop, but there was no answer at the house in Rome he said he would be staying at on this date. Remember my last night with him. Touch myself. Think of Victor. I hate Rickie Lee Jones. Turn the radio on instead. Wash my hair. I turn the volume up. Bad station. Top 40. Static. But then I hear a song that I remember listening to when I was seeing Victor. It was a dumb song and I didn't like it at the time but it suits the moment now and makes me cry. I want to write this feeling down, or draw it out, but then I feel like that would make the whole thing seem impure and artificial. I decide it will only cheapen the feeling and so I lay there in the white brightness and think of memories the song brings me. Of Victor. Victor's hands. Victor's leopard-skin pants. Ripped army boots and . . . his pubic hair? His arms. Watching him shave. At the Palladium, how handsome he looked in a tuxedo. Making love in his apartment. Brown eyes. What else? He starts to fade. I get scared. I get scared because while I'm laying here it suddenly seems as if he doesn't exist anymore. It seems as if only the song that's playing does, not Victor. It's almost as if I had made him up last summer.

SEAN Terror in the Dining Halls. Part IVXVV. The girl who fucked Mitchell last night and who I want to fuck again is standing over at the Beverage Center. I can see her very clearly from where I sit. She's talking to her overweight lesbian (probably) potter friend. Wearing a dress that I really can't describe. I guess you'd call it a kimono maybe but shorter and with a sweatshirt over it. It's bulky but you can still tell that she has a good body and it doesn't look like she's wearing a bra so her tits look nice. I sort of know this girl; after we'd spent the night together, I talked to her at a Friday night party in Franklin. She might be in one of my classes but I'm not sure since I don't go often enough to tell. But, whatever the story is, she is next.

Dinner again and I'm sitting with the usual crew: Tony, Norris, Tim, Getch. The goddamn House Pigs, our house band, woke me up at four this afternoon, rehearsing above my room. I took a shower, aware when I was blow-drying my hair that I missed two classes today and that I have to find a major before the end of the month. I paced the room, smoking, listening to old Velvet Underground hoping it would drown the House Pigs out, until it was time for dinner. They were still playing when I left for Commons.

Jason was serving and I told him I talked to Rupert and that I could get him the four grams by tomorrow night, but that he should take his sunglasses off because they make him look too suspicious. He only smiled and gave me an extra slab of meat, or turkey, or pork or whatever the hell it was he was serving, which was cool considering, I guess. So, I'm looking at that girl, wondering if she's the one who's been putting those notes in my box and I get excited—even if it's not her. But then her fat friend says something to her and they both look at our table and I look down and pretend to eat. I think she's a Sophomore and I'm pretty sure she lives in Swan but I'm not going to ask anyone at this table. I don't want to take the fun out of the pursuit. Tim's a bonehead for getting Sara pregnant and he doesn't care. I screwed Sara a couple of times my second year. In fact most of the guys at the table had. It seemed almost like a joke that Tim just got stuck with the short end of the stick, the deal. But no one's too upset or morose about the whole thing. Even Tim makes jokes about it.

"So many girls are having them there might as well be a CWS job for it," he laughs.

"I'd seriously do it for fifty bucks," says Tony.

Getch is playing with an Etch-a-Sketch and says, "Gross man. That is just gross."

"Are you talking about the food or the abortion jokes?" I ask.

Tony explains: "Drano in a Water Pik."

Getch says, "Great, we're making jokes about it."

"Come on," I tell Getch. "Cheer up."

"Why aren't you upset, man?" Getch asks Tim, staring at him in a way only a Social Science major could.

"Look," says Tim. "I've been through this shit so many times before, it doesn't even faze me."

Getch nods, but looks like he doesn't really understand, but he shuts up, and looks back at the Etch-a-Sketch.

"How do you know it's even yours?" asks Tony, who just came back from a student council meeting, stoned.

"I know," Tim says, like he's proud of being so confident.

"But how do you *know?* The bitch could be fucking you over," says Tony, a big help.

"You can *tell*," says Tim. "You can look at her and just know she's not lying."

No one says anything.

"You can *feel* it," he reiterates.

"That's, uh, really mystical," Tony says.

"So when is she getting the fetus ripped out of her?" Norris asks.

The whole table moans collectively and Tim's laugh is guilty but helpless and it makes me queasy. The girl finally gets a Coke and walks out of the main dining room, looking confidently hot.

"Wednesday, guy," Tim borrows a cigarette and cups his hands even though there is no possibility of the match going out. Precautions, I guess. "It would've been Tuesday, but she has this primal dance piece on Tuesday so it has to be Wednesday."

"Show must go on," I smile, grim but loose.

"Yeah," says Tim, a little anxious. "Right. And then she's going to Europe, which is a total *relief*."

The table, including Tim, has already lost interest in this already old (known since last night, for latecomers, lunch) piece of gossip, so other conversations ensue, about other important subjects. I ask Norris if he can get me some coffee when he gets up.

"You want cream in it?" he asks.

"Yeah. Cream in it," I tell him. Old joke.

"Hey Sean, you're . . . pretty funny."

"Yeah, I'm a pretty funny guy."

"Does anyone know where we can get Ecstasy tonight?" Tim asks.

"Where's the party tonight?" Getch asks.

I spot my roommate, he's back from New York.

"Ça va," he says as he passes by.

"Ça va," I say, then "Ribbet."

"At End of the World and probably The Graveyard," Tony tells him. Tony's head of Rec Committee too. "All donations toward alcohol will be greatly appreciated."

"Isn't it too cold to be outside?" asks Getch.

"Dress warm, pussy." Tony pushes his plate away and starts on his salad; even though I like Tony, that European salad thing bugs me.

"Pussy? Who said pussy?" asks Tim. "I haven't heard that term since eighth grade."

"Fuck off," Tony says. He's pissed because he didn't get the part in some stupid Drama Division production, even though he's a sculpture major, and even though he's a good guy and all, it bugs me that he gets sulky over something so lame. I want to fuck Sara again. She gives incredible head, I remember. Or was that someone else? Or was Sara the one with the coil I almost slit my dick open on? Considering what the situation is now, she probably wasn't the one with the I.U.D., but even if she was I might just take a chance again, if it was offered to me.

"Anyone know what the movie is tonight?" asks Getch.

"Beats me," says Tony.

Norris comes back with the coffee and whispers, "Creamed in it."

I sip it and smile. "Delicious."

"I don't know. *Night of the Dead Baby*? I don't know," says Tony.

"Can we shut up?" asks Tim.

"I heard from Roxanne that The Carousel's closing," I offer the table.

"No way. Really?" Norris asks.

"Yeah," I say. "At least that's what Roxanne says."

"Why?" Getch asks.

"Freshman and Sophomores don't drink anymore," Tony says. "Sucks, doesn't it."

"I think it sucks too," Getch says. He always looks cheesy to me for some reason. I can't explain it. He shakes the Etch-a-Sketch.

I say, "Rock'n'roll."

Tim laughs, "The horrah, the horrah."

Tony says, "It's just another example of this place going to shit, that's all."

I tell him, "Deal with it."

Tony's losing his patience, getting all political. "Listen, do you realize that we're getting a fucking weight room? Why? Do you understand? Can you explain? I can't. Do you realize that I just came out of a student council meeting where the Freshman reps want fraternity houses installed on campus? Do you understand that? Do you want to *deal with it?*"

I cringe. "It's all dumb."

"Why?" Tim asks. "I think a weight room's a good idea."

"Because," I explain, hoping to cool Tony down, "I came here to get away from jock idiots and frat assholes."

"Listen," Tim says with an ugly leer, "Girls work out on that shit for those inner thigh muscles man." He grabs at my leg and laughs.

"Yeah, well," I'm suddenly confused. "Still, a weight room." I don't really care.

Tony looks at me. "Who are you to talk, Sean? What are you majoring in? Computers?"

"Reagan's Eighties. Detrimental effect on underclassmen," Tim says, shaking his head.

It really doesn't piss me off as much as he wants it to. "Computers," I mimic him.

"What *are* you majoring in?" He's daring me, the big fucking baby, finish your salad, asshole.

"Rock'n'roll," I shrug.

He gets up, disgusted. "What are you, a parrot?"

"What's up his ass?" someone asks.

"Didn't get that part in the Shepard play," Getch says.

Deidre appears out of nowhere, to save the day? Not quite.

"Peter?"

The table looks up and falls silent.

"I thought my name was Brian," I say, without looking at her.

She laughs, probably high. I can see her hands, her fingernails aren't painted black anymore. It looks like cement color. "Oh well, yeah. How are you?" she asks.

"Eating." I point at the plate. All the guys are looking at her. This is a highly uncomfortable situation.

"You going to the party tonight?" she asks.

"Yeah. I'm going to the party tonight. You going to the party tonight?" Meaningless.

"Yeah." She seems nervous. The guys are intimidating her. She was actually okay last night, just too drunk. She's probably good in bed. I look over at Tim, who's checking her out. "Yeah, I am."

"Well I guess I'll see you there." I look at Norris and roll my eyes up.

"Okay," she says, lingering, looking around the room.

"Okay, see you there, bye," I mutter. "God."

"Okay, well," she coughs. "See you."

"Go away," I say under my breath.

She goes to another table. The guys aren't saying anything. I'm embarrassed because she's not that great looking and they all know I screwed her last night and I get up to feed more coffee to my impending ulcer. Rock'n'roll.

"I need a double bed," Tim says. "Anyone got a double bed?"

"Don't smoke pot," someone else says.

"Yabba Dabba Do," Getch says.

The feeling is neither icy nor hot. Yet there is still no in-between. Just this bland pulse that fixates in my body at any given time of the day. I have decided to put notes in his box every day. I imagine him pinning these notes somewhere, perhaps pinned to a white wall in his room, a room I wish to live in. Are these devices sufficient? I ask myself, sickened, left punctured and cowering after I deliver these notes into his box, his pocketbed. My will is an ambulance on emergency call. But I often try to forget him (I have not met him, will not meet him until later, have not dared open my mouth to confront him, sometimes I want to scream, sometimes I think I am dying) and I try to forget this beating from my heart, but cannot and get sick. The space I follow is black and arid. *My obsession (I do not know if it can even be considered that, that word does not seem quite right) though futile or ridiculous to you takes the mystery from nothing. It is simple. I watch him. He reveals himself in dark contours. Everything I believe in floats away when I witness him, say, eating, or crossing the boundaries of a crowded room. I feel a scourge. I have his name written on a sheet of pale blue paper that is tissue thin, fallen poplars I've drawn surround the letters. Everything reminds me of his being: there is a dog that lives across the hall from me. Its owner registered it as a cat (canines are forbidden at this place) and took a fuzzy photo of it and it is small and white-violet and has gremlin ears. I fed it Bon Bons once. I take that person's actions as a hint and because of that I speak to no one. He is beautiful, though you might not think so. There is something circular about him, like moths fluttering in the clear Arizona night. And I know we will meet. It will come easy and soon. And my resentment— my terrified, futile resentment—will float away. I write another note after dinner. He must know it is me. I know his brand of cigarette. I saw him buy a Richard and Linda Thompson tape in town once. I was standing, looking through a bin I didn't care about, and he didn't notice me. I listened to them in high school. When Linda and Richard were still together. They broke up, like John and Exene, like Tina and Ike, Sid and Nancy, Chrissie and Ray. That will not happen to me. His name is a word on top of a page and it signifies a poem started, stated, started but unfinished since the typewriter will not type anymore. I kiss my hand and smell it and smell him, oh I pretend it is his scent. His. His. I don't dare go to his house or pass his room. I will walk by him and not even look. I will pass him in the dining hall with a nonchalance that shocks even me.*

PAUL I tried to talk to Mitchell at the party at End of the World tonight. He was standing by the keg filling a plastic cup. I already had a beer and was standing alone, where The Graveyard started. I poured the beer out and walked over to the keg. "Hi, Mitch," I said. It was cold and my breath steamed. "What's going on?"

"Hi, Paul. Nothing much." He was filling two cups. Couldn't the helpless bitch get her own fucking beer? "What's going on with you?"

"Nothing. Can we talk?" I took the tap from him.

He stood there holding the two beers.

"What do you want to talk about?" he asked with that famous blank stare.

"Just about what's going on," I said, concentrating on the beer and foam coming out of the tap. A girl came by and waited. I gave her a look but she wasn't looking at me, only at my hands, impatiently.

"I warned you, Paul. Remember that," Mitchell said.

"Yeah, I know," I said and laughed quickly. My cup wasn't even half-full but I handed the girl the tap anyway. "Wait, you warned me about what?" I asked. I could see Candice standing by the edge of End of the World, behind her and down, the Valley of Camden, lights in the town. I didn't understand how he could prefer *that* because Mitchell was, admittedly, too good-looking for her. It was beyond my comprehension. I took a gulp of beer.

"I *warned* you." He started walking.

"Wait." I followed him. He stopped by one of the speakers. The Pretenders were coming loudly from them. A small group of people were dancing. He said something I couldn't hear. I knew what he was going to say, but I didn't think he had the nerve to say it. Had I been warned? Probably, but not in any verbal way. In the way he would recoil if I touched him in public or after he came. Or if I bought him a beer at The Pub and the way he would throw a fit and tell me that he'd pay for it and push a dollar across the table. How all he would talk about was wanting to go to Europe, take a term off, and then how he would always add, stress, *alone*. I *had* been warned and I hated to admit it to myself. But I followed him over to where Candice stood anyway. He gave her the beer. She looked so trashy or maybe she looked pretty and I was having a hard time accepting this. Mitchell was wearing a T-shirt (was it one of mine? probably) and an Eddie Bauer sweater and he scratched at his neck nervously.

"You two know each other?" he asked.

"Yeah, hi," she smiled and he held her beer while she lit a cigarette.

"Hi," I smiled, genial as ever. Then threw her a severe look when she wasn't looking, hoping that Mitchell would catch it, but he didn't.

The three of us stood there at End of the World, past that came the slope that headed down toward the valley, and then the middle of Camden. It wasn't steep but if I was to push her, accidentally say, inconspicuously, over the knee-high stone protector, it would cause more than slight damage. The Pretenders turned into Simple Minds and I was grateful because I could not have stood there if there had been no music. Parties are, in their own right, perfect grounds for confrontation, but not this one. I had lost this one. I had probably lost it a long time ago, maybe even that last night in New York. Someone had strung dim yellow lights up and they illuminated Mitchell's face, making it seem pasty, and washed-out. He was gone. The scene of us standing there was too real and too pointless. I wandered away.

SEAN The girl's name is Candice. I'm standing by the keg with Tony who's giving Getch a long speech on the effects of drinking too much beer and I watch her and block Mitch Allen out of my line of vision. She's dressed too nicely for a Friday night party and out here on Commons lawn she looks classy, really nice, maybe too conservative and uptight in that Jappy sort of way, but also in a good, sexy way, like you look at her and you know she'd be wild in bed or something. At any rate she looks too good for Mitch, who isn't really all that handsome as far as I can tell. He always reminded me of a high school dork who was trying too hard. I wonder if she really likes fucking him. Then I think maybe they're not even fucking. Maybe I can just go over there and start talking to her and maybe she'll accept my offer and tell Mitch that she'll see him later. And thinking about all this is killing me, almost. Down another beer and another Jap, Roxanne, comes over to the keg, and stands next to me. Then this girl is walking away from End of the World, following him. They can't be leaving, I'm thinking, it's too early. But they aren't leaving, they're just walking away from someone. Too early for *what?* I wonder to myself. They'll just go back to his room eventually (she probably has a roommate) and she'll let him fuck her. I'm so horny I'm not even excited, just weak. I look at Roxanne, who I owe lots of money to. She's wearing too much jewelry and looking okay. I wonder if she'll fuck me tonight. If there's even a slight possibility. She's smoking a joint and hands it to me. "What's going on?" she asks.

"Drinking beer," I explain.

"Is it good? Are you drinking a good beer?" she asks.

"Listen," I tell her, getting to the point, "Do you want to go back to my room?"

She laughs, drinks her beer, bats her thickly mascaraed eyelashes and asks me why.

"Old times?" I shrug. I hand her back the joint.

"Old times?" She laughs even harder.

"What's so funny? Jesus."

"No, I don't, Sean," she says. "I have to pick up Rupert anyway." She's still smiling.

The bitch. There's a bug, a moth in her beer. She doesn't see it. I don't say anything.

"Lend me a couple bucks," I ask her.

"I don't have my purse with me," she says.

"Right," I say.

"Oh, Sean. You're still the same," she says, not being mean, but it makes me want to hit her (no, fuck her, then hit her). "I don't know if that's good or bad."

I want her to drink that bug. Where did Candice go, damnit? I look back at Roxanne, who's still got that goddamned smile, thinking to herself, happy that I asked her, happier that she has the power to say no. I look at her and am genuinely repulsed.

"Do you have any morphine?" I ask her.

"Why?" she asks, spotting the bug, pouring the beer out onto the lawn.

"Take some. You look like you could use it," I tell her, walking away.

"I have something for you to pick up, sweetheart," is the last clear thing I hear.

My line was neither quick or effective and I cannot believe I actually saw that girl for a while. It was when she started dealing coke so she could lose weight. It had worked, sort of. I think she still has a fat ass, and can look dumpy, and has dried-out black hair and writes awful poetry and I'm pissed off that I let her get into that position of denying me. I go back to my room and slam the door a couple of times. Rommate's gone, snap on the radio. I pace. "Wild Horses" comes on the local station. I flick the tuner. "Let It Be" is on the next station. On the next is "Ashes to Ashes," then some Springsteen dirge, then Sting crooning "Every Breath You Take," and then when I turn it back to the local station, asshole D.J. announces he's going to play all four sides of Pink Floyd's "The Wall." I don't know what comes over me but I pick the receiver up and hurl it against the closet door, but it doesn't break and I'm grateful even if it is a cheap stereo. I kick it, then grab a box of tapes, unwind one I don't like and smash it with my boot heel. Then I take a crate of singles I own and make sure I have them on tape before I snap them all into two, then, if possible, into four. I kick at the walls on roommate's side and then break a doorknob on the closet door. Then I go back to the party.

LAUREN Me and Judy. Stretching canvas. My studio. Judy just did her nails so she is not really, as one says, into it. So we stop. Another Friday night. She brought two Beck's over and some pot. I like Judy. I do not like mother. Mother called earlier. After dinner. It depressed me so completely that I could only walk around in a stupor and smoke cigarettes until I came down to the studio. My mother had nothing to say to me. My mother had no pressing information to pass on to me. My mother was watching movies on the VCR. My mother is crazy. I asked her about the magazine (she runs it), about my sister at R.I.S.D., about finally (big mistake) my father. She said she didn't hear me. I did not ask her again. Then she mentioned that Joana (father's new girlfriend) is only twenty-five. And since I didn't groan or throw up or try to kill myself, she said that if I approve of what he's doing why don't I just stay with *him* over Christmas. By that time the call had already degenerated so completely I told her that I had a class to go to at midnight and hung up and went to the studio and looked at all the shit, the completely shitty shit I'd been doing all term. I was supposed to be doing the posters for the Shepard play but the dyke who was directing it really bothers me, so maybe I'll give her one of these unfinished pieces of shit. I cry out, "It's all shit! Judy look at this. It's *shit!*"

"No, it's not." But she's not looking.

"You're not looking. Oh god." I open my second pack of the day and it's not even eleven. Last thing I have to worry about is lung or breast cancer. Thank god I'm not on the Pill.

"I'm changing majors," I say. Look at what I've done. Jackson Pollock freed the line, remember that, someone told me in Advanced Painting yesterday. How can I free this shit? I wonder. I stand back from the unfinished canvas. I realize that I would rather spend my money on drugs than on art supplies. "I'm changing my major. Are you listening?"

"Again?" Judy says, all concentration on rolling another joint. She laughs.

"Again? Did you have to say that?"

"Don't make me laugh or else I can't do this."

"This is ridiculous," I say.

"Let's go to the party." Whining. Judy whining.

"Why? We have everything we need here. Warm beer. Music. And even better, no boys."

I change the tape. We have been listening to Compilation Tape #2 we made Freshman year. Bad/Good memories come from it. Michael Jackson ("How many songs off 'Thriller' can you name?" Victor asked me once. I lied and said only two. After that he said he loved me . . . where was that? Wellfleet Drive-in, or were we walking down Commercial Street in Provincetown?), Prince (having sex in the campus van parked outside a Friday night party with good-looking Boy from Brown), Grandmaster Flash (we danced to "The Message" so many times and we never tired). Tape depresses me. Pull it out. Put something else, Reggae Tape #6, in.

"When is Victor coming back?" Judy asks.

I can hear music coming from Commons and End of the World and it sounds tempting. Maybe we should go. Go to party. There was always the book of sexual diseases with gruesome explicit photographs in them (some of the close-ups, pink, blue, purple, red blisters were beautiful in an abstract minimalist sort of way), which always works as a deterrent to a Friday night party. Victor would be a deterrent too. If he was here. We'd probably go to the party and have a good time. Flip through the book. Close-up of girl who was allergic to the plastic in her diaphragm. Yuck. Maybe we would have a good time. I picture poor handsome Victor in Rome or Paris, alone, hungry, somewhere, desperately trying to get in touch with me, maybe even screaming at some mean operator in broken Italian or Yiddish, near tears, trying to reach me. Gasp and lean up against the posts in the studio and then throw head back. Too dramatic.

"Who knows?" I hear myself saying. "What does this stuff remind you of?" I ask her, standing back. "Degas? Seurat? Renoir?"

She looks at the canvas and says, "Scooby Doo."

Okay, it's time for The Pub. Get a pitcher of Genny and if we haven't forgotten to cash a check, maybe some wine coolers to get drunk/sick on, then a pizza or bagel? Judy knows it. I know it. When the going gets tough, the tough go drinking.

So we go to The Pub. Someone has written in black letters Sensory Deprivation Tank on the door and I don't find it funny. Not many people are here because of the party. We get a pitcher and sit in the back. Listen to the jukebox. I think about Victor. A joint left unsmoked is in Judy's bag. And we have the same conversation that we always have on partyless Friday nights in The Pub. Conversations that only recently, now that I'm a Senior, am I tiring of.

J: What's the movie tonight?

Me: *Apocalypse Now?* or *Dawn of the Dead*, maybe. I think.

J: No. Not *again,* god.

Me: So, who are you in love with?

J: Franklin.

Me: I thought you said he was a geek, a bore. Why?

J: There's no one else to like.

Me: You said he was a geek, though.

J: I really like his roommate.

Me: Who's that?

J: Michael.

Me: Why don't you go for Michael?

J: He's maybe gay.

Me: How do you know?

J: I slept with him. He told me he likes boys. I don't think it would work out. He wants to be a ballerina.

Me: If you can't be with the one you love, honey . . .

J: Fuck their roommate instead.

Me: Are we going anywhere or not?

J: No, I don't think so. Not tonight.

Me: What's the movie tonight?

PAUL I first met Sean when I was standing by the keg, watching Mitchell and Candice leave. They walked past me and Mitchell smiled good-night and waved half-heartedly. As did Candice, which I could take as either a kind, pity gesture or as a victorious, gleeful salute. (Victorious? Why? Mitchell would never tell her about me.) I watched them walk away and started to refill my cup. I looked over and remember seeing Dennis Jenkins, this scrawny, ugly dramafag staring at me. (Dennis Jenkins was one of many reasons why I despised being a Drama major). I sighed and told myself that if I went to bed with him tonight I would kill myself in the morning. I finished filling the cup, which was mostly foam since the keg was running out, and when I looked up Sean Bateman was standing there, waiting. I had known Sean like everyone knows everyone else at this place, meaning we had probably never spoken to each other but knew of each other's cliques, and we had mutual acquaintances. He was handsome in a vague, straight way, always spilling beer and playing video games or pinball in The Pub, and I wasn't much interested, at first.

"Hi, Sean," I said. If I hadn't been more than slightly drunk I probably would have said nothing; nodded and walked away. I was fairly sure he was majoring in Mechanics.

"Hi, Paul," he smiled, staring off.

He seemed nervous and I followed his gaze to the darkness of the college, back to the houses on campus. I don't remember, or know, why he was staring off like that. Maybe he was just nervous and too shy to talk to me. Behind him people were leaving End of the World and heading either back home or to The Graveyard.

"Do you know that girl with Mitchell?" he asked, which I took as a lame conversation starter.

"You mean Candice," I said, gritting my teeth. "Her name is Candice."

"Yeah. That's right," he said.

"I was in a class with her but I failed it," I said, getting wistful.

"I was in that class too. So did I," he said, surprised.

In that instant, looking back, mutual rapport was established.

"I didn't ever see you in there," I said, suspiciously.

"That's why I failed it," he admitted; a sheepish smile.

"Oh," I said, nodding.

"I can't believe *you* failed it," he said.

I hadn't failed it. I had actually gotten an incomplete, which I finished over the summer. In fact it was an incredibly easy, undemanding class (Ethnic Chamber Drama) and I was shocked anyone could fail it, whether you showed up or not. But Sean seemed impressed by this and I kept it up.

"Yeah, I failed two others," I said, trying to gauge his reaction.

"You did?" His mouth, the lips were full and red, sexy, maybe sensitive but not really, fell open.

"Yeah." I nodded.

"Boy, I'd never think that *you'd* fail anything," he said, making it sound like a compliment.

"You'd be surprised," I said. The first outright flirting of the conversation. It comes easily at Friday night parties.

"My type of guy," he laughed, self-deprecatingly. Then he remembered that he came for the beer, or had he? He reached for the tap, but it was all gone.

I stood there, looking him over. He was wearing jeans and boots and a white T-shirt and a fairly tacky leather jacket with fur trim: the casual American boy look. And I was thinking it would be quite a coup to get this person into bed. Then I sighed and realized I was being so stoopid. The party was ending and I was getting depressed and the keg was sputtering, so I cleared my throat and said, "Well, see you around."

And then he said the strangest thing. The thing that started it all off. I wasn't that drunk to misunderstand and I was taken aback at such a bold proposition. I didn't ask him to repeat his invitation. I simply rephrased what he had asked me: You wanna get a quesadilla?

"You want to go and get a quesadilla?" I asked. "You want to go out to dinner tomorrow night? Mexican? Casa Miguel?"

And he was so shy, he looked down and said, "Yeah, I guess." He looked bewildered almost. He was hurt. I was touched. The Supremes were singing, "When the Love Light Starts Shining Through His Eyes." And even though it seemed like he wanted to go *now*, we arranged to meet tomorrow night at Casa Miguel in North Camden at seven.

SEAN The party is starting to end and I've had my eye on Candice the whole goddamn time. But the moment comes and she leaves with Mitch and I'm not as upset or surprised as I expected. I am also considerably loaded and that helps. The last people are hanging out, and the last people hanging out at these parties waiting to find someone to go home with always depress me. It reminds me of kids being picked last for teams in high school. It's weak. Really improves one's sense of self-worth. But I don't give a fuck in the end. I walk over to the keg and Paul Denton's standing by it and somehow the keg has run out and Tony's selling bottled beer for two bucks apiece over in his room and I don't want to spend the money and I'm not in any mood to snake it from the guy and I suspect that Denton's got some bucks so I ask him if he wants to go with me and get a case of beer and the guy is so drunk he asks me if I want to have dinner with him tomorrow and I guess I'm drunk too and I say sure even though I don't know why the fuck I'm saying that, confused as hell. I walk away and end up going to bed with Deidre again which is sort of . . . I don't know what it sort of is.

LAUREN Wake up. Saturday morning. Tutorial on the postmodern condition. Believe it or not. At ten. In Dickinson. It's October already and we've only had one session. I doubt there's anyone else in the class. I was the only one at the first meeting a month ago and Conroy was so drunk that he lost the rollsheet. Go up to brunch. Pass Commons lawn. People who've probably been up all night are clearing the debris away. Maybe they are still partying, still having a good time. Eternal End of the World Keg Party? The kegs are being rolled away. Sound equipment packed up. Lights being taken down. Should have gone. Maybe. Maybe not. Stop by Commons. Coffee. No mail from Victor. Walk up to Dickinson. And . . . guess what. Conroy's asleep on the couch in his office. Office reeks of marijuana. Marijuana pipe on desk next to bottle of Scotch. Sit at the desk, not surprised, unfazed and smoke a cigarette, watch Conroy sleep. Getting up? No, he's not. Put the cigarette out. Leave. Victor recommended this course to me.

SEAN I get up early, for a Saturday, sometime after breakfast. I take a shower and kind of remember about this tutorial I happen to be up in time for. I smoke a couple of cigarettes, watch the Frog sleep, pace. I can't believe I have a roommate whose name is Bertrand. I go up to Tishman because there's nothing else to do. Saturdays suck anyway and I've never been to this class so it can't be all that boring. I get to Tishman but it's the wrong building. Then I remember that it might be in Dickinson but I go to the wrong room but then I find the right room even if it looks like the wrong room. It's the teacher's office and there is no one here. I'm not that late either, and I wonder if maybe they've changed rooms. If they have, then I'm dropping this class, I'm not going to put up with that kind of bullshit. The office smells like pot though, so I stick around in case someone comes back with more. I sit at the desk, look for signs of what this class is all about. But I can't find any. So I go back to my room. The Frog is gone. Maybe I'll check out the AA meeting in Bingham, but it's not there and after hanging out in the living room, waiting, smoking, pacing, I go back to my room. Maybe I'll take a ride, go to Manchester. Saturdays suck.

I was in a class yesterday (terminable, because of you) and I noticed Fergus's back (though if it had been your back I would have noticed it sooner) and I wrote to the person next to me (a person I had never seen or witnessed, a person who does not know and does not care about me, a person who would spread her legs for you—perhaps already has, everyone has, everyone has, to me—) that Fergus has a sexy back and she wrote something down and it said "Yeah . . . But look at his face." The simple dumb cruelty of it all! That stupid response made me want to cry out and I thought of you. I left another note in your box, yet another tepid warning of desires in my heart. You probably think that I am a babbling insane creature but I am not. I repeat, I am not. I only want You. There must be something you want from me. If only You knew. These notes I leave are hard to compose. I have refrained desperately from spraying them with my perfume—trying to grab at any of your senses: aural, oral, nasal, etc. After I deliver these notes into your box I clench my teeth and squeeze my eyes shut, my hands feel like terrible claws, a patient in an eternal dentist's chair. It takes courage though. An irritating and tugging courage. The touch of you, or my imagined touching, seems both repellent and oddly succulent. It stings. These feelings sting. My eyes are always ready for you. They want to grapple and lay you down in fluffy white sheets of linen, safe, in your arms, strong arms. I would take you to Arizona and have you meet my mother even. The seeds of love have taken hold and if we won't burn together, I'll burn alone.

PAUL   I didn't make it to Casa Miguel on that Saturday night for that first date in early October. I was in my room getting dressed, so unsatisfied with what I was wearing that

I had changed four times in the space of thirty minutes. It was getting ridiculous and near seven and since I didn't have a car I was going to call a cab. I changed once more, turned off the Smiths tape and was on the verge of leaving when Raymond burst into my room. His face was white and he was panting and he told me, "Harry tried to kill himself."

I knew something like this was going to happen. I just had a feeling that there would be some obstacle, major or minor, that was going to prevent this evening from happening. I had a feeling all day that there would be something that would screw this night up. So I asked, "What do you mean Harry tried to kill himself?" I stayed calm.

"You've got to come to Fels. He's there. Oh shit. Jesus, Paul. We've got to do something." I had never seen Raymond so keyed-up. He looked like he was going to cry and he gave this event (a Freshman suicide? oh, please) a dimension of unwarranted emotion.

"Call Security," I suggested.

"Security?" he yelled. "Security? What in the hell is Security going to do?" He reached for my arm and grabbed it.

"Tell them a Freshman tried to kill himself," I told him. "Believe me, they'll be there within the hour."

"What the hell are you talking about?" he shrieked, still grabbing at me.

"Stop it," I said. "He'll be fine. I have an appointment at seven."

"Will you please come on!" he screamed and pulled me out of the room.

I grabbed my scarf off the coatrack and managed to close my door before I followed him down the stairs and over to Fels. We walked down Harry's hallway and I started getting scared. I was nervous enough about the date with Sean (Sean Bateman—I had whispered the name to myself all day, chanting it almost, in the shower, in my bed, the pillow above my face, between my legs) and even more nervous that I was going to be late and ruin it. *That* put me in more of a panic than this alleged suicide: dumb Freshman Harry trying to off himself. How did he do it, I wondered, heading toward his door, Raymond making weird breathing noises next to me. Try to O.D. on Sudafed and wine coolers? What provoked him? C.D. player conk out on him? Did they cancel "Miami Vice"?

Harry's room was dark. Light came from a small metallic black Tensor lamp on his desk, below a poster of George Michael. Harry was laying on his bed, his eyes closed, wearing typical Freshman garb: Bermudas (in October!), Polo sweater, Hi-Tops, his head lolling back and forth. Donald sat by his side trying to make him throw up into the wastebasket next to the bed.

"I brought Paul," Raymond said, as if that was going to save Harry's life.

He walked over to the bed and looked down.

"What did he take?" I asked, standing in the doorway. I checked my watch.

"We don't know," they both said at the same time.

I walked over to the desk and picked up a half-empty bottle of Dewar's.

"You don't know?" I asked, irritated. I smelled the bottle as if it were a clue.

"Listen, we're taking him to Dunham hospital," Donald said, trying to lift him up.

"That's in fucking Keene!" Raymond shouted.

"Where else *is* there, asshole?" Donald cried out.

"There's a hospital in town," Raymond said, and then, "You imbecile."

"How am I supposed to know these things?" Donald cried out again.

"I have to meet someone at seven," I told him.

"Fuck the meeting. Get your car, Raymond," Donald shouted in one breath, lifting Harry up. Raymond rushed past me and down the hallway. I heard the backdoor of Fels slam.

I went over to the bed and helped Donald lift Harry, who was surprisingly light, from the bed. Donald raised

Harry's arm and for some reason took the cashmere vest he was wearing off and tossed it in the corner.

"What are you doing?" I asked.

"That's my vest. I don't want it ruined," Donald said.

"What are we doing?" Harry coughed.

"See, he's alive," I said, accusingly.

"Oh Jesus," Donald said, shooting me a look. "It'll be okay, Harry," he whispered.

"He seems fine to me. Maybe drunk," I said.

"Paul," Donald said in his maddening lecture tone, seething yet the lips barely moving, "He called me up before dinner and said he was going to kill himself. I came over here after dinner, and look at him. He's obviously taken something."

"What did you take, Harry?" I asked, slapping him a little with my free hand.

"Come on, Harry. Tell Paul what you took," Donald coaxed.

Harry said nothing, just coughed.

We dragged him, reeking of Dewar's, down the hallway. He was passed out and his head hung down limply. We got him outside just as Raymond pulled up in his Saab, next to the backdoor of Fels.

"Why did he do this?" I asked as we tried to get him into the car.

"Donald, you drive," Raymond said, getting out of the Saab and helping us lay him down in the backseat. The motor was running. I was getting a headache.

"I can't drive a stick," Donald said.

"Shit!" Raymond screamed. "Then you sit in back."

I got in the passenger seat and Raymond started moving the car before I could shut my door. "Why did he do it?" I asked again, when we were past the Security gate and halfway down College Drive. I was considering asking them to drop me off in North Camden but I knew they'd never forgive me, so I didn't.

"He found out he was adopted today," Donald said from the backseat.

Harry's head was on his lap and he started coughing again.

"Oh," I said.

We passed the gates. It was dark out and cold. We were going in the opposite direction of North Camden. I checked my watch again. It was a quarter past seven. I pictured Sean sitting alone at the uncrowded bar at Casa Miguel, nursing a frozen Margarita (no, he would never drink that; I pictured some Mexican beer instead), disappointed, and driving back (wait, maybe he didn't have a car, maybe he walked there, oh Jesus) alone. There were very few cars out now. There was a line in front of the Cinemas I & II, townies waiting for the new Chuck Norris film. Housewives and professors' wives walking out of Price Chopper, wheeling carts. Shoppers at the Woolworth's on Main Street, huge shafts of fluorescent light pouring onto the parking lot. The Jam were on the cassette deck and, listening to the music, it struck me how small this town actually was, how little I actually knew about it. I could see the hospital that I had never been to before in the distance. We were almost there, a smallish brick structure that sat next to a vast, empty parking lot, near the end of town. Beyond that, the woods, a forest that stretched for miles. No one was saying anything. We passed a liquor store.

"Could you stop? I need cigarettes," I said, checking my pockets.

"Can I remind you that we have someone O.D.ing in the backseat?" Donald said.

Raymond was hunched over the wheel, looking worried, like he could use a cigarette and was seriously considering it.

I ignored Donald and said, "It'll just take a minute."

"No," Raymond said, though he seemed unsure.

"He's not O.D.ing," I said, almost furious, thinking about an empty bar in North Camden. "He's just a Freshman. Freshmen don't O.D."

"Fuck you!" Donald said. "Oh shit, he's throwing up. He's gonna throw up."

We could hear the retching sounds in the darkness of the

Saab and I turned around to get a better look. Harry was still coughing and looked sweaty.

"Open the window," Raymond screamed. "Open the fucking window!"

"You two should really calm down. He's not throwing up," I said, pissed-off but sad.

"He's gonna throw up. I just know it," Donald was shouting.

"What do you call that sound?" Raymond inquired about the retching, shouting at me.

"Dry heaves?" I shouted back.

Harry started to mumble to himself, then he started to retch again.

"Oh no," Donald said, trying to lift Harry's head up to the window. "He's going to throw up again!"

"Good," Raymond shouted back. "It's good if he throws up. Let him throw up."

"I can't believe you two," I said. "Can I change this tape?"

Raymond drove up to the Emergency entrance and stopped the car with a screech. We all got out and pulled Harry from the backseat and with his feet dragging carried him to the front desk. The place was empty. Muzak was coming from invisible speakers on the ceiling. A young fat nurse looked at us and smirked, probably thinking, oh boy, another Camden College prank. "Yes?" she asked, not looking at Harry.

"This guy's O.D.ing," Raymond said, walking over to the desk, leaving Harry in Donald's clutches.

"O.D.ing?" she asked, getting up.

Then the doctor on duty came out. He looked like Jack Elam, some old fat guy with thick glasses, mumbling to himself. Donald lay Harry on the floor. "Thank God," Raymond murmured, in a way that sounded like he was relieved this whole situation was in someone else's hands and not his. The doctor leaned over to check Harry's vital signs. I knew the guy was a quack when he didn't ask any of us anything. None of us said a word. It irritated me that Raymond and Donald not only made me miss this all-important meeting but also that they were wearing the same long wool jacket I was wearing. I had bought mine first at the Salvation Army store in town for thirty dollars. It was Loden wool. Then the next day the two of them ran down and bought the two remaining, probably donated by someone on the faculty who was going West, to teach in California or somwhere. The doctor grunted and raised Harry's eyelids. Harry laughed a little, then jerked around and lay still.

"Will you get him into the Emergency room." Raymond's face was red. "Hurry. Isn't there anyone else here?" He looked around, frantic in a practiced way. Like someone who's worried, but not really, about getting into Palladium or something.

The doctor ignored him. His shock of gray-white hair was unsuccessfully greased back and stiff, and he kept grunting. He checked Harry's pulse, found nothing, and then unbuttoned Harry's shirt and placed the stethoscope to his tan, bony chest. We all stood there in the empty hospital. The doctor checked the pulse again and grunted. Harry was moving around a little, a drunken smile on his young Freshman face. The doctor checked for a heartbeat, for any sign. He used the stethoscope again. The doctor finally looked at the three of us and said, "I'm not getting any pulse."

Donald threw a hand over his mouth and backed into the wall behind him.

"He's dead?" Raymond asked, disbelieving. "Is this a joke?"

"Oh shit, I can see him moving," I said, pointing at the rise and fall of his chest. "He's not dead. I can see him breathing."

"He's dead, Paul. Shut up! I knew it. I knew it!" Donald said.

"I'm sorry about this, boys," the doctor said, shaking his head. "How did this happen?"

"Oh God," Donald wailed.

"Shut up before I slap you," I told him. "*Look*. He's not dead."

"Boys, I'm not getting a heartbeat or a pulse. The pupils look dilated to me." The doctor wheezed with the strain of getting up, and pointing at Harry, "That boy's dead."

None of us said anything. I looked over at Raymond, who wasn't looking too worried anymore, and he gave me a glance that said this-quack-is-a-fucking-lunatic-let's-get-the-hell-out-of-here. Donald was still upset, his back facing us. The nurse was looking over the desk, disinterested.

"I don't know what to tell you boys," the doctor said. "But your friend is dead. He's simply not alive."

Harry opened his eyes and asked, "I'm not dead am I?"

Donald screamed.

"Yes, you are," Raymond said. "Shut up."

The doctor didn't seem too shocked by Harry's state and grunted as he knelt down next to Harry and took his pulse again. "I'm telling you, there's no pulse. This boy is *dead*." He was saying this even though Harry's eyes were open, blinking. The doctor used his stethoscope once more. "I'm not getting anything."

"Wait a minute," I said. "Uh, listen. Doctor. I think we're going to take our friend home, okay?" I approached him cautiously. I knew we were in Hospital Hell or somewhere similar. "Is that, like, okay, with you?"

"Am I dead?" Harry asked, suddenly looking better, cracking up.

"Tell him to shut up!" Donald screamed.

"I'm pretty sure your friend is dead," the doctor grunted, a little confused. "Maybe you want me to run some tests."

"No!" Raymond and I said at the same time. We stood there watching the supposedly dead Freshman, Harry, laugh. We said nothing. Even though Dr. Phibes kept insisting he wanted to run some tests on "your friend's corpse," we finally took the Freshman home, but Donald wouldn't sit in the backseat with him. It was almost eight-thirty by the time we got back to campus. I had blown it.

SEAN Today, I hang out, ride my motorcycle into town, walk around, buy a couple of tapes, then come back to Booth and watch *Planet of the Apes* on Getch's VCR. I love the scene where an ape bullet has made Charlton Heston mute. He escapes and frantically runs around Ape City and as the net closes over his head he is raised triumphantly by The Gorillas and he finds his voice and screams, "Get your stinkin' hands off me you damn dirty apes!" I've always liked that scene. It reminds me of nightmares I had in elementary school or something. Then, when I'm about to take a shower, I find the Duke of Disease (gross grad of '78 or '79) doing his friggin laundry in my bathroom. And he doesn't even go to school here. Just visiting an old teacher. I have to run after the asshole with a can of Lysol. I get another note in my box after dinner tonight. They don't say anything really except, like, "I love you" or "You're Sexy," stuff like that. I used to think they were jokes that Tony or Getch were putting in my box, but there's been too many of them to take as a joke. Someone is *seriously* interested in me. My interest has *definitely* been aroused.

Then it's back in Booth after dinner watching TV in Getch's room and some tall greasy-haired hippie turned professional-college-student-type named Dan, who had been fucking Candice last term, is there talking to Tony. Anyway, it's about eight-thirty and the room is cold and I feel feverish. Tony and this guy get into a heated argument about politics or something. It's frightening. Tony, in a pre-drunken state, is pissed off that his point was lost, and Dan, smelling like some twenty-year-old unwashed rug, keeps referring to leftist writers and calling the N.Y.C. police force "Nazis." I tell him that I was once beaten up by the city police. He smiles and says, "Here's a case in point." I was joking. I feel weird, my body aches. I watch people argue about Nazis. I enjoy it. Saturdays suck.

Now, I'm at the party and I can't find Candice, so I hang around, by the keg, talk to the D.J. Go to the bathroom but some asshole has thrown up all over the floor and I'm about to leave when I bump into Paul Denton, who's walking down the hallway, and I vaguely remember talking to him last night, and I nod to him as I'm walking away from the vomit-covered toilet, but he walks up to me and says, "Oh, I'm so sorry about tonight."

"Yeah," I say. "I'm sorry."

"Did you stay?" he asks me.

"Stay? Yeah," I say. Whatever. "I stayed."

"God, I'm really sorry," he says.

"Listen, it's okay. It really is," I tell him.

"I've got to make it up to you," he's telling me.

"Okay. Sure," I say. "I've gotta take a leak, okay?"

"Oh sure. I'll wait," he smiles.

After pissing off the vomit from the toilet seat I head back down the hall and Denton's still standing there with a fresh beer for me. I thank him, what else can I do, and we walk back to the living room where these asshole frat guys from Dartmouth have crashed the party. I have no idea how the fuck they got onto campus. Security must have let them in as a joke. So these stupid rich frat guys all dressed up in Brooks Brothers come up to me while I'm waiting for Denton to get another beer and one of them asks me, "What's going on?"

"Not much," I tell him. It's the truth.

"Where's that Dressed To Get Screwed party?" one of them asks.

"That's not until later," I tell him.

"Tonight?" the same one asks.

"Next term," I lie.

"Oh shit man. We thought *this* was The Dressed To Get Screwed party," they say, really disappointed.

"It looks like a Halloween party if you ask me," one of them says.

"Freaks," one of them says, looking around, shaking his head. "Freaks."

"Sorry, guys," I say.

Denton comes back with a beer and hands it to me and we all talk. They get really excited when the D.J. spins old

Sam Cooke and one of them grabs a not-bad-looking Freshman and dances with her when "Twisting the Night Away" comes on. It makes me sick. The remaining Dartmouth jerks do a little frat handshake. They're all wearing green for some reason. Denton's looking at them closely and asks, "Aren't you all a little far away?"

"It's not that far a ride," one of them says.

Then Denton asks, "Well, what's it like on the outside?"

It's pretty weak that Denton's even acknowledging these jerks but I don't say anything.

"It's cool," one of them says, eyeing some ugly girl. Our student body president.

"You guys are really in the middle of nowhere," one of the more brilliant ones says.

Denton laughs and says, "Kind of."

"Hanover's a real sprawling metropolis," I mutter loudly.

"I swear this looks like a fuckin' Halloween party," one of them says again and they're pissing me off and okay, maybe it does look like one but it doesn't give these assholes any right, so I have to tell them, "No, it's not a Halloween party. It's the Get Fucked party."

"Oh yeah?" They all raise their eyes up and nudge each other. "We're ready."

"Yeah. Bend over and get fucked," I find myself saying.

They look at me like I'm crazy and walk off telling me how "perverted" I am. I don't even know why I bothered to say that. I look over at Denton and he's laughing, but when he sees that I'm not, he stops. It gets late and Candice is nowhere to be found and the keg runs out. Denton says why don't we go to his room since he has beer there. And I'm a little wasted so I say why not. I make sure I bring the pot I picked up earlier this afternoon when I was at Roxanne's scoring for some Freshman girls in McCullough. We leave the party and head for Welling.

PAUL   After we returned from our little excursion to the hospital, I went back to my room and wondered what I should do. I first called Casa Miguel and had Sean paged. He wasn't there. He had already left. I sat on my bed and smoked a couple of cigarettes. I then went to The Pub, cautiously at first. I didn't look around the room until I had made my way to the bar. Harry was already there, recovered, getting even more smashed by the jukebox with David Van Pelt. I got a beer, but didn't drink it, then followed some people over to Booth (it was getting too cold for parties at End of the World) to confront Sean. It was a party, after all.

The party was in full-swing when I got there. Raymond was standing around but I didn't want to talk to him. He came over anyway and asked if I wanted a drink.

"Yeah." I craned my neck to look over the dance floor.

"What do you want? I know the bartender."

"Rum and anything."

He walked off and then I spotted Sean. From where I stood in the darkened living room of Booth I could see him in the light coming from the bathroom down the hallway. He was standing in the doorway and had a beer in one hand and a cigarette in the other and he was trying to kick something off his boot. He saw me for an instant and then shyly turned away. I was feeling guilty about our meeting last night—telling him I had failed three classes last term. I only told him that because I thought he was great-looking and I wanted to sleep with him. I hadn't failed any classes that term. (Sean later admitted to me that he had failed all four. In fact, I couldn't imagine anyone failing not only four classes at Camden, but even one. I guess the thought seemed so irrational to me that I found him even more attractive in some perverse way.) He had been coming on to me the night before, there was no doubt about that and that's all that really mattered. From where I stood he looked a little like a rock star caught unknowingly in a video. Maybe a little like Bryan Adams (without the acne scars, though, sometimes, admittedly, that can be sexy). I went over to him and told him how sorry I was.

"Yeah," he said, looking modestly at the ground, still trying to kick something off his boots. I wondered suddenly if he was Catholic. My spirits rose: Catholic boys will usually do anything. "I'm sorry too."

"Did you stay there?" I asked him.

"Stay there? Yeah, I guess," he admitted, embarrassed, confused. "I stayed."

"I'm really, really sorry," I said.

"Oh, don't worry about it. It's okay. Some other time," he said.

I felt so shitty about ruining his date that a rush of sympathy (or horniness: the two were interchangeable) went through me and I said, "I'll make it up to you."

"You don't have to," he said, though you could tell he had not wanted to say that.

"I know I don't, but I want to. I really insist."

He looked down and said he had to use the restroom and I said I'd wait.

I wondered if we were going to sleep together tonight, but then I tried to push the thought away and pretended to be rational about the whole thing. In the meantime, four gorgeous Dartmouth guys came into the party. When I went back to the keg to get another beer for Sean (if nothing else, I was going to succeed in getting him drunk) they all walked over to him and started a conversation. Jealously I hurried back. When I handed him the beer, almost protectively, the one that was the best-looking went off dancing with the student body president ("The Vagina Lady," Raymond always seemed to call her). The Dartmouth boys thought that this was the annual Dressed To Get Screwed party and they were quite disappointed that they had driven all the way from Hanover to come to the Camden Early Halloween Ball. They said this sarcastically and I thought it was a little mean. But I asked them, flirtatiously, "Aren't you all a little far away?"

"It's really not all that far away, I guess," the blond said.

"So, what's going on in the real world?" I asked, laughing.

"It's cool," the one with a slight double-chin said.

"The same stuff," another one said.

"You guys are kind of in the middle of nowhere, aren't you?" the blond asked. They were all looking at the dance floor, nodding their heads.

"Kind of," I said.

Then Sean made some rude comment that I couldn't hear. I realized then that I was making Sean jealous by talking to these guys, so I immediately stopped talking to them. But it was too late. He was so jealous that he ended up telling them off. He told them it was the Get Fucked party and that they should bend over and get fucked. I hoped I wasn't playing too hard to get, but it was sort of erotic to hear him say that, yet I still showed no emotion. I was afraid that the Dartmouth guys were going to beat him (actually, me) up but they just walked away, too stunned to say anything, their suspicions about this place confirmed by Sean's brash actions. After a while, when it was nearing midnight, I asked him if he wanted to come by my room. I had asked Raymond to stop at Price Chopper on the way back from the hospital so I could pick up a six-pack, especially for this occasion. But I wasn't sure if we'd even get around to drinking it since he was fairly drunk by now anyway. I first made sure he was interested by asking him if he wanted to go to his room first.

"We could," he said. "My roommate's gone a lot. His girlfriend lives off-campus, so he's there a lot." He was slurring his words. He bumped into someone's drink, oblivious.

"Do you have any alcohol?" I asked, laughing.

"I have alcohol?" he asked himself. "Do I?"

"You do?" I asked.

"I don't . . . have any," he said, starting to laugh also.

"Let's go to my room," I said. "I have beer."

We walked out of Booth, past the Dartmouth guys. Someone had stuck pieces of paper with the word "Asshole" on them to their backs. We started for Welling.

"Are you a Catholic?" I asked him.

We walked a little while before he finally answered. "I don't remember."

LAUREN I don't know why I sleep with Franklin. Maybe it's because Judy likes him, or is just sleeping with him, occasionally. Maybe it's because he's tall and has brown hair and reminds me of Victor. Maybe it's because we're at a Sunday night party and it's dark and I'm bored but what am I doing at Booth anyway. I should know better. Maybe it's because Judy went to the movies over in Manchester. Maybe it's because when I asked the boy from L.A. after poetry class to meet me at the Beverage Center at dinner tonight he didn't show and when I saw him later at Booth he told me he thought I meant the Beverly Center. I don't know. Maybe it's because Franklin's . . . just *there*. But he's not the only possibility. There's the cute French guy who comes up to me and tells me he's in love with me. But he also reminds me that maybe I should go to Europe and just find Victor and bring him back home. But then what would that do? We talk, Franklin and me. But not about much. Some great-looking but utterly bland

Dartmouth guys crash the party (How can you tell they're from Dartmouth? Franklin asks. They're wearing green, I explain. Franklin nods, impressed, and wonders what our school color is. Easy, I guess. Black.) I really hope (but not really) that Judy comes back so I won't end up doing this. We dance to a couple of oldies. He pays for drinks he brings me. When he sweats he's really handsome. What am I talking about? This is Judy's geek. But then I get mad at him: what a jerk to cheat on Judy like this. But I get drunk and too tired to argue and I crumple into his arms and he doesn't quite know what to do with me. I decide to leave it all up to him. We walk back to his room. How easy this all is. Will Judy ever know? Will she even care? Doesn't she like his roommate instead? Michael? That's right. I look over at Michael's side of the room: a fern, Hockney print, poster of Mikhail Baryshnikov. Definitely not for you, Judy. Forget him. It makes me remember a boy I was in love with last term, part of last summer. B.V. The time Before Victor. And maybe *that's* why I go to bed with Judy's lover. But she should have been here to stop him. And maybe he shouldn't have touched my neck that way, a cruel but familiar sensation. Even before he's in me I know that I will never sleep with him again. And maybe Franklin reminds me of that lost boyfriend, which is good but maybe bad and now we're in bed, actually on the bed.

"What about Judy?" I ask, reaching back and feeling the knots and blades in his shoulders.

"She's in Manchester." He has strong fingers.

It seems a sufficient answer.

PAUL   I used the dead best friend story. It seemed better than using the girlfriend with cancer story or the favorite aunt who committed suicide after the favorite uncle died story, both of which seemed overly melodramatic. I told him about "Tim" who died in a "car accident" on a "road near Concord" killed by "a drunken gas station attendant." I told him this after we finished the first beer, when I was adequately drunk.

He said, "Gee, I'm sorry."

I kept my head lowered, tingling with excitement. "It's so terrible," I said.

He agreed, excused himself for a minute to go to the restroom.

I bolted up and checked myself in the mirror then took one of his cigarettes that were lying on my desk, a Parliament. Then I sat back down in a suitable, casual position on the bed and turned on the radio. Nothing good was on so I put a tape in. When he came back he asked me if I wanted to smoke some pot with him. I told him no, but that it was okay if he wanted some. He sat in the chair next to the bed. I was sitting on the edge of the bed. Our knees touched.

"Where did you spend your summer?" I asked.

"Oh, last summer?" he said, lighting the small pipe with a lighter that barely worked.

"Yeah."

"Berlin."

"Really?" I was impressed. He'd been to Europe.

"Yeah. It was okay," he said, looking for another lighter.

"How are the clubs there?" I asked, reaching into my pocket. I handed him some matches.

"Good, I guess," he laughed and sucked in on the pipe. "Clubs?"

"Yeah? Do you speak German?" I asked.

"German? No," he said, laughing. His eyes were very red. He took his jacket off.

"You don't?"

"No. Why?"

"Well, I just assumed since you spent the summer in Berlin, I thought . . ." my voice trailed off and I smiled.

"No. Berlin, New Hampshire." He was studying the pipe; he sniffed it, then filled it with more pot. It smelled bad, I thought.

"There's a Berlin here?" I asked.

"Sure is," he said.

I watched him refill the pipe, inhale, then hand the pipe to me. I shook my head and pointed at the Beck's in my hand. He smiled, scratched at his arm and let out a thick stream of smoke. I had only my desk light on so it was dark in the room and beginning to get hazy, dreamlike, smokey. I watched his growing intensity as he refilled the pipe, his fingers delicately fingering what looked like dried moss to me. (He assured me it was "top grade weed.") And it struck me then, that I liked Sean because he looked, well, slutty. A boy who had been around. A boy who couldn't remember if he was Catholic or not. That appealed to something basic in me though I didn't know what.

I took another Parliament and asked him to sit on the bed.

"I have to go to the restroom first," he smiled shyly and left.

I took my jacket off and put another tape into the cassette player. Then I decided to take my shoes off. I checked myself in the mirror once more and ran a hand through my hair. I opened another beer even though I didn't need it. He came back five minutes later. What was he doing in there, I wondered.

"What took you so long?" I asked.

He stood there and closed the door, then leaned against it for balance.

"I had to make a phone call." He started to laugh.

"To who?" I asked, smiling.

"To Jerry," he said.

"Jerry who?" I asked.

"Jerry Garcia," he said, still smiling.

"Who's Jerry Garcia?" I asked. His roommate? "Does he live in Booth?"

He didn't say anything and stopped smiling. Was he a lover? What?

"I'm just fucking with your mind," he said, whispered actually.

There was a long silence. I drank the beer. We listened to the music. I started to shake. Finally I said, "I didn't expect you to come."

"I didn't either," he said, confused, shrugging.

"Come here." I motioned for him.

He looked down. He touched the back of his neck.

"Come here," I said, patting the bed.

"Um, let's talk for a little while. What did you get on your S.A.T.s?" He was nervous and shy and I didn't like feeling as if I was the instigator.

"Come *here*," I urged.

He started moving toward the bed, slowly.

"Um," he started nervously. "What do you think about . . . nuclear weapons? Nuclear war?"

"Here." I moved over so there was room but not too much.

Something romantic was on the tape. I forget what it was exactly, maybe Echo and the Bunnymen or "Save a Prayer" but it was something that sounded lush and slow and appropriate. He sat down next to me. And I looked at him and said, "You're no different. You're just like me, right?" I was still shaking. So was he. My voice trembled. He didn't say anything.

"You're no different," I said again. It wasn't a question anymore. I leaned closer. He smelled like pot and beer and his eyes were watery and bloodshot. He looked at his boot, turned to me, then looked down again. Our faces were almost touching and then I kissed the side of his mouth and pulled back, waiting for a reaction. He was still looking at his boots. I touched his leg. He was breathing hard. Our eyes met for something like five seconds. The music seemed to be getting louder. My face felt hot and red. I moved my hand up. He spread his legs slightly and he looked at me, daring. I kissed him again. His eyes closed.

"Don't pretend we're not doing this," I told him.

I moved my hand up the denim, unsure if it was at his knee or thigh or close to his crotch. I leaned over slowly. "Come here," I said. I tried to kiss him again. He moved back. I moved closer. He moved his head a little towards me, eyes on the ground. And then his mouth was on mine. He stopped and breathed in and then kissed harder this time. Then we both leaned back, flat, on the bed, him slightly on top of me. We kept kissing. I could hear a toilet flushing, then footsteps padding down the hallway. I raised one of my legs carefully, then reached down and unbuttoned his jeans, then pushed my hand underneath his shirt. His body was thin and tight and he was moving on top of me. His pants and underwear pulled halfway down, mine also, rubbing against each other, our hands interrupting occasionally, hands we had licked or spit on. The springs in the mattress squeaked rhythmically as our bodies moved together in the darkness. I kissed his hair, the top of his head. The springs and our breathing, which came in hard sighs and gasps, were the only sounds in the room once the tape clicked off. We came together, or close enough, and lay like that for a long time, barely moving.

SEAN Go to Denton's room. We drink some cold ones and smoke some pot and talk but I can't deal with the friend's death story and the Duran Duran music and his weirdo stares so we talk a little while longer and I get wasted. Then I leave and wander around campus. There's a keg in Stokes, since the party in Booth died. See some graffiti written about myself in the bathroom and make an attempt to remember if it's true. The guy from L.A. is standing in the hallway wearing shorts and sunglasses and a Polo shirt. He doesn't smile when I pass him by, just says, "Hey dude." One of the girls I scored for earlier, who has short spiked hair and who wears a lot of black kohl and who's holding her pet snake named Brian Eno, leaning against a lava lamp, calls me over, and we talk about the snake. Her friends join us, all on Ecstasy, but they don't have any left. I'm too wasted to complain. Getch is there radically stoned and tells me that kids who die of crib death are the smart ones, since they have an intuition of how terrible life is and choose this option out. I ask him who passed this info his way. The music's really loud and I'm not sure whether he tells me it was Freud or Tony. I leave, walk around campus, look for cigarettes, look for Deidre, for Candice, even Susan. Then I'm in Marc's room, but he's left, gone, history, vapor.

LAUREN Laying in bed. Franklin's room. He's asleep. Not a good idea. Judy could enter any second. I should leave before gay roommate comes back and I can't stop thinking about you Victor. Dear, dear Victor, I'm in the arms of someone else tonight. I remember a night last term. It was a Wednesday and there you were sitting in your room, writing your silly paper for a silly class, and I was sorry about being the cause of a delay in your essay. Oh Victor, life is weird. I was typing in your room and I was misspelling so many words but I didn't want to interrupt and annoy you with correcting things over each other. Oh my God. That sounds like a profundity to me! Life is like a typographical error: we're constantly writing and rewriting things over each other. Are you the same here as when you're in Europe? I wonder. Last summer you told me you would be. It would upset me terribly if you weren't; if I was there with you and you were off on some other planet somewhere. That would not be good. You wanted to get pizza and not go to the Wet Wednesday party in Welling that night, because you wanted to catch "Dynasty" and the Letterman show. I remember that night very well. I kept staring at your *Diva* poster. I should have never gotten semi-drunk halfway. It was a bummer. I really liked the song that was playing. That was really wonderful that you were listening to that tape I made for you all on your own, of bands from Paris, but remembering that song depresses me, especially since there is a Frenchman somewhere in Booth who's in love with me. Oh Victor, I miss you. That night last term when you didn't want to go to the party and I did because there was a boy there I was in love with and still seeing and you said he was a fag so it didn't count and you were half-right but I didn't care. I smoked cigarettes instead.

"Do you have a match?" I asked you.

You shuffled through a very nice leather jacket. "Yeah." Threw matches at me.

"Thanks," I said and turned back to the typewriter to write a seemingly meaningless note to you. You. You, who was busy scribbling nonsequiturs to a black man that always wore sunglasses that reflect your eyes even if it was storming outside. What class was that? Electronic Jazz?

Hmmmm, I thought, what are those papers on your desk, upside down? But being that I respected your privacy I didn't touch them or ask about them. I'm sure you didn't want me to know about their existence anyway. There was a roll of toilet paper on your desk, a Baggie full of excellent Hawaiian pot, and a copy of *The Book of Rock Lists*. I wondered what it all meant. I was running out of paper. Perhaps I should have asked if you were going to be done soon but I just stared at you instead.

"What do you want?" you asked as I stared at you, checking on your progress.

"Paper," I said, not wanting to stop your train of thought.

"Here," you tossed me a piece of composition paper.

"Are you almost finished?" I questioned.

"What time is it?" you asked, realizing that you told me you'd be done by ten.

"You have one minute left," I told you.

"Shit," you said.

So went our days, Victor. It always seemed that there was just one minute left, all the time. . . . That doesn't make any sense, especially since we don't often do, well, I guess that that might be wrong and, well. . . .

(Oh Jesus, me and Franklin, what about Judy? This is not good.)

Well . . . perhaps I shouldn't place value judgemints. Paul got very angry at me once because I couldn't spell judgemint (see?) Shit. Juhgment. That's wrong too. Actually, now I understand why he got angry. Jaime was reading the letter and I knew you were in love with her and not with me (though you would be by summer) and you could have cared less if I went out with the fag or not. Jaime asked who the letter was for. I told her it was for you. Jaime was a slut. That's my opinion. She's a . . . well, forget it. It isn't worth it. I am very tired. That's what I am. Tired of everything. Anyway, dear Victor this is enough. I'm going to stop thinking about you. I never signed that letter. I never even gave it to you. Don't remember what it even said. I just hope you remember who I am. Don't you forget about me. . . .

How tense sounding, I think of myself. I look over at Franklin.

Immobile, unmoving, I spend the rest of the night with him, in bed.

But I do not go up to breakfast with him.

BERTRAND Je ne pouvais m'empêcher de m'approcher de toi à la soirée. J'ai bu trop de tequila et j'ai peut-être fumé trop de pot mais ça ne veut pas dire que je ne t'aime pas. Cependant après te l'avoir dit, j'ai marché jusqu'à la fin du monde et j'ai vomi. Hier nous nous sommes séparés avec Beba, ma petite amie. Toi, tu étais une des raisons pour ça (alors Beba ne sait pas que je te désire) mais pas la seule. C'est que depuis longtemps que je me sens séduit par toi. Je ne suis pas fou, mais tu m'intéresse et j'ai pris quelque photos de toi que j'ai fait quand tu ne regardais pas. Je ne peux pas croire que tu ne m'as pas remarqué. Si tu étais venue avec moi hier soir, je t'aurais rendue heureuse. J'aurais pu te rendre très heureuse. Et j'aurais pu te rendre plus heureuse que ce type avec qui tu es partie hier soir. En mettant les choses au pis je pourrais toujours retourner à Paris et vivre avec mon père. De toute façon, L'Amérique est chiante. Toi et moi faisant l'amour dans la villa de mon père à Cannes. Et quitter mon boulot de redacteur à *Camden Courier*. Peut-être as-tu vu mes articles? "Comment prévenir le Herpes" et "Les effets positifs de l'extase." Tu ne m'obsède pas. Je pourrais avoir n'importe quelle fille que je veux ici (et j'y ai passé près), mais tes jambes sont parfaites, meilleures que toutes celles des autres filles et tes cheveux sont si blonds et doux, meilleurs encore de tous et ta figure est parfaite elle-aussi. Je ne sais pas si tu as eu une opération de nez mais ton nez est parfait. Tes traits sont vraiment parfaits. Je vais peut-être essayer encore une fois. Mais ne pars pas la prochaine fois. Rappelle-toi que je pourrais te rendre très heureuse. Je sais bien baiser et j'ai la Carte American Express de platine. Je suppose que tu l'as aussi. Tes jambes sont splendides, et meilleures que celles de toute autre fille. De quelle couleur sont tes yeux? Les photos que j'ai prises sont toutes en noir et blanc. Je voudrais suivre les mêmes cours que toi, mais je fais de la photo et toi . . . quoi? Les beaux-art? Tu es sexy. Si je savais que quelqu'un s'est épris de toi comme moi, et toi, tu éprouvais le même sentiment envers lui, je partirais. Je rentrerais chez moi. Aucun doute.

PAUL The days went by so quickly that time seemed to stop. During the next weeks I was only with him. I stopped going to Acting II, Improv Workshop, Set-Building, and

Genetics. None of them made a difference anyway. At least not in the way he did. I was in a dreamlike trance but it was tension-filled and satisfying. I was always smiling, looking like a perpetual drunk even though I quit drinking as much beer as I usually consumed since I did not want to obtain a beer-belly. I drank vodka instead.

What did the two of us do? I mostly hung out with him and no one else. I didn't introduce him to Raymond or Donald or Harry and he didn't introduce me to his friends. He taught me how to play Quarters and I learned how to flip that coin with such skill and dexterity into those plastic cups filled with keg beer that when we would play, either with Tony or just alone, he would end up getting smashed and I'd sit there slightly sober, sipping warm Absolut, staring. And he would be shocked that I had caught on so quickly and he would practice alone to keep up with me.

It was a time when I would notice old lovers at parties and not squirm, since I felt so confident about this new romance. Whenever I would pass one by in Commons or at a party or when Sean and I were in town or sitting by the End of the World watching fall turn into winter, I wouldn't blush or look away. I would nod a hello, smile, and go back to whatever I was doing without flinching. At parties when I helped Recreation Committee set up (only doing it because of Sean) by rolling kegs in and setting the speakers up, I wouldn't flirt or even want to look at anyone else. Not that I wouldn't notice people I had slept with. No, they seemed to stand out even more, and I was only relieved that I wasn't with them, but that I was with Sean instead.

Since his roommate Bertrand ("a stuck-up Frog," he'd say) was either shopping in New York on weekends or over at his girlfriend's place off-campus, we had the room to ourselves, which was good and bad. Good, since it was in a house where there was usually a party, any party, on any night of the week and so it was nice to get drunk in Booth, in the living room, or if it wasn't snowing or raining or cold, out by the front porch, then walk up the stairs to that room at the end of the hall. It was also bad because he was afraid people would hear us so he would get paranoid and have to drink a lot more before even any sort of foreplay could be initiated.

After sex (during sex he was crazed, an untamed animal, it was almost scary) we would both be starving and then we'd drive on his motorcycle to Price Chopper. He always had an extra helmet. I'd put my arms around his firm slim waist and he'd race down College Drive toward the market. Once there he would play a few games of Joust at the video machines near the front door and I'd buy the sliced cheese, the bad salami he liked a lot, the rye bread for him, the whole grain wheat for me, and, if it was before two, the inevitable six-pack of Genny or Bud. I liked Beck's but he said it was too expensive and he didn't have enough money. Most of the time he liked to shoplift. He loved to do it so much that I would have to calm him down. We'd only do it in the middle of the night when no one was there, just one checkout line open and the nightshift boys unpacking canned goods in back, with Rush coming from the speakers that during the day carried Muzak. I'd be wearing my long Loden wool coat I got at the Salvation Army in town and he'd be wearing his leather jacket with the tacky fur trim that had a surprising amount of pocket room and we'd pass through the checkout line without any hassling, my coat and his jacket weighed down with cigarettes, bottles of wine, Häagen Dazs ice cream, shampoo, and he would stop, just to be daring, and buy one piece of Bazooka gum. One night I saw an old lady who was too thin and who barely had any hair left and she was sorting out coupons and I almost didn't want to steal the Swiss Chocolate Almond Häagen Dazs and the Ben & Jerry's Heath Bar Crunch but Sean wanted it so badly that I couldn't say no, since he stood there, defiant, sexy in tight jeans, his jaw set, his hair shiny but matted with sweat due to our lovemaking and casually tousled. How could I say no?

He didn't tell me a lot about himself but I wasn't particularly interested in his background anyway. We'd either get drunk at The Pub on campus (sometimes we'd go there after dinner and stay until we closed the place) or we'd drive to The Carousel on Route 9 and sit and drink alone at the bar and those were the only times he'd say anything. He told me all about growing up in the South and that his parents were farmers and that he had no brothers, a couple of sisters and that he was on financial aid and that he was majoring in Literature, which was strange since there were no books in his room. It was also strange that he was from the South since he didn't have a trace of an accent. But these weren't the things I liked about him. His body wasn't as nice as Mitchell's, which had been systematically worked out, and last summer, in New York, he had gone to a tanning salon so his skin color was a combination of pink and brown, except for the shocking whiteness where his underwear had blocked out the ultraviolet rays. Sean's body was different. It was in good, solid condition (probably from working on the farm as a boy) with barely any hair (a little on his chest) and hung well (well hung? I never knew how to use that expression anyway). He had. brownish wavy hair he parted to one side that could of used some mousse but I didn't press it.

I liked him for his motorcycle too. Even though I had grown up in Chicago I had never ridden one before and the first time I had been on one with him I laughed my head off, dizzy with excitement, the danger of it amusing me. I liked the way we fit on it, sometimes my hands on his thighs, often below, and he wouldn't say anything, just drive faster. He drove like a madman anyway, through lights, through stop signs, going around corners in the rain at what seemed like eighty miles an hour. I didn't care. I would just hold on tighter. And after that, riding drunk on the way back to campus from drinking at The Carousel in the windy New England night, he would pull up to the Security gate and wait for the guards to let us in. He would act as sober as possible, which really didn't matter since he knew all the Security guards anyway (I've found that people on financial aid usually do). We would go to his room or my room if the Frog was in, he'd fall on my bed, kicking off his boots and telling me I can do anything I want. He didn't care.

STUART What would he do if I came over one night with a bottle of wine or some pot and said, "Let's have an affair?" I have moved to Welling House, across from Paul Denton's room.

Dennis was the one who really pushed the move on me since he couldn't stand the awful Freshman yuppie roommate I had been stuck with, even though I was a Senior, since I had forgotten to tell them I was coming back last term. Luckily I was first on the waiting list for a single, so when Sara Dean left because of her "urinary tract infection" or "mono" (depending on who you ask, since everybody in the world knew she had an abortion and freaked) I moved in immediately. Unfortunately, so did Dennis, who lived off-campus but who was too much of an alcoholic to walk (driving was out of the question) home after parties and long nights at The Pub, so I'd let him sleep in my room where we'd have long fights about why I wouldn't sleep with him. He would get back at me by showing up to the room, on Sunday nights with a case of Dewar's and a group of his fellow actors, and they'd spend long hours rehearsing Beckett (always in white face) or Pinter (for some strange reason, that too, in white face) and they'd get loaded and all pass out, which meant I had to move downstairs to the living room, or wander the hallways, which was all right with me since I was always hoping to run into Paul Denton.

The first time I met Paul was in an acting class and we had to do an improv scene together and I was so bowled over by how handsome he was that I botched the scene up and I think he could tell. I was so embarrassed that I dropped the class and made sure to keep out of his way. He'll probably loathe the fact that I moved in across from him and ignore me, but at least we'll get to share the same bathroom.

SEAN Sitting in class, staring at the desk, someone's carved "Whatever Happened To Hippie Love?" I guess the first girl I kind of liked at Camden was this hippie I met my Freshman year. She was really stupid but so gorgeous and so insatiable in bed that I couldn't help myself. I had met her once, before I fucked her, at a party off-campus my first term. The hippie had offered me some pot and I was drunk so I smoked it. I was so drunk in fact and the pot was so bad that I threw up in the backyard and passed out in some girl's car who had brought me. I was embarrassed but not really, even though the girl who drove was pissed off since I lost it again all over the backseat of her Alfa Romeo on the way back to campus, and was jealous since she could tell that the hippie and I had been making eyes at each other all night, and had seen the hippie even kiss me before I left to throw up in back.

I really got to meet her the following term when another person I knew when I first came to Camden (and who had been a hippie but quit) introduced us at a party at my urging. I cringed, mortified, when to my shock I realized I had been in the hippie's Intro to Poetry Workshop my first term and this girl on the first day of class, so high her head looked like it was on springs, like some doped-up jack-in-the-box, raised her hand and said slowly, "This class is a total mindfuck." I dropped the class, disconcerted, but still wanting to fuck the hippie.

This was the Eighties, I kept thinking. How could there be any hippies left? I knew no hippies when I was growing up in New York. But here was a *hippie*, from a small town in Pennsylvania, no less. A hippie who was not too tall, who had long blond hair, features sharp, not soft like one would expect a hippie's features to resemble, yet distant, too. And the skin smooth as brown marble and as clean. She always seemed clean; in fact she seemed abnormally healthy. A hippie who would say things like, "None of your beeswax," or commenting on food, "This is really mellow chili." A hippie who would bring her own chopsticks to every meal. A hippie who had a cat named Tahini.

JIMI LIVES was painted in big purple letters on her door. She was constantly stoned. Her favorite question was "Are you high?" She wore tie-dyed shirts. She had beautiful smallish firm tits. She wore bell-bottoms and tried to learn how to play the sitar but she was always too stoned. She tried to dress me up one night: bell-bottoms, tie-dyed shirt, headband. Didn't work. It was extremely embarrassing. She said "beautiful" constantly. She didn't have any goals. I read the poetry she'd write and lied that I liked it. She had a BMW 2002. She carried a bong in a tie-dyed satchel that she had made herself.

Like all rich hippies (for this hippie was extremely

wealthy; her father owned VISA or something) she spent a lot of time following The Dead around. She'd simply split school for a week with other rich hippies and they'd follow them around New England, stoned out of their minds, reserving rooms and suites at Holiday Inns and Howard Johnsons and Ramada Inns, making sure to always have enough Blue Dragon or MDA or MDMA or Ecstasy. She'd come back from these excursions ecstatic, claiming that she was indeed one of Jerry's long lost children; that her mother had made some sort of mistake before she married the VISA guy, that she truly was one of "Jerry's kids." I guess she was one of Jerry's kids, though I wasn't sure which kind.

There were problems.

The hippie kept telling me I was too stiff, too uptight. And because of this the hippie and I broke up before the end of term. (I don't know if that's the real reason, but looking back it seems weird that we even bothered since the sex was so good.) It came to an end one night when I told her, "I think this is not working." She was stoned. I left her at the party after we made out in her room upstairs at Dewey House. I went home with her best friend. She never knew or realized it.

The hippie was always tripping, which bothered me too. The hippie was always trying to get me to trip with her. I remembered the one time I did trip with her I saw the devil: it was my mother. I was also sort of amazed that she even liked me in the first place. I would ask her if she'd ever read much Hemingway. (I don't know why I asked her about him since I never had read that much.) She would tell me about Allen Ginsberg and Gertrude Stein and Joan Baez. I asked her if she had read *Howl* (which I had only heard about through some crazy class called Poetry and the Fifties, which I failed) and she said, "No. Sounds harsh."

The last time I saw the hippie I was reading an article on the postmodern condition (this was when I was a Lit major, before I became a Ceramics major, before I became a Social

Science major) for some class I failed in some stupid magazine called *The New Left*, and she was sitting on the floor of the smoking section, stoned, looking at the pictures in the novelization of the movie *Hair* with some other girl. She looked up at me and giggled then slowly waved. "Beautiful," she said, turning a page, smiling.

"Yeah. Beautiful," I said.

"I can dig it," the hippie told me after I read some of her haiku and told her I didn't get it. The hippie told me to read *The Tale of Genji* (all of her friends had read it) but "You have to read it stoned," she warned. The hippie also had been to Europe. France was "cool" and India was "groovy" but Italy wasn't cool. I didn't ask why Italy wasn't, but I was intrigued why India was "groovy."

"The people are beautiful," she said.

"Physically?" I asked.

"Yeah."

"Spiritually?" I asked.

"Uh-huh."

"How spiritually?"

"They were groovy."

I started liking the word "groovy" and the word "wow." Wow. Spoken low, with no exclamation, eyes half-closed, fucking, how the hippie said it.

The hippie cried when Reagan won (the only other time I'd seen her cry was when the school dropped the yoga classes and replaced them with aerobics), even though I had explained patiently, carefully, what the outcome of the election was going to be, weeks in advance. We were on my bed and we were listening to a Bob Dylan record I had bought in town a week earlier, and she just said, sadly, "Fuck me," and I fucked the hippie.

One day I asked the hippie why she liked me since I was so different from her. She was eating pita bread and bean sprouts and writing on a napkin with a purple pen, a request for the comment board in the dining hall: More Tofu Please. She said, "Because you're beautiful."

I got fed up with the hippie and pointed to a fat girl

across the room who had written something nasty about me on the laundry room wall; who had come up to me at a Friday night party and said, "You'd be gorgeous if you were five inches taller."

"Is *she* beautiful?" I asked.

She looked up, bean sprout stuck on lower lip, squinted and said, "Yeah."

"That bitch over there?" I asked, pointing, appalled.

"Oh her. I thought yóu meant that sister over there," she said.

I looked around. "Sister? What sister? No, *her*," exasperated, I pointed at the girl; mean-looking, fat, black sunglasses, a bitch.

"Her?" the hippie asked.

"Yeah. Her."

"She's beautiful too," she said, drawing a daisy next to the message on the napkin.

"What about him?" I pointed to a guy who it was rumored had actually caused his girlfriend to kill herself and everyone *knew*. There was no way in hell the hippie could think that *he*, this fucking monster, was beautiful.

"Him? He's beautiful."

"Him? Beautiful? He killed his fucking girlfriend. Ran her over," I said.

"No way," the hippie grinned.

"Yes! It's true. Ran her straight over with a car," I said, excited.

She just shook her lovely, empty head. "Oh man."

"Can't you make distinctions?" I asked her. "I mean, our sex is great, but how can everything, everyone be beautiful? Don't you understand that that means no one is beautiful?"

"Listen, man," the hippie said. "What are you getting at?"

She looked at me, not grinning. The hippie could be sharp. What *was* I getting at?

I didn't know. All I know was that the sex was terrific.

And that the hippie was cute. She loved sweet pickles. She liked the name Willie. She even liked *Apocalypse Now.*

She was not a vegetarian. These were all on the plus side. But, once I introduced her to my friends, at the time, and they were all stuck-up asshole Lit majors and they made fun of her and she understood what was going on and her eyes, usually blue, too blue, vacant, were sad. And I protected her. I took her away from them. ("Spell Pynchon," they asked her, cracking up.) And she introduced me to her friends. And we ended up sitting on some Japanese pillows in her room and we all smoked some pot and this little hippie girl with a wreath on her head, looked at me as I held her and said, "The world blows my mind." And you know what?

I fucked her anyway.

PAUL   He liked me. He would sing "Can't Take My Eyes Off of You" by Frankie Valli. It was on the jukebox at The Carousel in North Camden and he would ask me to play it a lot. The townies would watch us suspiciously, Sean shooting pool, drinking beer, me shuffling over to the jukebox, slipping quarters in it, punching F17, the first strains coming on, shuffling back to where Sean sat, now by the bar, motorcycle helmets propped up by our drinks, and he'd lip-synch it. He even found the single and put it on a tape he made for me when I was in bed with a hangover. It was in a bag he brought over that included orange juice, beer and French fries and a Quarter Pounder from McDonald's, still warm.

When he didn't want to go to class and when he didn't want me to go either and he found it too boring to simply not go and sit around, I'd follow him to the infirmary and once there he would have fake attacks; fairly well-planned and -acted fits and imaginary seizures. He would then receive medicine and the two of us would leave (I'd complain that my migraines were acting up), excused from classes for the day, and we'd go into town to an arcade called The Dream Machine and play this totally anal retentive video game he loved to play called Bentley Bear or Crystal Bear or something like that. Afterwards we'd walk through town together. I'd look around for a double bed and he'd look for cough syrup with codeine in it so he could get high (this was after he smoked all the pot; what a hick, I know, I know). He'd find the cough syrup and actually get stoned on it ("I *am* hallucinating," he'd announce) and we'd drive back to campus on his bike as it got dark in the late afternoon. By then, classes had already ended. And back in his room, which was usually a mess (at least his side), I'd sit around and play tapes and watch him stumble around and spin, high. He was always so animated around me, but so reserved and serious in front of other people. In bed, too, he'd alternate between being melodramatically loud and then a parody of the strong silent type: either grunting softly or emitting a weird quiet laughter, then it was suddenly loud rhythmic "yeah's" or yelling muffled obscenities, on top of me, me on top of him, both of us hungover, the stale smell of beer and cigarettes everywhere, the empty cups with the quarters stuck on the bottom of them scattered around the floor and the always-present odor of pot, hanging thick in mid-air, reminded me of Mitchell strangely enough, but he was already fading away, and it was hard to remember what he even looked like.

Sean liked to say "Rock'n'roll" a lot. For example I would say, "Well, that was a pretty good movie" and he'd say "Rock'n'roll." Or I'd ask, "What do you think of Fassbinder's early work?" and he would reply "Rock'n'roll." He also liked the term, "Deal with it." For example, I'd say, "But I want you to," and he'd say, "Deal with it." Or, "But why do you have to get stoned before we do it?" and he'd say, "Deal with it," without even looking at me. He also liked his coffee really faggy—tons of cream, lots of sugar. I'd have to drag him to the movies they showed that term and he'd have to get stoned first. He liked *Taxi Driver*, *Blade Runner*, *The Harder They Come*, and *Apocalypse Now*. I liked *Rebel Without a Cause*, *Close Encounters of the Third Kind* and *The Seventh Seal*. ("Oh shit, subtitles," he moaned.) We both didn't like *Everything You Always Wanted to Know About Sex*.

Of course I started finding the notes someone was leaving in his box. Pathetic, girlish yearnings. Whoever it was, offering "herself" to "him." And though I wasn't sure if he was actually responding to this nitwit I still would take them out of his box and either throw them away or keep them and study them and then put them back. I would watch the girls who'd flirt with us in The Pub and I'd watch the ones who would sit next to him, asking for a light even though they had matches in their pockets. And, of course, there would be a lot of girls around since he was so good-looking. And though I hated them, I also realized that I had the power in this game since I was also good-looking and had some semblance of a personality, something Sean lacked utterly. *I* could make them laugh. *I* could lie and agree with their stupid observations about life, and they'd lose immediate interest in him. Sean would sit there, shallow as a travel agent's secretary, that one strip of eyebrow furrowed and confused. But it was a hollow victory and I'd look at the girls and wonder who was leaving the notes. Didn't that person realize we were fucking each other? Didn't that mean anything to anyone anymore? Obviously not. I thought it was this one girl. I thought I saw her put something in his box. I knew who she was. I found out where her box was and when no one was looking put a couple of cigarettes out in it. My warning. He never mentioned it. But then I realized that maybe it wasn't a girl leaving the notes. Maybe it was Jerry.

LAUREN Conroy, who I bump into at the American Cartoon Exhibit in Gallery 1, asks why I wasn't at the tutorial last Saturday. No use arguing. "I was in New York," I tell him. He doesn't care. I'm with Franklin now. Judy doesn't care. She's seeing the Freshman, Steve. Steve doesn't care. She fucked him the night she went to Williamstown. I don't care. It's all so boring. Conroy who doesn't care tells me to tell the other person in class to come on Saturday. It's some Senior guy. So after I leave a reminder in this guy's box, Franklin and I go to The Pub and get a little drunk and Franklin tells me what the symbolism in *Cujo* means and then we go to my room. I have received no mail from Victor. The idea crosses my mind that Victor might just be dead. Conversation I overheard at lunch the other day.
    Boy: I think we should stop this.
    Girl: Stop what? This?
    Boy: Maybe.
    Girl: Stop it? Yeah.
    Boy: Maybe. I don't know.

Girl: Was it because of Europe?

Boy: No. I just don't know why.

Girl: You should stop smoking.

Boy: Why don't you stop . . . stop . . .

Girl: You're right. It's not working.

Boy: I don't know. You're really . . . You *are* pretty.

Girl: You *are* too.

Boy: The meek shall inherit the earth.

Girl: The meek don't want it.

Boy: I like the new Eurythmics song.

Girl: It's the drugs, isn't it?

Boy: Do you want to go back to my room?

Girl: What Eurythmics song?

Boy: Was it because of who I slept with?

Girl: No. Yes. No.

Boy: The meek don't want it? What?

I have not painted in over a week. I am going to change my major unless Victor calls.

PAUL   My mother called from Chicago and told me that her Cadillac had been stolen while it was in the parking lot of Neiman Marcus. She mentioned that she was flying to Boston on Friday, which was the next day, and would be there for the weekend. She also mentioned that she wanted me to be there with her.

"Wait. That's tomorrow. I have classes all day," I lied.

"Darling, you can miss one class to meet your mother and the Jareds."

"The Jareds are coming?"

"Didn't I tell you? Mrs. Jared is coming and so is Richard. He's taking the weekend off from Sarah Lawrence," she said.

"Richard?" Hmmm, that ought to be interesting, I was thinking, but tomorrow was The Dressed To Get Screwed party and there was no way I was going to leave Sean here unguarded. "You have got to be kidding," I told her. "Is this a joke?"

I was leaning against a wall in the phone booth of Welling. I had been in town all day, most of it spent in an arcade with Sean who was trying to get the high score on Joust and was failing miserably. We smoked pot and had three beers each at lunch and I was tired. There was a cartoon someone had drawn next to the phone: in a cage was a hot dog that had sad eyes and a mean, pursed mouth and spindly arms grabbing at the bars. The hot dog was asking "Where's me muddah?" and beneath that someone had written: "A term for the wurst."

"Now, can you take the bus down Friday into Boston, or the train?" she asked, knowing damn well that Friday meant *tomorrow*. "How much does that cost? From Camden to Boston?"

"I have money. That's not a problem. But *this* weekend?" I asked.

"Darling," she managed to sound serious, even long-distance, "I want to talk."

"What about Dad?"

There was a pause, then, "What about him?"

"Is he coming too?" I asked, then added, "I haven't spoken to him in a month."

"Do you want him to come?" she asked.

"No. I don't know."

"Don't worry about it. I will see you at The Ritz-Carlton on Friday. Right, dear?" she hurriedly asked.

"Mom," I said.

"Yes?"

"Are you sure you want to do this?" I was relenting. Suddenly she depressed me so badly that there wouldn't have been any way to say No under any circumstance.

"Darling, yes. Now don't worry. I will see you Friday, right?" She paused and then said, "I want to talk. There's things we have to talk about."

Like what? "Fine," I sighed.

"Call me if there are any problems?"

"Yes."

"Goodbye. Love," she said.

"Yeah, you too," I said.

She hung up first and I stood there for a minute and then slammed my fist against the wall and stormed out of the booth. My mother's timing had never been worse.

I can tell by the way he moves that he knows. In some way he has caught on and I'm no longer left in the dark about the messenger who is me. I know he knows. The way he looks around a room, the dining hall, the way he walks past Commons. Everything about him. And I think,

I just think, that he knows it's me. I've seen him look me in the face; those sultry dark eyes scan the rooms he's in and they come on me. Is he too afraid to come up to me and tell me how he feels? I listen to "Be My Baby" and dance sad dances and sing His name while I listen and hug myself. I know he likes me. I know it. And tomorrow night at the ball it will be complete. The final answer will be . . .

(I called my mother today . . . she wasn't feeling well . . . I received a nice comment from a glowering teacher. . . .)

A teacher asked us today in class if a person can die of heartbreak. He was serious. He is also a devil. My idea of hell is being locked in a room away from you but able to see you and smell you. Shut up, shut up, I tell myself over and over again. If I taught a class I would tell you, "You must sleep with me and love me to pass." I have to learn to write my notes to Him neater. I sit so still thinking of Him. Afraid to breathe. Sometimes I think I will scream. Mary, I tell myself, tomorrow is the night. What do you think about? Who do you think about? Me? Alone? Who has seen you naked, I think to myself. Who have you slept with and loved, is another one. How many cigarettes have you smoked, also crops up. Two, today? True? Shrewjewblue-brewcrewdrewrabbitfrufru. Song for poor Mary. Nobody likes me. Everybody hates me. Guess I'll go eat some worms. Oh! Lay! Your! Hands! On! Me!

I am in a class now with only forty minutes left. I think I'm going to throw up. I have to see You. I am frustrated, I tell myself calmly, because I want to moan and writhe with You and I want to go up to you and kiss Your mouth and pull you to me and say "Love you love you love you" while stripping, while sex commences. I want to kill the ugly girls who sit around you at The Pub but cannot. I hear a Bread song and suddenly you appear. Someone came up to me and said "Undo the karma, undo the karma," and I thought of you. I could leave and go somewhere, I guess. Take a vacation . . . where? Concentration . . . on what? Penn Station? Masturbation? I have seen this couple walk-

ing around and they seem to be very unhappy and I want to touch you. I want you to touch them. Do you like those boring naive coy calculating girls? A poster I saw the other day in a room I peeked in on: When two snake rattlers fight, it is according to strict rules. Neither uses poison fangs, the object is only to force the opponent's head to the ground and hold it there for a few seconds, thus establishing superiority. Then the grip is released and the loser dismissed. Who can turn the world on with her smile? Who can take a nothing day and suddenly make it all seem worthwhile? Well, it's you girl and you should know it, with each little glance and every movement you show it. Love is all around, no need to fake it, you can have it all, why don't you take it, your gonna . . . Sometimes I hate Him. Tomorrow night.

PAUL We were lying in my bed since the Frog was back. Sean sat up and leaned against the wall and asked me to hand him the cigarettes that were on the floor. I lit one for myself then gave them to Sean.

"What's wrong?" he asked. "No. Let me guess. Paul's tense, right?"

"Ten points for Sean."

He got up, disgusted, and put on his boxer shorts.

"Why do you wear boxer shorts?" I asked.

He ignored me and continued getting dressed, cigarette dangling from his lips.

"No, I mean, I really never noticed that before, but you wear *boxer* shorts."

He pulled on a T-shirt and then tied up his paint-splattered boots. Why were they paint splattered? Did he fingerpaint or something?

"Do you have them in different colors? Say, mauve? Or maybe tangerine?"

He finished dressing then sat on the chair next to the bed.

"Or do they only come in that . . . asphalt gray?"

He just stared at me. He knew I was acting like a fool.

"I knew a guy named Tony Delana in ninth grade who wore boxer shorts."

"That's a real scorcher, Denton," he said.

"Yeah?"

"So you don't want to go to Boston tomorrow, is that it?" he asked.

"Now, you have twenty points." I put my cigarette out in an empty beer bottle that was on my nightstand and shook it.

Sean just looked at me and said, "I don't like you that much. I don't know why I'm here."

"I'm sorry about that," I say, getting up and putting on a robe. I smelled the robe. "I've got to do my laundry."

I scanned the room for something to drink, but it was late and we had finished all the beer. I reached over him and held a bottle up to the light to see if there was anything left in it. There wasn't.

"You're going to miss The Dressed To Get Screwed party," his voice was low and ominous.

"I know." I tried not to panic. "Are you going?" I finally asked.

"Sure," he shrugged, moved over to the mirror, still in the chair.

"What are you going to wear?" I asked.

"What I usually wear," he said, staring at himself. The narcissistic little sonofabitch.

"Is that right?" I looked around the room. I didn't know what I was looking for. I wanted a drink. I walked over to the stereo and looked behind it. There was a half-empty Beck's next to the speaker. I sat back on the bed.

He stood up. "I'm gonna go."

"Where to?" I asked. I casually tasted the bottle. It was warm and flat and I made a face but drank it anyway.

"All night study room," he said. The narcissistic lying little sonofabitch.

He walked to the door and I ended up blurting out, "I don't want to go to Boston for the weekend. I don't want to see my mother. I don't want to see the Jareds," (though I probably did want to see Richard) "and I don't want to see Richard from Sarah Lawrence" (hoping to make him jealous) ". . . and . . ." I stopped.

He stood there, saying nothing.

"And I don't think I want to leave you here . . ." Because I don't trust you, I didn't say.

"I'm gonna go," he said. He opened the door and looked back. "I'll take you to the bus station tomorrow. What time does it leave?"

"I think eleven-thirty." I took another sip of the beer, then coughed. It tasted terrible.

"Okay, meet me at my bike at eleven," he said, heading out.

"Eleven," I said.

"Night." He closed the door and I could hear his footsteps echo down the hallway.

"Thanks, Sean."

I started to pack, wondering what Richard looked like now, trying to remember when I saw him last.

SEAN   Someone walks into The Pub, looks for someone, can't find them and leaves, the door closes behind them. It wasn't Lauren Hynde, the completely beautiful girl who had been leaving notes in my box, the only reason I'm in The Pub tonight, waiting to confront her. I saw her slip one in last Saturday, when I was up in Commons. I couldn't believe it. I was so shocked that it was actually someone good-looking that I spent the last week in a sort of daze. Now I'm sitting at a table with four or five or six people, kind of listening to some lame conversation, looking for the girl. They're all talking about what's going on at the sculpture studio, about sculpture teachers, and sculpture parties, about Tony's latest sculpture, even though they have no idea what it *says*. Tony told me it was supposed to be a steel vagina, but none of these idiots can figure it out.

"It's so disturbing, lyrical," this girl with a serious problem says.

"Very potent. Undefinable," her friend, some dyke from Duke who's visiting, who looks like she's had way too much MDA, agrees.

"It's Nimoy. Pure Nimoy," Getch says.

My attention drifts. Somebody else walks in, somebody who if I remember correctly gave me a totally unprovoked kiss on the lips at the last Friday night party. Peter Gabriel still plays on the jukebox.

"But it's Diane Arbus with none of the conviction," one of the girls says and she's *serious*.

Denton gives me a steely look from across the table. He probably agreed with that.

"But the revisionist theory on her seems completely unmotivated," someone else gleefully replies. There's a pause, then someone asks, "What about Wee Gee. What do you think about Wee Gee, for Christ sakes?"

Vaguely horny I order another pitcher and a pack of Bar-B-Que potato chips, which give me indigestion. Peter Gabriel turns into more Peter Gabriel. The girl who kissed me on the lips last Friday leaves after buying a pack of cigarettes and in some warped way I'm disappointed. She's not that pretty (slightly Asian, Dance major?) but I'd probably fuck her anyway. Back to the conversation.

"Spielberg has gone too far on this one," the angry mulatto intellectual with the neo-Beatnik casual but hip look plus beret who has joined the table hisses.

Where has he gone? Does he just hang out in the Canfield apartment and drink like a maniac and split on parents weekend and have a whole bunch of friends visiting him every term from boarding school? What the fuck does he do with his life? Little Freshman girls confiding in him and long walks around the dorms after dinner?

"Simply too far," Denton agrees. He's serious, not joking.

"Simply too far," I say, nodding.

The table behind ours, Juniors arguing about Vietnam, some guy scratching his head, joking but not really, says, "Shit, when was *that?*" someone else saying, "Who gives a shit?" and this fat, earnest-looking girl who's on the verge of tears, bellows, "I do!" Social-Science-Major-Breakdown. I turn back to our table, with the Art Fucks because they seem less boring.

The dyke from Duke asks, "But don't you think his whole secular humanism stems from the warped pop culture of the Sixties and not from a rigorous, modernist vantage point?" I turn back to the other table but they've dispersed. She asks the question again, rephrasing it for the intense mulatto. Who in the hell is she asking? Who? Me? Denton just keeps nodding his head like she's saying something incredibly deep.

Who *is* this girl? Why is she alive? Wonder if I should leave right now. Get up and say, "Goodnight fuck-ups, it's been a sheer sensation and I hope I never see any of you again," and leave? But if I do that they'll end up talking about me and that seems worse and I'm seriously drunk. Hard to keep my eyes open. The only pretty girl at our table gets up, smiles and leaves. Someone says, whispers loudly, "She fucked . . . are you ready?" The table leans inward, even me. "Lauren!"

The table gasps collectively. Who's Laurent? That

French guy who lives in Sawtell? Or is it the alcoholic girl from Wisconsin who works in the library? It can't be *my* Lauren? It can't be *that* one. There's no way she's a lesbian. Even if she is, it turns me on a little. But . . . maybe she's been putting the notes in the wrong box. Maybe she meant to put them in Jane Gorfinkle's box, the box above mine? I don't want to ask which Lauren they mean even though I want to know. I look over at the bar, try to get my mind off it, but there are at least four girls I have slept with standing there. None of them are looking over at me. Businesslike and impersonal they sip beers, smoke cigarettes

oh, what the fuck. I finally snap, get out of there, leave. As simple as that. I'm out the door. Fels is close by. I have some friends who live there, don't I? But thinking about it bores the fuck out of me so I just walk around the dorm for a while and then split. Sawtell is next? Nah. But that girl, that girl who kissed me . . . I think she lives in Noyes, a single, room 9. I go to her door and knock.

I think I hear some laughter, then a high-pitched voice. Whose? I feel like a fool but I'm a drunk, so it's cool. The door opens and it's the girl who left the table, not the girl who kissed me, and she's wearing a robe and behind her I can see some hairy, pale guy in bed, lighting up a big purple bong on a futon. Jesus, this really sucks, I'm thinking.

"Um, doesn't Susan live here?" I ask, turning red, trying to keep it cool.

The girl looks back at the guy in bed. "Does Susan live around here, Loren?"

The guy sucks in on the bong. "No," he says, offering it to me. "Leigh 9."

I leave, fast. I walk out, fast. I'm outside, it's cold. What am I going to do? I think. *What is this night* unless I do *something?* Is this just going to be *nothing?* Like every other fucking night? Something goes through my head. I decide to go to Leigh 9, where Susan lives. I knock on the door. I can't hear much but Springsteen's "Nebraska" album. Great music to fuck by, I'm thinking. It takes a while but Susan opens the door, finally an answer.

"What's going on, Susan? Hi. Sorry to be bothering you at this hour."

She looks at me strangely, then smiles and says, "No problem, come in."

I walk in, hands in my jacket pockets. There are two Xeroxed maps of Vermont . . . actually it's New Hampshire, or maybe Maryland, up on the wall, above the computer and the bottle of Stoli. I'm too drunk to do this I realize as I stagger in, take a deep breath. Susan closes the door and says, "Glad you stopped by" and locks the door and her locking the door just depresses me; it makes me realize that she wants to fuck too and that that's what's expected of me and it's my own fault and it's really Lauren Hynde I want and I think I'm going to pass out and she looks really desperate, really young.

"Where have you been?" she asks.

"Movie. Wild Italian movie. But it's all in Italian so you can't watch it stoned," I say, trying to be rude, turn her off. "Subtitles, you know."

"Yeah," she smiles kindly, still in love with me.

"What I mean, like, um, why are those maps, um . . . Yeah, like what are those maps doing up there?" I ask. What a dwid.

"Maryland's cool," Susan says.

"I want to go to bed with you, Susan," I say.

"What?" She pretends she didn't hear me.

"You didn't hear me?"

"Yeah. I did," she says. "You didn't feel that way the other night."

"So, how do you feel about it?" I ask, letting that comment fly right over my head.

"I think it's kind of ridiculous," she says.

"How? I mean, why do you think so?"

"Because I have a boyfriend," she says. "Remember?"

Actually, I don't, but I blurt out, "That doesn't matter. You don't have to not screw because of *that*."

"Really?" she asks skeptically, but smiling. "Explain."

"Well, you see, it's like this." I sit on the bed. "It's like this . . ."

"You're drunk," Susan says. God, the name Susan is so ugly. It reminds me of the word sinus. She's daring me. I can almost smell how wet she is. She wants it.

"Where have you been all my life?" I ask.

"Did you know I was born in a Holiday Inn," I think she says.

I stare at her, really confused, really fucked-up. She's next to me on the bed now. I keep staring.

I finally say, "Just get naked and lay or stand, I don't care, on the bed and, like, it doesn't matter if you were born in a Holiday Inn. Do you understand what I'm saying?"

"Perfectly," she says. "Are you still an Art major by any chance?"

"What?" I ask. My eyes are tearing. She's dimming the lights and it's all really happening, boyfriend or no boyfriend. I'm drunk but I'm not drunk enough to say no. In the bathroom in Commons today someone had written "Robert McGlinn has no penis and no testicles" about fifteen times above the toilet.

She turns to me, her flesh glowing green because of the lighted words from the computer screen, and says nothing. I lay back and she starts sucking my dick and trying to stick a finger up my ass. It feels good and she's really into it and I'm thinking what do you talk about in situations like this? Are you Catholic? Did you ever like the Beatles? Or was it Aerosmith you asked girls? High school girls you met who wore black armbands the day Steven Tyler got married. High school sucked. She's sucking still, her lips moist but hard. I reach under her shirt, massage her tits. She has a little stubble under her arm and it doesn't really turn me off. It doesn't turn me on all that much either, but it doesn't turn me off.

"Wait . . . wait . . ." I try to pull my underwear off all the way, then the jeans, but I'm on the bed and she's sucking me and trying to push my legs farther apart and even though I'm sort of grossed-out by the whole thing, it feels too good to complain. She lifts her head up. "Diseases?" she asks. "Nope," I say though I should just say yeah crabs and end this. She lays across me and we start kissing, deep, intensely. I lift her shirt up over her head, line of green saliva attached to our lips as she brings her head up. I touch the side of her face, then unbutton my shirt, kick my pants off. "Wait, turn the light off," I tell her.

She grins. "I like it on." She places her hands on my chest.

"Well, like, fuck that. I want it off. Deal with it."

"I'll turn it off." She does. "Is that better?"

We start kissing again. Now, what's going to happen, I wonder. Who's going to initiate the dreaded fucking? What would her parents say if they knew that this is all she does here? Write haiku on her Apple, drink vodka like some crazed alcoholic fish, screw constantly? Would they disown her? Would they give her more money? What?

"Oh baby," she moans.

"You like this?" I whisper.

"No," she moans again. "I want the lights *on*. I want to see *you*."

"What? I don't believe this."

"I want to know what the fuck I'm doing," she says.

"I don't see how you can be confused," I tell her.

"I'm into neon," she says, but she doesn't turn it back on. I push her head down.

She starts sucking my cock again. I start to get her off with my hand. She gives decent head. I tell her "Wait—I'm gonna come . . ." She lifts her head. I go down on her, slowly, kiss her tits (which are sort of too big) and then past her stomach to her cunt, spread, swollen, three fingers easing into it, licking it at the same time. Bruce is singing about Johnny 69 or someone and then we're fucking. And I come—spurt spurt—like bad poetry and then what? I hate this aspect of sex. It's always someone wanting and someone giving but the giver and the wanter are hard to deal with. It's hard to deal with even if it goes good. She hasn't come, so I go down on her again and it tastes vaguely seedy and then . . . where do you go once you've come? Disillusionment strikes. I can't stand doing this and I'm still hard so I start to fuck her again. She's groaning now, humping up, down, up, and I put my hand over her mouth. She comes, licking my palm, snorting. It's over.

"Susan?"

"Yeah?"

"Where's the Kleenex?" I ask. "Do you have a towel or something?"

"Did you come yet?" she asks, confused, lying in the darkness.

I'm still in her and I say, "Oh yeah, well, I'm gonna come. In fact I'm coming now." I moan a little, grunt authentically and then pull out. She tries to hold me, but I just ask for some Kleenex.

Susan says, "I don't have any," and then the voice cracks, she starts to cry.

"What? What's wrong?" I ask, alarmed. "Wait. I told you I came."

LAUREN Victor hasn't called. I've changed my major. Poetry.

What do Franklin and I do? Well, we go to parties: Wet Wednesday, Thirsty Thursday, parties at The Graveyard, at End of the World, Friday night parties, pre–Saturday-night party parties, Sunday afternoon parties.

I try to quit smoking. Write letters to Victor in computer class that I never send. Franklin always seems to be broke. He wants to sell blood to get some cash, maybe buy some drugs maybe sell some drugs. I sell some clothes and old records in Commons one afternoon. We spend a lot of time in my room since I've got a double bed. I've stopped painting completely. Since Sara left (even though the abortion by her account wasn't traumatic enough to excuse her absence) I watch her cat, Seymour. Franklin hates the cat. I do too, but tell him I like it. We hang out in the Sensory Deprivation Tank. Sometimes Judy and Freshman and me and Franklin go to the movies in town and no one cares. What is going on? I ask myself. We drink a lot of beer. The boy from L.A., still wearing shorts and sunglasses and nothing else, came on to me at one of the parties last week. I almost went home with him but Franklin intervened. Franklin is an idiot, really unintentionally hilarious. I have come to this conclusion, not by reading his writing, which is science fiction, which is "heavily influenced by astrology," which is terrible, but by something I don't understand. I tell him I like his stories, I tell him my sign and we discuss the importance of the stories but . . . I hate his goddamned incense and I don't know why I'm doing this to myself, why I'm being such a masochist. Though of course it's because of a certain handsome Horace Mann graduate who's lost in Europe. I try to quit smoking.

(. . . no mail from Victor . . .)

But I like Franklin's body and he's good in bed and easy to have orgasms with. But it doesn't feel good and when I try to fantasize about Victor, I can't.

I go to computer class. I hate it but need the credit.

"Did I tell you I was strip-searched in Ireland?" Franklin will mention at lunch.

I will look straight ahead and avoid eye contact when he says things like that. I pretend I don't hear him. He doesn't shave sometimes and he gives me beard burns. I am not in love with him, I'll chant under my breath at dinner, with him sitting across from me with other oily Lit majors all dressed in black and exhibiting a dry yet caustic wit and I'll be blown away by how nondescript he is. But can you remember really what Victor looked like? No, you can't, can you? It freaked him out badly that I put a note on my door that said "If my mother calls I'm not here. Try not to take a message either. Thanks." I try to stop smoking. I forget to feed the cat.

"I want to trip with my father before he dies," Franklin said at lunch this afternoon.

I didn't say anything for a very long time and then he asked, "Are you high?" and I said "High" and lit another cigarette.

SEAN There is no way I'm driving the dude to the bus station. I can't believe he even asked me. I'm hungover as hell and feel like I'm going to throw up blood and I woke up on the floor of someone's room and it's cold and I'm in a bad mood and I owe Rupert five hundred bucks. He's pissed off supposedly, and has threatened to kill me. I can't believe I'm up this early. I bought an onion bagel at the snack bar and it's cold but I'm still wolfing it down. He's standing there already, with his bag and sunglasses and long coat, reading some book. I mumble a good morning.

"Just get up?" he asks, smirking.

"Yeah. Missed my guitar tutorial. Shit." I climb on the bike and try to start it. I hand him the onion bagel. I turn the ignition. I decide to just fake it; pretend the bike won't start. He won't be able to tell.

"You shaved," I say, trying to make conversation; get his attention away from the bike.

"Yeah. I was getting a little scruffy there," he says.

"Doing it for Mom? That's real nice," I say.

"Uh-huh," he says.

"Nice," I say.

"Can I have a bite of your bagel?" he asks.

No way. I don't want to give him a bite of my bagel. I say, "Sure."

I start the bike up, jiggle the keys, then let it die again. Put my foot on the accelerator; turn it off with a flick of the wrist. Then start it up again. The bike makes a sputtering sound, the engine dies.

"Oh shit," I say.

I pretend to try it again. The bike, of course, just won't start.

"Shit." I get off the bike and lean down. He's watching me closely.

"What's wrong?" he asks.

I don't know what to say so I say, "Needs a jumpstart." Smile to myself.

"Jumpstart? Christ," he mutters, checking his watch.

I get back on the bike and do the trick again. The bike just will not start.

"It's not gonna start," I tell him.

"What do I do?" he asks.

I sit there, look out over Commons, finish the cold bagel, yawn. "What time is it?"

"Eleven," he says.

He's a liar. It's only ten-forty-five. I go along with it. "Your bus leaves at eleven-thirty, right?"

"Right," he says.

"That's enough time to find someone who'll give me a jumpstart." I yawn again.

He's looking at his watch. "I don't know."

"I'll find someone. Getch'll do it."

"Getch has Music for the Handicapped now," he tells me.

I knew that. "Does he?" I ask.

"Yes."

"I didn't know that," I say. "I didn't know Getch took that."

"I'm taking a cab," he says.

Thank God. "Okay," I say.

"Don't worry about it," he says.

"Sorry guy," I say.

"It's all right." He's irritated. He gets off the bike and tucks the copy of the book he's reading in the dufflebag, straightens his sunglasses.

"I'll see you Sunday, okay?" he says, asks.

"Yeah. Bye," I say.

Go back to my room and drink some Nyquil to get to sleep. I heard that junkies use the stuff when they can't find any heroin or methadone. It does the job. The only problem is that I dream about Lauren, and she's all blue.

PAUL   It was a Friday morning and I was waiting by Sean's bike in the student parking lot. It was only ten-thirty and the bus station in town was maybe a five minute drive from campus but I wanted to get there early. When I was sixteen I was supposed to meet my parents in Mexico. They had flown down the week before and told me that if I wanted to come I could get a ticket and meet them down in Las Cruces. When I got to O'Hare to catch the flight down to Mexico City I found out I missed it. When I went back to my car I found a parking ticket on the windshield. I stayed home and had a party and ruined the couch from Sloane's and saw eleven movies and skipped school all that week. And that's probably why I get so paranoid before going on a trip. Ever since then, I arrive at airports and train stations and bus terminals much earlier than needed. Even though it was ten-forty and I knew I'd probably make the bus to Boston, I still couldn't concentrate on the copy of *The Fountainhead* I was reading or anything else. Last summer Mitchell told me I was an illiterate and that I should read more. So he gave me a copy of *The Fountainhead* and I began it, rather reluctantly. When I told Mitchell one day at some cafe that I didn't like Howard Roark, he said he had to go to the restroom, and he never came back. I paid the check. I remember that my parents bought me a stuffed iguana and smuggled it through customs for me. Why?

Sean arrived and noticed that I'd shaved, flirting, like a bastard. His bike wouldn't start, so I decided to take a cab to the bus station. He was nice about it and I felt sorry for him that his bike wouldn't start, and he looked like he was really going to miss me and I decided that I would call him when I got to Boston. Then I remembered The Dressed To Get Screwed party and knew that he was going to get laid; that everyone does. By the time the cab brought me to the bus station I was chain-smoking and bending my copy of *The Fountainhead* so hard that it became permanently creased. But the bus was late anyway when it arrived at eleven-forty-five, so I had nothing to worry about in terms of making it. Myself, some young fat lady with a blue jacket with dice on the back of it and her blond dirty-faced little boy, and a well-dressed blind man were the only people getting on at Camden. Since there was no one else on the bus I took a seat in the smoking section, near the back. The fat woman got on with her son and they sat up front. It took a while for the blind man to get on and the driver helped guide him slowly to a seat. I hoped that the blind man wouldn't sit next to me. He didn't. I was relieved.

The bus pulled out of Camden and started up Route 9. I was glad that there was no one else on the bus today going to Boston. It would be a nice, calm trip. Opening the book, I stared out the window, and got the feeling that maybe this weekend in Boston wouldn't be too awful. Richard would be there, after all. I was even a little interested in what my mother wanted to talk to me about. Her stolen Cadillac? It was probably a company car anyway. Easy to replace, nothing to worry about. It certainly didn't merit a visit to Massachusetts though. I took off the sunglasses since it was overcast and lit a fresh cigarette, tried to read. But it was too nice out not to stare past the window at the mid-October countryside, still signs of fall everywhere. Reds and dark greens and oranges and yellows all passed by. I read some more of the book, smoked some more cigarettes, wished that I'd brought my Walkman.

After about an hour the bus pulled into some town and made a stop at a small station where an old couple got on and sat near the front. The bus pulled out of the station and continued back on the highway for a mile or so and then stopped in front of a huge group of people, kids from the college nearby, standing in front of two green benches. I tensed up and realized as the bus slowed down and pulled close to the curb that these students were actually going to board the bus. I panicked for a moment and quickly moved to an aisle seat.

When the kids from the college got on, I took my sunglasses off and then put them on again and looked down at the book, hoping that they wouldn't realize I was a student from Camden. Fifty or sixty of these kids piled into the bus and it got unbearably loud. Most of them were girls dressed in pinks and blues, Esprit and Benetton sweatshirts, snapping sugarless gum, Walkmans on, holding cans of caffeine-free Diet Coke, clutching issues of *Vogue* and *Glamour*, looking like they stepped out of a Starburst commercial. The guys, eight or nine of them, were mostly good-looking and they sat in the back, near me, in the smoking section. One was carrying a big Sony cassette player, the new Talking Heads blasting from it, issues of *Rolling Stone* and *Business Week* being passed back and forth. Even after all these Pepsi rejects got on, there was still no one sitting next to me. I started feeling completely self-conscious and thought, god I must look pretentious, sitting in the back, Wayfarers on, black tweed coat ripped at the shoulder, chain-smoking, faded copy of *The Fountainhead* in my lap. I must scream "Camden!" But I was still grateful that no one sat next to me.

But just as the bus pulled away I noticed The Boy, looking exactly like Sean, looking very out of place, standing near the front of the bus, trying to make his way to the back. He had tangled longish hair and a week's growth of beard. He was wearing a Billy Squier T-shirt (oh my god) and holding a bulging pillow sack. I couldn't get over the resemblance and my heart stopped, then skipped a little before it resumed its normal beat. I looked around the bus and got the awful feeling that this Sean look-alike, who also had grease-stained hands, holding a wrinkled copy of *Motor Trend* (did this guy go to Hampshire?) was going to have to sit next to me. The boy passed the empty seat I was sitting next to and looked around the back of the bus. One of the college boys, wearing a Members Only jacket and leafing through a *Sports Illustrated*, Hi-Tops kicked up on the seat in front of him, talking about how he lost his Walkman in Freshman Econ class, shut up, and when he did that all the guys looked over at The Sean Boy and snorted derisively rolling their eyes. I was thinking please don't sit next to me. . . . He looked so much like Sean.

He knew the college boys were making fun of him and he moved over to me.

"Is that seat taken?" he asked.

And for a minute I wanted to say yes, but of course that would have been ridiculous, so I shook my head and swallowed hard and stood up to let The Boy sit down. The seats were close together and I had to move over to the edge of mine to accommodate us. He had the same color hair on his head and arms and he also had one eyebrow and tight ripped jeans. It was hard to deal with.

The bus pulled away from the curb before everyone was seated and hurled back onto the highway. I tried to read the book but couldn't. It started to rain, the sound of the Talking Heads coming from the gleaming cassette player, the girls passing Diet Pepsi and nachos back and forth and trying to flirt with me, the incessant yapping from the college boys in back, smoking clove cigarettes, an occasional joint, talking about how some slut named Ursula was fucked by some guy named Phil in the back of some guy's Toyota Nissan named Mark and how Ursula lied to Phil and said it wasn't his baby but he paid for the abortion anyway and it was all so irritating I couldn't even concentrate on anything. And by the time we were near Boston I was so angry with my mother for asking me to come that I just kept staring over at The Sean Boy, who, in turn, stared out the window, smoothing the creases out of his ticket with his grease-stained hands, his Swatch ticking loudly.

SEAN I get another note in my box today from Lauren Hynde. It says "I will meet you tonite—once the sun sets—E-L-O-V will no longer be spelled this way. . . ." I can't wait until the party, until "the sun sets" so I try to talk to Lauren at lunch. She's standing, smoking a cigarette, by the desserts, with Judy Holleran (who I screwed last term and who I occasionally score for; she's also really fucked-up, she's been in psychological counseling forever) and I come up behind them slowly, and suddenly I want to touch Lauren, I'm about to touch her, gently, on the neck, but the Frog roommate, who I haven't seen in days, excuses himself and reaches for a croissant or something and lingers. He notices me and says "Ça va." I say "Ça va." Lauren says "Hi" to him and she blushes and looks at Judy and Judy smiles too. He keeps looking at Lauren and then goes away. Lauren's telling Judy how she lost her I.D.

"What's going on?" I ask Judy, picking up a plate of melon.

"Hi, Sean. Nothing," she says.

Lauren's looking over the cookies, playing hard to get. It's so obvious I'm embarrassed.

"Going to the party tonight?" I ask. "Once the sun sets?"

"Totally psyched," Judy says, sarcastic as hell.

Lauren laughs, like she agrees. I bet, I'm thinking.

The geek from L.A. grabs an orange from the fruit tray and Lauren looks down, at what? His legs? They're really tan and I've never seen him with his sunglasses off, big deal. He lifts his eyebrows in recognition. I do the same. I look back at Lauren and I'm struck by how great-looking she is. And standing here, even if it's only for something like a millisecond, I overload on how great-looking this girl is. I'm amazed at how her legs affect me, the breasts, braless, beneath a "We Are the World" T-shirt, thighs. She looks over at me in what seems like slow motion. I can't meet her blue-eyed gaze back. She's *too* gorgeous. Her perfect, full lips locked in on this sexy uncaring smile. She's constructed perfectly. She smiles when she notices me staring and I smile back. I'm thinking, I want to *know* this girl.

"I think it's supposed to be a toga party too," I say.

"Toga? Jesus," she says. "What does this place think it is? Williams?"

"Where's the party?" Judy asks.

"Wooley," I tell her. She can't even fucking look at me.

"I thought we already had one," she says, and inspects a cookie. Her fingers are long and delicate. The nails have clear polish on them. Her hand, small and clean, scratches at her perfect, small nose, while the other hand runs through her blond, short hair and then back over her neck. I try to smell her.

"We did," I say.

"A *toga* party," she says. "You've got to be kidding. Who's on Rec Committee anyway?"

"I am," I say, looking directly at her.

Judy pockets an oatmeal cookie and takes a drag off her, Lauren's, cigarette.

"Well, Getch and Tony are gonna steal some sheets. There's a keg. I don't know," I say, laughing a little. "It's not really a *toga* party."

"Well, it sounds really happening," she says.

She leaves abruptly, taking a cookie, and asks Judy, "I'm going into town with Beanhead, wanna come?"

Judy says, "Plath paper. Can't."

Lauren leaves without saying anything to me. Obviously embarrassed, flustered, by my presence.

Tonight, I think. I go back to the table.

"The weight room opened today," Tony says.

"Rock'n'roll," I say.

"You're an idiot," he says.

Once the sun sets, I'm thinking.

PAUL I got off the bus with the other college students and the blind man and the fat woman with the blond kid and got lost amid the flotsam in the large terminal in Boston. Then I was outside and it was rush hour and overcast and I looked around for a cab. There was a sudden tap on my shoulder and when I turned around I was confronted by The Boy Who Looks Like Sean.

"Yeah?" I lowered my sunglasses. I was experiencing an adrenaline rush.

"Man, I was wondering if I could borrow five bucks," he asked.

I got dizzy and wanted to say no but he looked so much like Sean that I fumbled for my wallet, couldn't find a five and ended up giving him a ten.

"Thanks man," he says, slinging the pillow case over his shoulder, nodding to himself, walking away.

I nodded too, an involuntary reaction, and started to get a headache. "I am going to kill her," I whispered to myself as I finally wave down a cab.

"Where to?" the driver asked.

"Ritz-Carlton. It's on Arlington," I told him, sitting back in the seat, exhausted.

The driver turned his neck and looked at me, saying nothing.

"The Ritz-Carlton," I tell him again, getting uneasy.

He still stares.

"On . . . Arlington . . ."

"I hear you," the cab driver, an old guy, muttered, shaking his head, turning around.

Then what the fuck are you staring at? I wanted to scream.

I rubbed my eyes. My hands smelled awful and I opened a package of Chuckles I bought at the bus station in Camden. I ate one. The cab moved slowly through the traffic. It started raining. The cab driver kept looking at me in the rearview mirror, shaking his head, mumbling things I couldn't hear. I stopped chewing the Chuckle. The cab had barely made it down one block, then turned and pulled over to the curb. I panicked and thought, Oh Jesus, what now? Was he going to kick me out for eating a goddamn Chuckle? I put the Chuckles away.

"Why have we stopped?" I asked.

"Because we're here," the driver sighed.

"We're here?" I looked out the window. "Oh."

"Yeah, that'll be one forty," he grumbled. He was right.

"I guess I forgot it was . . . so, um, close," I said.

"Uh-huh," the driver says. "Whatever."

"I hurt my foot. Sorry," I pushed two singles at him and tripped in the rain getting out of the cab and I just know Sean's going to fuck someone at the party tonight and I'm in the lobby now, soaked, and this just better be good.

He doesn't know it but I had seen Him over the summer. Last summer. I spent my summer vacation on Long Island, in the Hamptons with my poor drunken father. Southampton, Easthampton, Hampton Bays—wandering the island with other Gucci-clad nomads. I stayed with my brother one night and visited a recently widowed aunt on Shelter Island and I stayed in tons of motels, motels that were pink and gray and green and that glowed in the Hamptons light. I stayed in these havens of shelter since I could not bear anymore to look at my father's new girlfriends. But that is another story.

I saw Him first at Coast Grill on the South Shore and then at this oh-so-trendy Bar-B-Que place whose delightful name eludes me at the moment. He was eating undercooked chicken and trying not to sneeze. He was with a female (a wench, definitely) who looked anorexic. Fag bartenders stood around them, looking bored, and I would order Slow Comfortable Screws to bother and tease them. "That's made with rum?" they'd lisp, and I'd lisp back Yes because you can't lisp No. Mouth-breathing waitresses came on to You, You, who were bronzed like a God, a GQ man, Your hair slicked back. I heard Your name called—a phone call. Bateman. They'd mispronounce it—Dateman. I was sitting, shrouded in darkness at the long sleek bar and I had just found out oh-so-discreetly that I had failed three out of four classes last term. Unfortunately I had forgotten to hand in, to even complete, the prerequisite "Some Papers," before I left for Arizona and hit the Hamptons. And there You sat. The last time I had seen You was at a Midnight Breakfast; You hurled a balled-up pancake at a table of Drama majors. Now You lit a cigarette. You did not bother to light the wench's. I followed You to the phone booth.

"Hey dude, like, didn't you speak to the dean and like, uh, tell them how unwrapped I am?"

I assumed it was Your psychiatrist.

You yawned and said, "I am concerned." .

There was an indefinite pause and then You said, "Just refill the Librium."

Another pause. You looked around, didn't recognize me from school. Me, sunburned and stiff and trying to drink but oh-so-sober. "I'm all set," You said.

You hung up. I watched as You nonchalantly threw bills on the table and walked out of the restaurant before the wench. The door closed on her, but she followed you anyway. You both sped away in a bright red Alfa Romeo and I got drunk and waited for Tonight.

Tonight. I've spent all afternoon in a bath full of scented water, preparing, cleansing, soaping, shaving, oiling myself for You. I have not eaten in two days. I wait. I am good at

*that. I listen to old soon-to-be-forgotten songs and wait for
Tonight and for You. Wait for that final moment. A mo-
ment so filled with such expectance and longing that I al-
most do not want to witness its occurrence. But I'm ready.
One fine day you'll want me for your girl, my radio cries.
That's right. Tonight.*

PAUL I walk up to the register desk and stand there, the
urge to flee, to go back to Camden, just walk the two
blocks, in the rain, to the terminal, just get on the bus, and
intercept Sean at The Dressed To Get Screwed party,
overwhelms me and I just stand there staring blankly at the
snotty, well-dressed men behind the desk until one glides
over and says, "Yes, sir?" I'm tempted to leave, split, do it.

"Yes, sir?" he asks again.

I snap out of it. I looked at him. It was too late. It was all
too late.

"I think my mother made reservations for the weekend.
The name's Denton."

"Denton, very good," the clerk said, looking me over
dubiously before he checked the files. I looked down at
myself, confused, then back at the clerk.

"Yes, Denton. Three days. That's two rooms, right?"
the clerk asked.

"I guess."

"Could you please sign this?" The clerk handed me something.

I filled in the address of Camden but I didn't know why. My hands were still wet. They stained the card.

"Will your mother be paying cash or with VISA, Mr. Denton?" the clerk asked.

I could have paid with my American Express but why the hell should I have done that? That would have been stupid; this whole thing was stupid. "VISA, I guess."

"Fine, Mr. Denton."

"I guess the rest of them are coming later." And don't call me Mister Denton. My name's Paul, you fools, Paul!

"Fine, Mr. Denton. Is that the only baggage you have?"

I was standing there wet, my life ruined. It was over with Sean. Another one bites the dust.

"Sir?" the clerk persisted.

"What?" I blink.

"I'll have someone take it up right away," he said.

I didn't even hear him, just "Thanks" and unbutton my coat and someone handed me a key and in a daze I walk into an open elevator and pushed a button for the ninth floor, no, someone else pushed it for me and some person walked me down a hallway and helped me find the two rooms.

I laid on the bed for a long time before I decided to get up. I open the doors that connected the suites and ponder which room looked better. I laid on one of the double beds in the other room and decide that the first room was more comfortable. I look at the other double bed, where Richard would sleep. I wondered if we'd fool around, since we had in high school, back in Chicago. I had almost gone to Sarah Lawrence because of him. He had almost gone to Camden, but then opted out and told me, "There's no fucking way I'm doing time in New Hampshire," and I had told him "I'd rather go to college in Las Vegas than Bronxville." Richard was definitely very good-looking, but getting together was a bad idea and, except for leaving Sean, was my main reservation about Boston. I turned the TV on and laid down again and then took a shower, the phone kept ringing, I kept hanging it up, got dressed, watched more TV, smoked more cigarettes, waited.

LAUREN I'm dreaming about Victor. It's a Camden relocation dream. People from school are milling about a salad bar on a beach. Judy is standing by the sea. The sea behind her is sometimes white, sometimes red, sometimes black. When I ask her where Victor is, she says, "Dead." I wake up. For a long, painful moment, between the point at which I have the nightmare, and the moment at which, hopefully, it is forgotten, I lie there, thinking about Victor. A very common morning.

I look around the room. Franklin is gone. The things around me depress me, seem to define my pitiful existence, everything is so boring: my typewriter—no cartridges; my easel—no canvas; my bookshelf—no books; a check from Dad; an airline ticket to St. Tropez someone crammed in my box; a note about Parents' Weekend being cancelled; the new poems I'm writing, crumpled by the bed; the new story Franklin has left me called "Saturn Has Eyes"; the half-empty bottle of red wine (Franklin bought it; Jordan, too sweet) we drank last night; the ashtrays; the cigarettes in the ashtrays; the Bob Marley tape unwound—it all depresses me immensely. I attempt to return to the nightmare. I can't.

Look over at the wine bottles standing on the floor, the empty pack of Gauloises (Franklin smokes them; how pretentious). I can't decide whether to reach for the wine or the cigarettes or turn on the radio. Thoroughly confused I stumble into the hallway, Reggae music coming thump thump from the living room downstairs. It's supposed to be light out, but then I realize it's four-thirty in the afternoon.

I'm leaving Franklin. I told him last night, before we went to bed.

"Are you kidding?" he asked.

"I'm not," I said.

"Are you high?" he asked.

"Beside the point," I said. Then we had sex.

PAUL I was thinking about taking another shower, styling my hair or calling Sean or jerking off or doing any number of things, when I heard someone trying to get into the room. I stood next to the door and heard my mother and Mrs. Jared babbling about something.

"Oh Mimi, help me with this damn lock." It was my mother bitching.

"Jesus, Eve," I heard Mrs. Jared's whiny voice answer back. "Where's the *bellboy?*"

I ran over to the bed and flung myself upon it and placed

a pillow over my head, trying to look casual. I looked ridiculous and stood up, tentatively.

"Damnit, Mimi, this is the wrong key. Try the other room," I heard, muffled, a complaint.

My mother knocked on the door, asking "Paul? Paul, are you in there?"

I didn't know if I should say anything, then realized that I had to and said, "Yes? Who is it, please?"

"It's your mother, for God's sake," she said, sounding exasperated. "Who do you think it is?"

"Oh," I said. "Hi."

"Could you please help me open this door?" she pleaded.

I walked over to the door and turned the knob, trying to pull it open, but my mother had screwed it up somehow and had locked it from the outside.

"Mother?" Be patient, patient.

"Yes, Paul?"

"You locked it."

Pause.

"I did?"

"You did."

"Oh my."

"Why don't you unlock it?" I suggested.

"Oh." There was a silence. "Mimi, get over here. My son tells me that I should unlock the door."

"Hello, Paul dear," Mrs. Jared said through the door.

"Hi, Mrs. Jared," I called back.

"It appears that this door is locked," she commented.

I pulled on it again but the door wouldn't open.

"Mother?"

"Yes, dear?"

"Is the key in the lock?"

"Yes. Why?"

"Why don't you turn it to the, let's say . . . left? Okay?"

"To the left?"

"Oh, why not."

"Try it Eve," Mrs. Jared urged.

I stopped pulling the door. There was a click. The door opened.

"Darling," my mother screamed, looking wigged out of her mind, coming toward me, her arms outstretched. She looked quite pretty, actually. Perhaps too much make-up, but thinner, and she's dressed to the hilt, her jewelry's clanking all over the place, but it was all in an elegant way, not tacky. Her hair, brunette, darker than I remembered, had been stylishly cut and it gave her the appearance of looking much younger. Or maybe it was that eye job, or the eye tuck, she had last summer, before we went to Europe, that gave me this impression.

"Mother," I said, standing still.

She hugged me and said, "Oh, it's been so long."

"Five weeks?"

"Oh that's a long time, dear," she said.

"Not really."

"Say hello to Mrs. Jared," she said.

"Oh Paul, you look so cute." Mrs. Jared said and hugged me also.

"Mrs. Jared," I said.

"So big and away at college. We're so proud of you."

"He's so handsome," my mother said, walking over to the window and opening it, waving the smell of cigarette smoke out.

"And tall," Mrs. Jared said. Yeah and I've fucked your son, I was thinking.

I sat down on the bed, refrained from lighting a cigarette and crossed my legs.

My mother rushed to the bathroom and immediately started to brush her hair.

Mrs. Jared took her shoes off and sat down opposite from me and asked, "Tell me Paul, why are you wearing so much black?"

STUART   After dinner and a shower, I had some friends over for wine and we all had a hair-dyeing party. While they were monopolizing the bathroom and washing their hair in the sinks, I walked across the hall to Paul Denton's room. I stood there for a long time, too nervous to knock. I read the notes that people had left on his door, then I ran my hand over it. I was going to invite him over and I was stoned enough to get up the nerve to do so. I knocked softly at first, and when there was no answer I knocked with more force. When no one opened the door I walked away, confused and relieved. I told myself I would talk to him at the party tonight; that was when I would make my move. I came back to my room and Dennis was sitting on my bed. His hair was wet and freshly dyed red and he was looking through the new *Voice* and playing my Bryan Ferry tape. I spent last night with him. I don't say anything. He tells me, "Paul Denton will never ever sleep with you." I don't say anything. Just get more drunk, turn the music up and dress to get screwed.

PAUL   "How was the flight?" I asked them.

"Oh lurid, lurid," Mrs. Jared said. "Your mother met this absolutely gorgeous doctor from the North Shore in first class who was going to Parents' Weekend at Brown and you know what your mother did?" Mrs. Jared was smiling now, like a naughty little girl.

"No." Oh, I couldn't wait.

"Oh Mimi," my mother moaned, coming out of the bath-room.

"She told him that she was *single*," Mrs. Jared exclaimed and got up and took my mother's place in the bathroom and closed the door.

There mustn't be any silence so my mother asked me, "Did I tell you about the car?"

"Yes." I could hear Mrs. Jared urinating. Embarrassed, I spoke louder, "Yes. Yes, you did. I think you did tell me about the car."

"Typical. It's all so typical. I was seeing Dr. Vanderpool and the two of us were going to lunch at The 95th and—"

"Wait. Dr. Vanderpool? Your shrink?" I asked.

She started brushing her hair again and asked, "Shrink?"

"Sorry," I said. "Doctor."

"Yes. My doctor." My mother gave me a strange look.

"Going out to lunch?" I reminded her.

"Yes," she said. I had thrown her off balance. She stood there, stumped.

"I thought this happened at Neiman's," I said, amused, but, oh shit, who cares?

"No. Why?" she asked, still brushing her hair.

"Forget it." I've forgotten I shouldn't be amused by things like that anymore. I mean, I've only been away, what, three years, right? The toilet flushed and I flinched, looking back at the TV, pretending that Mrs. Jared didn't even take a piss.

"Well . . ." My mother was looking at me like I was a real weirdo. A real KooKoo.

"Go on," I urged. "Go on."

"Well," she continued. "I came out of his office and it was gone. Completely gone. Can you believe it?" she was asking me.

"Typical," I told her. Just pretend she's not crazy and things will go smoothly.

"Yes." She stopped brushing her hair, but continued gazing into the mirror.

The bellboys broug͟ ͟ ͟ ͟ ͟ ͟ ͟ ͟
That's right. Of course,͟ ͟ ͟ ͟ ͟ ͟ ͟ ͟
two people, sure. There͟ ͟ ͟ ͟ ͟ ͟ ͟ ͟
pieces of Louis Vuitton,͟ ͟ ͟ ͟ ͟ ͟ ͟ ͟
Gucci, Mrs. Jared's.

"How's school?" my mo͟ ͟ ͟ ͟ ͟ ͟ ͟ ͟
bellboys (who were not se͟ ͟ ͟ ͟ ͟ ͟ ͟
allusions that they were).

"Fine," I said.

"Classes," she reminded hersel͟ ͟ ͟ ͟ ͟

"All right."

"What are you taking?" she aske͟ ͟ ͟ ͟

I must have told her this, given h͟ ͟ ͟ ͟ ͟ ͟ ͟ ͟ ͟
at least five times. "Classes. Just cl͟ ͟ ͟ ͟ ͟ ͟ ͟ ͟ Improv.
Scene Design. Classes. Drama."

"How is that lovely friend of yours? Michael? Monty?
What?" she asked, unzipping one of the bags and looking
through it.

I couldn't believe she did shit like that. She damn well
knew his goddamn name but I couldn't even get angry, so
I laid back and sighed his name. "Mitchell. His name was
Mitchell."

"Yes. Mitchell. That's it."

"How is he?" I asked.

"Yes."

"Fine." I started to worry about Sean again. Sean at the
party. Sean fucking someone. Who? That girl leaving notes
in his box? Or worse . . . what if he went home with Raymond or Harry or Donald? What am I doing here?

"When is Richard coming in?" I asked, changing the
subject.

"I don't know," my mother whispered, suddenly concerned. "Mimi?"

"I'd say sixish," Mrs. Jared said. "I told him that we had
dinner reservations downstairs at nine, so he knows when
to be here."

What am I doing here? My mother wants to speak to me
about nothing. It's only a ploy to get me here so she can

s and eat and smoke and live
else. My mother and Mrs. Jared
om. "We'll leave this room to you
alk and whatever. . . ." It sounds omi-
cious and what am I doing here? I look over
y of *The Fountainhead* on top of the TV set, a
der of Michael? Monty? I watch a cartoon. My
other and Mrs. Jared split a Seconal or whatever and
start to worry about what they're going to wear tonight. I
watch more cartoons and curse Sean and order room service. I decide to get drunk early.

SEAN After I got drunk this afternoon I looked for
Lauren at dinner tonight. She wasn't there. I looked for her
after Getch and Tony and Tim and I fixed up Wooley. I
looked for her after I put my toga on. (Since I'm on Wreck
Committee I've got to wear a toga but I put my leather
jacket on over it so it looked hip.) I even looked for her
room, walking around campus in the dark, trying to remember which house she lived in. But it was too cold to
look, so I stopped and watched TV in Commons, and drank
some beer instead. I didn't know what I was going to say to
her once I found her. It was just that I wanted to *see* her.
And thinking about her like that, searching all over the
place for her, I went back to my room and jerked off, fan-

tasizing about her. It was something completely spontane-
ous, something I couldn't help doing. It was like walking
past a beautiful girl on the street, someone you can't help
but look at, someone you can't suppress whistling at, someone who gets you that excited, that horny. That's how I
was feeling about Lauren, my toga raised above me, touching myself feverishly in the darkness. What does she like,
I was thinking. Questions raced through my mind—does she
go wild during sex, does she come easily, does she freak out
about oral sex, does she mind a guy coming in her mouth?
Then I realized I won't go to bed with a girl if she won't
do that. I also won't go to bed with a girl if she can't or
won't have an orgasm because then, what's the point? If
you can't make a girl come why even bother? That always
seemed to me to be like writing questions in a letter.

PAUL   I call Sean up. Someone answers the Booth phone.
   "Yeah?" Person is obviously stoned.
   "Can I talk to Sean Bateman? I think he lives upstairs,"
I ask.
   "Yeah." Really long pause. "If he's asleep should I wake
him?"
   "Yes. Please." The idiot probably *is* asleep.
   I look at myself in the mirror and turn away. Next door,
either my mom or Mrs. Jared is taking a shower. The TV
is still on. I reach over and turn the volume down.

"Yeah? Hello?" Sean says.

"Sean?"

"Yeah? Who is this? Patrick?"

Patrick? Who the hell is Patrick? "No. It's Paul."

"Paul?"

"Yeah. Remember me?"

"No. This better be good," he says.

"I just wanted to know what's going on," I say. "Who's Patrick?"

"No, Paul. That's not it. What did you want?"

"Were you asleep?"

"No, of course I wasn't asleep."

"What are you doing?"

"I was just about to go to the party," he says.

"With who?" I ask. "With Patrick?"

"What?"

"With who?" I ask again.

"I thought you asked me that," he says.

"Well?"

"The person who's been leaving notes in my box," he says loudly, laughing.

"Are you?" I ask, sitting up.

"No, I'm not. Christ, you call me up to check on who I'm going with to the party?" he yells into the phone. "You're sick!"

"I thought . . . I had a very vivid . . . image of you."

"You're also a bad judge of character," he says, calming down.

"I'm sorry," I say. "I apologize."

"It's okay." I can hear him yawn.

"So . . . who *are* you going with?" I ask, after a while.

"No one, you idiot!" he yells.

"I was only joking. Calm down. Can't you take a joke?" I ask. "Don't people from the South have a sense of humor?"

There's a long pause and then he says, "When we're around funny people."

"Scorcher, Sean. Scorcher."

"Rock'n'roll. Deal with it," he mutters.

"Yeah." I try to laugh. "Deal with it."

"Listen, I'm going to the party, okay?" he says, finally.

"Well. . . ."

"I'll see you next week," he says.

"But I'm coming back on Sunday," I say.

"Right. Sunday," he says.

"I'm sorry for calling," I say.

"Sunday. Bye." He hangs up.

I hang up too, then touch my face, and drink another beer; wonder why Richard's late.

LAUREN   Judy's room. Judy and I decide to wear togas to The Dressed To Get Screwed party. Not because we want to all that much, but just because we look better in the togas. At least, *I* look better in the toga than in the dress I was going to wear. Judy looks good in anything. Besides I don't want to go back to my room to get the dress since Franklin might be there, though he also might not, since I told him I thought *The Fate of the Earth* was the most boring book he's made me read yet (worse than *Floating Dragon*) and he had this violent seizure (capital S: he shook, he turned red) and stormed out. Plus I don't want to see if my mother called back. She called earlier today and demanded to know why I haven't called her in over three weeks. I told her I forgot my Calling Card number. But I'm in a good mood anyway, mostly because Vittorio, my new poetry teacher says I show a lot of promise and because of that I've been working on more poems, some of them pretty good; plus Judy and I might buy some Ecstasy tonight and that seems like a good idea and it's a Friday and we're in front of her mirror trying make-up on and "Revolution" is on the radio and I feel okay.

Judy says that someone put a cigarette out in her box the other day.

"It's probably the Freshman, Sam," I say.

"His name's Steve," she says. "He doesn't smoke. None of the Freshmen do."

I stand up, look at the toga. "How do I look? Do I look like an idiot?"

Judy checks her lips, then her chin. "No."

"Fat?"

"Nope." She moves away from the desk and over to the bed where she finishes rolling a joint, singing along with "Revolution." She tells me that she went off the Pill on Monday and says that she's already lost weight and I guess she looks thinner. Health Services supplied the diaphragm.

"Health Services is disgusting," Judy says. "That doctor is so horny that when I went in for an earache he gave me a Pap test."

"Are we going to buy the Ecstasy or not?" I ask.

"Only if he takes American Express," she says. "I forgot to cash a check today."

"He probably does," I murmur.

I look good, standing in front of the mirror, and it makes me sad that I'm surprised by this; that I haven't really gotten excited or dressed up to go out to a party since Victor left, and when was that? Early September? Party at the Surf Club? And I don't know why, but "Revolution" on the radio reminds me of him, and I still have mental pictures of him, standing around Europe, somewhere in my mind that resurface at the strangest moments: like a certain soup served at lunch, or flipping through *GQ* or seeing a jeans commercial on TV. Once, it was a book of matches from Morgan's in New York that I found beneath my bed last Sunday.

Judy's ready to light the joint but she can't find any matches so I go next door to the boy from L.A.'s room. Someone's written "Rest In Peace Called" in big red letters on his door. I can hear The Eagles playing inside but no one answers when I knock. I find some matches in the bathroom from Maxim's and bring them back to Judy. "Revolution" ends and another Thompson Twins song comes on. And Judy and I smoke pot, get high, make bloodys, try to list all the guys we've slept with at Camden but the list gets screwed up by hazy memory and the pot and the nervous expectations a Friday night party brings, and often we just write down "Jack's friend" or "Guy from Limelight" and the whole thing depresses me and I suggest we head over to Wooley. Maybe I should sleep with that French guy, like Judy keeps saying. But there are other options, I keep telling myself. What? I ask myself. The orgy in Booth tonight? But I'm high and feeling good as we leave Judy's place and from upstairs in her hallway we can hear the music calling to us from across Commons, accompanied by shrieks and muffled shouts in the night.

But then Judy has to ruin it as we're walking out of her house, the night autumn cold, both of us shivering in our togas, heading toward the music at Wooley.

"Have you heard from Victor?" she asks.

I hated saying it, but did anyway. "Who?"

PAUL Richard arrives sometime around eight. I'm sitting in the "boys'" room, in some plush chair, already dressed in this gray suit and silk red tie I bought at Bigsby and Kruthers, watching MTV, smoking, thinking about Sean. My mother and Mrs. Jared are in the other room getting dressed for dinner. Richard opens the door, wearing a tuxedo and sunglasses, hair greased back, walks in, lets the door slam and shouts, "Hi ya, Paul!"

I stare at Richard only slightly shocked. His long blond hair is now short, cropped and dyed a bright platinum blond that, because of the rain or mousse, looks dark. He's wearing a ripped white tuxedo shirt, one black sock, one white sock, and black Converse Hi-Tops, and a long over-coat with a Siouxsie and the Banshees decal stuck on the back. A tiny diamond stud earring in the left ear, the Way-farers still on, black and shiny. He's only carrying one small black bag with Dead Kennedys and Bronski Beat stickers on it, and in the other hand a very large cassette player and a bottle of Jack Daniel's, almost empty. He staggers in, then leans against the doorway, catching his balance.

"Richard," I say. I'm starting to feel that my entire world is beginning to turn into an issue of *Vanity Fair*.

"When are we gonna eat?" he asks.

"Richard? Is that you?" his mother calls from the other room.

"Yeah. It is," he says. "And my name's not Richard."

My mother and Mrs. Jared walk into the room, both in the middle of getting dressed and they stare at Richard who looks like a total Sarah Lawrence asshole but, maybe, sexy.

"It's Dick," he says lewdly and then, "Like, when's dinner?" He takes a deep swig from the Jack Daniel's bottle then belches.

SEAN Tense scene with Rupert.

Rupert shaved his head. I had to stop by Roxanne's place before the party to score for some Freshman idiots and the fucker had shaved his head. He was doing coke on the floor in the living room and staring at himself in the mirror, Hüsker Dü was blasting and some Brazilian guy was sitting on the couch fooling around with a portable Casio machine when I walked in.

"What's going on?" I shouted over the music. I walked over to the stereo and turned the volume down.

"You're gonna have to sell that bike of yours," Rupert growled, wiping the mirror off with his finger and then sucking on it.

"Yeah?" I laughed nervously. "What's going on?"

"Where's the money, chump?" he asked.

"Take American Express?" I joked.

Rupert threw his big white bald head to one side, a couple of razor cuts dried black made it look even creepier, and laughed for too long. I wondered if the Brazilian shaved Rupert's head. The thought made me queasy. "Oh, Bateman, you're not funny."

"Funny guy," I said.

"And because you're not funny, I'm going to give you some time." He stood up. He looked big, almost menacing but in a wimpy way and came near me.

"How much do I owe you?" I asked, backing away a little.

"I'm not gonna remind you, Bateman," he said, running his hand over the shiny head. He looked over at the gun case, considering which ones were loaded, but he was too coked out to do anything to me.

"There's an orgy in Booth tonight," I said, though I didn't care. I was going to be with Miss Hynde anyway, and the thought of kissing her momentarily got me excited and calmed me down at the same time and all I said was, "Need to score for some Freshmen."

"I need my money," Rupert said, pissed but judging from

his tone of voice would probably let it slide. He walked over to the desk near the gun case and opened a drawer.

"You know I'm broke," I said. "Stop picking on poor boys."

"What about the bike?" Rupert smiled, walking over to the stereo and turning the volume up but not as loud as it was before.

"What about it?" I asked.

"You're such a jerk," he sighed.

Before I left I asked him, "Where's Roxanne?"

"She's fucking the Brazilian," Rupert shrugged, pointed. He handed me a bag.

The Brazilian waved.

"How hip can you get?" I said.

"Yeah, walk on the wild side," Rupert said, turning away from me.

I grabbed the stuff, left, hopped on my bike and was back to school by ten.

LAUREN It's stupid but I called Victor. From The Dressed To Get Screwed party. I had one number left that he said he might be at in New York, and like an idiot I stood in the phone booth downstairs in Wooley, crying, wearing that awful-looking toga, and watching the party start, waiting for Victor to answer. I had to call twice because I really had forgotten my Calling Card number and when I finally got it right and the phone started ringing fuzzy and far away, I broke into a sweat. I started shaking, my heart beating like crazy, waiting for Victor's happy, surprised voice. A sound I hadn't heard in over eight weeks. Then I realized that I shouldn't be nervous and that this was just a really sad scene. I hadn't planned on calling this number. I had gone to the phone booth not with the intention of calling Victor, but because Reggie Sedgewick had come up to me, completely naked, and asked, "I want you to . . ."

He looked ugly and pathetic and was staring at the porno movie that was being shown on the ceiling and I was looking for the bar, and said, "Yes?"

And he said, "I want you to . . . suck my cock."

And I looked down at it and then back at his face and said, "You've got to be out of your mind."

And he said, "No baby. I want you to suck my cock, really."

And I thought of Victor and started for the phone booth. "Suck your own," I said, near tears, walking blindly for the door.

"You think I'd be asking you if I could?" he called out, pointing at it, drunk out of his mind or, even worse, maybe sober.

I got so depressed I just yelled "Fuck off!" and almost slammed the door of the phone booth and made the call, only slightly mortified that I knew the number from memory. When I gave the operator the final number of the Calling Card, and during the silence that followed, I knew it was over. I knew it standing in that phone booth waiting for Victor to answer at this strange, hostile number. I knew it was over even before I met Sean Bateman later that night. How long had I been deluding myself so completely, I wondered as the first ring came over the line. I felt ashamed of myself and I needed a cigarette and the phone kept ringing and Reggie Sedgewick started knocking on the door blubbering an apology and someone answered the phone and it was Jaime and I hung up and went back to the party, pushing Reggie out of the way. I was determined to get some fun out of this night.

So I got drunk, then met Sean, then watched Stuart Jackson dance to an old Billy Idol song, then got high in Gina's apartment. In that order.

PAUL The four of us—me, Richard, Mrs. Jared, my mother—are sitting in the middle of the dining room at The Ritz-Carlton. Classical music is being played by an expert pianist. Waiters dressed in new expensive tuxedos move quickly, gracefully, from table to table. Elderly women with too much make-up on, slumped lazily, drunkenly in the red velvet chairs, stare and smile. We're surrounded by what Mrs. Jared likes to call, "old, very old money," as if the Jared's money was new, very new. (Yeah, those banks have been in the family for only about a century and a half, I refrain from saying.) The whole thing is just really unnerving, especially since Richard, even after a shower and a new suit, hair still greased back, sunglasses still on, as of yet, hasn't sobered up. He looks, unfortunately, pretty hot. He sits across from me, making lewd gestures that I pray neither mother will notice. His foot is now in my crotch but I'm too nervous to get hard. He's drinking champagne Kirs and he's downed about four, all of them carefully and with what looks to me a definite sense of purpose. He'll alternately stare at his glass or raise his eyebrows up suggestively at me, then dig his shoeless foot into my crotch and I'll squirm and make faces and my mother will ask if I'm okay and I'll just cough, "Ahem." Richard stares at the ceiling, then starts humming some U2 song to himself. It's so quiet in this elegant, tacky, big cave that I'm afraid people are staring at us and, if not us, then at least at Richard, and they probably are and there's nothing to do but just get drunker.

After Mrs. Jared asks Richard for the sixteenth time to take his sunglasses off and he refuses, she finally uses the reverse psychology bit and says, "So Richard, tell us about school."

Richard looks at her and reaches into his pocket pulling out a Marlboro and grabbing the candle from the middle of the table, lights it.

"Oh, don't smoke," Mrs. Jared says disapprovingly, as he places the candle back.

I've refrained all evening from smoking and am seriously dying of a violent nicotine attack and I eye Richard's cigarette hungrily. I am trying to rip my napkin in half.

"My name's not Richard," Richard reminds her, quietly.

Mrs. Jared looks at my mother and then at Richard and asks, "Then, what is it?"

"Dick," he says, making it sound like the filthiest name imaginable.

"What?" Mrs. Jared asks.

"Dick. You heard me." Richard takes a long drag from the Marlboro and blows it across the table at me. I cough and sip my drink.

"No. Your name is Richard," Mrs. Jared corrects.

"Sorry," Richard shakes his head. "It's Dick."

Mrs. Jared pauses. She's slipping. She has not eaten much and has been drinking steadily, even before dinner began, and now she calmly asks, "Well, Dick . . . how *is* school?"

"Sucks cock," Richard says.

I'm sipping champagne when he says this and burst out laughing, spraying my plate. I quickly place the napkin I'm trying to rip apart over my mouth, attempt to swallow but start coughing instead, then choking. My eyes water and I breathe in, gasping.

"What are you taking . . . Dick?" Mrs. Jared asks, looking at me, trying to hold her composure, a stare of reprimand fixed on her face. I wipe my mouth and shrug.

"I don't know. Gangbanging 111. Freebasing tutorial," Richard shrugs, laughing, digging his foot even harder against my crotch. I cough again and grab at his foot beneath the table. "You like that?" he asks.

"What else?" Mrs. Jared is clearly trying not to act nonplussed, but her hand trembles as she finishes the rest of her drink.

"Oral Sex Workshop," Richard says.

"My God," my mother whispers, and she hasn't said a word all night.

"What's that like?" Mrs. Jared asks, still calm. Reverse psychology not working.

"I got a joke," Richard says, still rubbing his foot against me, puffing on the cigarette. "You all wanna hear it?"

"No," my mother and Mrs. Jared say at the same time.

"Paul wants to," he says. "See, Julio Iglesias and Diana Ross meet at this party and they go back to Julio's place and they fuck—"

"I do not want to hear this," Mrs. Jared says, waving a passing waiter away after pointing at her empty glass.

"Neither do I," my mother speaks again.

"Anyway, they fuck," Richard continues, "and afterwards, Diana Ross, who's come about fifty times and wants more of Julio's dick, says—"

"I don't want to hear this either," my mother repeats.

"She says," Richard goes on, getting louder, " 'Julio you gotta fuck my pussy again, I loved it so much' and Julio says 'Okay baby, but I need to sleep for a leetle beet—' "

"What has happened to you?" Mrs. Jared asks.

" 'But, you must keep one hand on my cock and the other on my balls' Julio says, 'and then after thirty minutes we fuck again, okay?' " Richard is getting animated and I'm just dying, tearing at the napkin.

"Oh my God," my mother says, disgusted.

"And Diana says," and now Richard does a really bad Diana Ross impersonation, " 'Why do I have to keep one hand on your cock and another on your balls, Julio?' "

"What has happened to you?" Mrs. Jared asks, interrupting again.

Richard's getting pissed off that she's interrupting and his voice gets louder and I just slump down deeper into the chair, let go of the napkin and light a cigarette. Why not.

"And Julio says, 'You wanna know why you have to keep one hand on my cock and one hand on my balls?' " He says this with a fierce leer on his face.

"What has happened to you?" Mrs. Jared is shaking her head and I feel sorry for her, sitting in this dining room, being abused by her son, dressed in that ugly outfit she probably got at Loehmann's.

Richard gets even angrier that she's interrupting his joke and I know what's coming and I don't even care who Sean is fucking tonight, at this moment. I just want the punchline to be over with, and Richard, the asshole, delivers it loud, staring at his mother: " 'Because the last time I fucked a nigger she stole my wallet.' " And then he sits back, drained, but satisfied. The table becomes hushed. I look around the room and smile and nod at one of the old ladies at the table across from ours. She nods approvingly and smiles back.

"What has happened to you?" Mrs. Jared asks for the fourth time.

"What do you mean, *what has happened to me?* What do you think?" Richard asks, followed by a gruff snort of contempt.

"I can see what that school has done to you," she says.

Great, I'm thinking. It's taken her three years to find this out? Actually Richard was always a rude jerk. I don't understand what the big surprise is now. I look down at my lap as the foot disappears. I finish my drink and suck on an ice cube, leaving the cigarette burning, unsmoked in the ashtray.

"That's really too bad, huh?" Richard sneers.

"Obviously I can see we should never have sent you there," Mrs. Jared says, and as much of an asshole as Richard's being, she's still a bitch.

"Obviously," Richard says, mimicking her.

"Do you want to leave the table?" she asks him.

"Why?" Richard asks, his voice rising, getting more defensive.

"Will you please leave the table," she says.

"No," Richard says, getting hysterical. "I will not leave the table."

"I am asking you to leave the table *now*," Mrs. Jared says, her voice getting quieter but more intense.

My mother watches this exchange in silent horror.

"No no no," Richard says, shaking his head. "I will not leave the table."

"Leave the table." Mrs. Jared is turning crimson with fury.

"Fuck you!" Richard screams.

The pianist stops playing and whatever quiet din of conversation there was in the dining room is killed. Richard pauses, then takes a last drag from his Marlboro, finishes his Kir, and gets up, bows and walks slowly out of the dining room, one of his feet shoeless. The maitre d' and the head waiter rush over to our table and ask if anything is wrong; if perhaps we want the check.

"Everything is fine now," Mrs. Jared says and actually musters a faint smile. "I'm really terribly sorry."

"Are you sure?" The maitre d' looks me over suspiciously as if I were Richard's twin.

"Positive," Mrs. Jared says. "My son is not feeling well. He has a lot of pressures . . . you know, with . . . with mid-terms coming up."

Mid-terms at Sarah Lawrence? I look over at my mother, who's staring off into space.

The waiter and the maitre d' look at each other for a moment as if they're not quite sure how to proceed, and when they look back at Mrs. Jared she says, "I would like another vodka Collins. Eve, would you like anything?"

"Yes," my mother says, stunned, shaking her head slowly, still horrified by Richard's exit. I wonder if I'll sleep with him tonight. "I mean . . . no," she says. "Well . . . yes." My mother is still confused and looks at me—for what? Help?

"Get her another one." I shrug.

The maitre d' nods and walks away, conferring with the waiter. The pianist resumes playing, slowly, unsure. Some of the people who were staring finally look away. I notice when I look down at my lap that I have almost succeeded in ripping my napkin in two.

After a while my mother says, "I think I want the next car to be blue. A dark blue."

No one says anything until the drinks arrive.

"What do you think, Paul?" she asks.

I close my eyes and say, "Blue."

SEAN   Lauren Hynde was standing with friends on the stairs. She was holding a cup of grain alcohol punch that was being served from a trashcan by this fat girl who was almost naked. Lauren was wearing a toga also (probably because I had mentioned it this afternoon) and it was cut low and her shoulders were brown and smooth and I got a rush, it knocked me out, from seeing that much skin. Suddenly, I wondered if she was a dyke. Standing there with Tony, watching her, her back, her legs, her face, hair, she was talking to some girls—ugly, undistinguished compared to her. Tony kept talking to me about his new sculpture and had no idea I was staring at this girl. He was only wearing underwear and had a mattress strapped to his back. I kept looking up at her and she knew it—she wouldn't look back, even though I was standing at the bottom of the staircase, directly below her. Centerfolds from porno magazines were glued to the walls everywhere and there was a movie being projected on the ceiling in the living room above the dance floor, but the girls in it were fat and too pale and it wasn't sexy or anything.

We ended up meeting in the bathroom. Getch was there leaning against the sink, on Ecstasy, and I think she was on it too, and Getch introduced us but we said we already knew each other, but only "sort of" she added. I got her some more punch even though I hated leaving her in the bathroom alone with Getch (but maybe Getch was gay, I was thinking) and I came back and Getch was gone and she was looking at herself in the mirror and I looked too, until she turned around and smiled at me. We talked and I told her I liked her paintings I saw in Gallery 1 last term (I was guessing) and she said "That's nice," (even though I really hadn't seen the paintings, but what the hell—I wanted to get laid) and then we went to the living room and she wanted to dance, but I couldn't dance very well, so I watched her dance to some song called "Love of the Common People" but then I got nervous that some jerk would start to dance with her if I didn't step in, so when "Love Will Tear Us Apart" by Joy Division came on, I moved in. But it wasn't the Joy Division version, it was someone else and it was popped-up and ruined, but I danced to it anyway since we were flirting like mad and she was so insanely beautiful that I couldn't understand why I hadn't fucked her before. I

was g
think o
dramafag s
in his underw
dominating the c
him—she was clapp
her a cigarette when
a Heineken bottle and w
since she was so drunk. I ga
waved the bottle in front of
Lauren had heard them since s
scrawny little geek jump all over t
the whole party on the sides scream
dancing, someone even threw him a ba
when I grabbed her arm and ran, headin
onto the cool dark lawn, leaving the party behi

EVE Mimi had two more vodka Collins and when the
three of us left the dining room and were taking the elevator upstairs, she fell against the elevator attendant and almost passed out. I walked her back to the room where she
took a Valium and went to sleep. Paul went into the other
room. I sat on the bed watching Eve sleep for quite some
time before I decided to tell him. I went into his room. He
had undressed already and was in bed, reading. Richard

ed up when I
he not wanted to
nted to come and see me?
ment and sorry for myself. What
uldn't be said in a hotel room and finally
y don't you get dressed?"

hy?" he asked.

"I thought maybe we'd go downstairs for a drink," I
suggested, casually.

"What for?" he asked.

"I want to talk to you about something," I told him.

He looked panicked and asked, "Why not here?"

"Let's go downstairs," I told him and went to get my
purse.

He put on a pair of jeans and a gray sweater and a ripped
black tweed coat that I didn't recognize, that I had not
bought for him. He met me in the hall.

We went downstairs to the bar and the host came up to
us and looked Paul over. "Yes, there are two of us," I said.

"I'm afraid there's a dress code," the host smiled.

"Yes? . . ." I waited.

"This young man is not following it," the host said, still
smiling.

"Where does it say there's a dress code?" I asked.

The host glared, still smiling and then walked over to a
white board and pointed to the bright blue lettering, first
to, "No Jeans," and then, "Tie Must Be Worn." I was getting a headache and I felt very tired.

"Forget it, Mom," Paul said. "We'll go somewhere else."

I said, "We are guests in this hotel."

"Yes, I realize that," the host explained, officiously I
thought. "But this applies to everyone."

I opened my purse.

"Would you like me to make reservations for later?" the
host asked.

"My son is dressed fine," I said, handing the host a
twenty dollar bill. "Just sit us in the back," I said wearily.

The host took the bill quickly and said, "Yes, there might be a table over in the corner, in the dark."

"In the corner, in the dark," I said.

He sat us down at a terribly small, dimly lit table in back, away from the large crowded bar, but I was too tired to complain and simply ordered two champagne Kirs. Paul tried to light a cigarette inconspicuously and all at once he looked so handsome sitting there, the light playing off his features, his hair blond and thick and combed back, his face lean, the nose regal and thin, that I wanted to hug him, make contact of some kind, but "Darling, I wish you wouldn't smoke" was all I could say.

"Mother, I'm sorry," he said. "But I need a cigarette. Badly."

I let it pass and the waiter brought the Kirs. I focused all my attention on the way the waiter quickly, nimbly opened each small bottle of Taittinger and poured them into the tall thin glasses. And how very beautiful it looked when the champagne slowly dissolved the reddish purple cassis on the bottom of each glass. Paul crossed his legs and tried to look at me once the waiter left.

"You know, your father and I first came here seventeen years ago for our fifth anniversary. It was in December and it was snowing and we would order these," I told him quietly, holding the glass up, tasting it.

He sipped his drink and seemed to relax.

I couldn't say anything for a long time. I finished what was in the glass and poured the rest of the champagne from the small green Taittinger bottle into it. I drank more, then asked about Richard.

"I wonder what happened to Richard tonight," I said, straining for conversation.

"Mid-terms," Paul said derisively, and then, "I don't know."

"Any ideas?" I asked.

"Walking?" he sighed. "I don't know."

"His mother says he has a new girlfriend," I mentioned.

Paul got very hostile very suddenly and rolled his eyes up. "Mom, Richard's bi."

"Bi what?" I asked.

"Bi," he said, lifting his hands as if to describe this condition. "You know. *Bi.*"

"Bilingual?" I asked, confused. I was tired and needed sleep.

"Bisexual," he said and stared at his glass.

"Oh," I said.

I liked my son very much. We were in a bar together and he was being polite and I wanted to hold his hand, but I breathed in and exhaled. It was too dark where we sat. I touched my hair and then looked at Paul. And for a very brief moment there it seemed as if I never had known this child. He sat there, his face placid, expressionless. My son— a cipher. How did it end up this way, I wondered.

"Your father and I are getting a divorce," I said.

"Why?" Paul asked, after a while.

"Because . . . " I stalled. Then said, "We don't love each other anymore."

Paul did not say anything.

"Your father and I have been living apart since you left for school," I told him.

"Where does he live now?" he asked.

"In the city."

"Oh," Paul said.

"Are you upset?" I asked. I thought I was going to cry but it passed.

Paul took another sip and uncrossed his legs. "Upset?" he asked. "No. I knew it was going to happen sooner or later." He smiled as if he remembered something private and humorous and it made me sad, and all I could say was, "We're signing the papers next Wednesday afternoon." And then I wondered why I told him this, why I gave him this detail, this piece of information. I wondered where Paul was going to be next Wednesday afternoon. With that friend, Michael, at lunch? And I wanted badly to know what he did at school—if he was popular, if he went to parties, who he slept with even. I wondered if he was still seeing that girl from Cairo, was it? Or Connecticut? He had mentioned something about her at the beginning of the year. I was sorry I brought him to Boston for the weekend and made him sit through that dinner. And I could have told him this in the hotel room. Being in the bar did not matter.

"What do you think?" I asked my son.

"Does it matter?" he said.

"No," I said. "Not really."

"Is this what you wanted to talk to me about?"

"Yes." I finished the champagne. There was nothing left to do.

"Is there anything else?" he asked.

"Anything else?" I asked.

"Yeah," he said.

"I suppose not."

"Okay." He put the cigarette out and did not light another one.

STUART I don't know what gets into me but I go to The Dressed To Get Screwed party in only my underwear, thinking my body looks okay, thinking I want to get Paul Denton's attention. So I do some coke with Jenkins and get completely fucked-up drinking that sickly sweet, sticky alcohol punch and when Billy Idol comes on I just go crazy and do this great number. The whole party loves it and they're all in a circle and I'm in the middle twirling and gyrating and jumping around, hoping he was watching me. I looked for him afterwards, turned on, dizzy and a little sick from dancing so hard, drunk, stoned, Dance majors coming on to me, and feeling pretty good. But, of course, I couldn't find him. He wasn't anywhere. He probably thought it was too uncool to come to these things anyway. But who *doesn't* go to The Dressed To Get Screwed party, besides that weird Classics group (and they're probably roaming the countryside sacrificing farmers and performing pagan rituals)? I ended up going home alone. Not really, I fooled around with Dennis a little while, but I fell asleep like I usually do on Friday nights: unscrewed.

It's party time and she is ready. The party is swirling and miraculous-seeming and she has dressed so carefully that she tries to avoid the living room and dance floor because if she gets messed up she thinks she will never see you, or you will never see her. This is why she is very careful as she roams the party looking for you. She enters the living room of this house, this tomb of destruction, songs she loves being danced out by sweat-drenched cap-

tives of the room's embrace. She is shocked not happy to see how many have decided to come wrapped in white sheets. Should she have? It is so very dark that she can only make out the paleness of unclothed bodies, a camera, a video crew in one corner capturing this night's images, other images, less graphic, flickering above them on the upperwalls, below the ceiling, a skinny boybody dancing enthusiastically in a circle made of those same sweat-drenched captives, near-naked people seem everywhere but it is not, strangely enough, or maybe it is strangely enough, erotic, and she walks by them, through the living tomb and into an area where pink beverage is being scooped from a cylindrical gray bin by a girl so fleshy that it makes her titter and she still doesn't see you. She searches hall-ways and bathrooms, finds couples fucking under the Oc-tober moon on the lawn, upstair bathrooms, upstair bed-rooms, roams the hallway, even the kitchen for god's sake, but she does not see you until she is back under the killing blue lights of the living room now illuminated. As fate has it you are dancing, swaying, with a beautiful girl she does recognize, but she does not think that you like her, but the music is too loud to feel anything really except—that you will give yourself to her. She stands next to a black box bigger than herself where music pours from, holding a pink drink and she loves the way your head is thrown back, moving, trying to keep the beat (you are not a good dancer) and the song ends, a new one overlaps it and it makes no sense at all. She follows you out of the room, you look back at the girl and decide to take her arm and the blue light makes your white sheets glow beneath the jacket you are taking off and she follows you to the light at the door and says . . . "Hello" . . . and never has a second hurt and ruptured, blistered so harshly because the music's too loud and you can't hear, don't even notice, and you take her hand instead and you are both leaving. You smiled, she thinks, at her. But by then she was hiding in the corner of the room, standing on the rolled-up carpet, the room a black-blue mass moving to the songs, her love *still silent and undeclared and it was time to make a decision. What can she do? Can she go to you and tell you things without you thinking of her as a crazy love maniac? No. Maybe it's not even that, but it is over. And she will not be with you. It's simple. But your smile actually echoes still, and it is too late. She stands in the corner, waiting, listening to the music, music that tells her nothing, doesn't even offer a clue as to what to do, just playing loudly, the same, excruciating, dumb beat that traps her, doesn't move her, and on the way out of this place, alone, she bumps into someone who has shaved their head and he sticks his tongue out at her, wagging it, yelling orgyinboothorgyinbooth but she doesn't listen, her face, still hot but numb with rejection, down, staring at the floor—it's over. It is time. Baldboy laughs at her. She walks away, by End of the World, looks down at the lights of the town. There won't be any more notes. It's last call.*

LAUREN   A lightbulb. I'm staring at the lightbulb above Sean's head. We're at Lila's and Gina's apartment in Fels. Two lesbians from the poetry workshop I recently joined. Actually, Gina in strict confidence told me that she's on the Pill, "just in case." Does that mean she's a lesbian technically? Lila, on the other hand, has confided in me that she's worried Gina will leave her since it's "in" to sleep with women this term. What do you say to someone? Well, what about next term? Actually, *what about* next term? You watch Sean too, you watch him roll a joint and he's pretty good at it which makes me want to sleep with him less, but oh who cares, Jaime answered the phone, right? and it's a Friday, and it was either him or that French guy. His hands are nice: clean and large and he handles the pot rather delicately, and I want him suddenly to touch my breasts. I don't know why I think this but I do. Not exactly handsome, but he's passable looking: light hair combed back, smallish features (maybe a little like a rat?), maybe too short, maybe too thin. No, not handsome, just vaguely Long Islandish. But a big improvement over that Kir-sipping Iranian editor you met at Vittorio's last party who told you you were going to be the next Madonna. After I told him I was a poet, he said he meant Marianne Moore.

"So, who's going to help us bomb the weight room?" Gina asks. Gina is part of Camden's "old guard" and the arrival of the weight room and an aerobics instructor has made her livid (even though she wants to sleep with the aerobics instructor—who, in my opinion, doesn't even have that nice a body). "Lila is devastated," she tells me.

Lila nods and rests her head on the Kathy Acker book she's been flipping through.

"B-U-M-M-E-R," I spell out, sighing. Look at the Map-plethorpe photo of Susan Sontag pinned above the sink and snicker.

Sean laughs and looks up from the joints as if I said something brilliant and it's not funny but because he laughs I laugh.

"Tim loves it," he says.

"Let's kill him and we'll call it art," Lila says. How does Lila know Tim, I wonder. Does Tim sleep with lesbians? I am drunk.

Still holding a glass of the pink punch it occurs to me that I am so drunk I cannot get up. I just tell Lila, "Don't get depressed," and then to Gina, "Do you have any coke?" too drunk to be ashamed.

"Depression becomes some," Lila says.

"No," Gina.

"You want some?" Sean asks.

"No."

Depression becomes some?

Can't argue with that so we light the first joint. Wish we had sex and it was over with so I could go back to my room with the down pillows and the comforter and pass out with some dignity. Lila gets up. Puts on a Kate Bush record and dances around the room.

"This place has really changed." Someone hands me the joint. I take a long, hard hit and look around the apartment and agree with whoever said that. Stephanie Myers and Susan Goldman and Amanda Taylor lived here my Sophomore year. It *is* different.

"The Seventies never ended." Sean the Philosopher Bateman this time. What a stupid thing to say, I'm thinking. What a strange and supremely stupid thing to say. He smiles at me and thinks it's profound. I feel sick. I want them to turn the music down.

"I wonder if everyone goes through this much hell at college," Lila ponders, dancing next to my chair, staring dreamily at me. Do I want to sleep with another girl? No.

"Don't worry darling," Gina says. "We're not at Williams."

Not at Williams. No, that's for sure. Smoke more grass. For some reason he's not looking at Gina. Lila sits down and sighs and resumes looking at the drawings in the Acker book. Go to Europe if you don't like it, I'm thinking. Victor, I'm thinking.

"Louis Farrakhan was supposed to visit but the Freshmen and Sophomores on student council voted against it," Sean says. "Can you believe that?" So he's politically conscious too. Even worse. He smokes more of the pot than Gina and I combined, someone's even brought out a bong. He holds it like Victor holds it. I look at him, nauseated, but it's too smoky and Kate Bush is too screechy and he doesn't notice. "They even want someone to redesign the school sign," he adds.

"Why?" I find myself asking.

"Not Eighties enough," Lila suggests.

"Probably want flashing neon," Gina.

"Get Keith Haring or Kenny Scharf," Lila grimaces.

"Or Schnabel," Gina cringes.

"Too passé," Lila mutters.

"Lots of broken plates and 'suggestive' smears," did Sean say this?

"Or getting Fischel to do the pamphlet. Some of the chic jet-setting nihilistic Eurotrash who live off-campus, nude, standing around with dogs and fish. Welcome to Camden College—You'll Never Be Bored." Gina starts laughing.

"I'm gonna redesign it," Lila says. "Win the money. Buy a gram."

What money? I'm thinking. Have I missed something. Am I out of it?

The grass is good but I have to light a cigarette to stay awake and during a break on the record we can all hear someone from the party next door scream, "That's phallic—yeah! yeah! yeah!" and we all look at each other, stoned, and crack up and I remember seeing Judy crying in a doorway upstairs at the party, in the bathroom, Franklin trying to comfort her, Franklin glaring at me as I left with Sean.

Now the inevitable.

We're in his room and he plays me a song. On his guitar. He *serenades* me and it's almost embarrassing enough to sober me up. "You're Too Good to Be True" and I start crying only because I can't help but think of Victor, and he stops halfway through and kisses me and we end up going to bed. And I'm thinking what if I went back to my room now, and what if there was a note on the door saying Victor called? What if there was just a note? Whether he called or not doesn't matter. Just to see a note, just to see maybe a V, and fuck the rest of the letters. If there was just a sign. It could make me elated for one week, no, one day. I put my diaphragm in at Gina's and Lila's apartment so there's no drunken forgetfulness on my part, no running to the bathroom in the middle of foreplay.

Sean fucks me. It's not so bad. It's over. I breathe easy.

SEAN We walked slowly back to my bedroom (she followed me like she knew this would happen, too eager, too stunned to speak) past the party which was still going on, across the Commons, and upstairs to Booth. I was so excited I couldn't stop shaking and I dropped the key when I tried to unlock the door. She sat on the bed and leaned against the wall, her eyes closed. I plugged in the Fender and played her a song I'd written myself and then segued into "You're Too Good to Be True" and I played it quietly and sang the lyrics slowly and softly and she was so moved that she started to cry and I stopped playing and knelt before the bed and touched her neck, but she couldn't look at me; maybe it was the grass we smoked at the dykes' who want to blow up the weight room, or maybe it was the Ecstasy I'm pretty sure she was on; maybe it was that she loved me. When I tilted her face up, her eyes were so grateful that . . .

. . . he had to kiss her quickly on the lips and . . . he got hard almost immediately after she started kissing back, still crying, her face slick, and he started to pull her toga off but there was an interruption that he was oddly grateful for. Tim came in without knocking and asked if he had a razor blade and he gave him one and Tim didn't apologize for interrupting since he was so coked-out and he made sure the door was locked after he left. But he was still strangely not excited. He turned back to her, and turned off the amp, then got on the bed.

She had already started taking her toga off and except for her panties she had nothing on beneath it. She had the body of a much younger girl. Her breasts were small but full, yet the nipples weren't hard, not even after he touched them, then kissed and licked them. He helped her remove the panties, saw how small her cunt was too, the pubic hair light and sparse yet when he squeezed it, hard then soft, slid a finger in, he didn't feel anything. She wasn't getting wet even though she was making soft little moans. He was semi-stiff, but still not excited. Something was missing. . . . There was a problem somewhere, a mistake. He didn't know what. Confused, he started to fuck her, and before he came, it hit him: he can't remember the last time he had sex sober. . . .

PAUL   I sit alone in my room, in a chair, in front of the TV, drinking beer I ordered up from room service, watching Friday night videos. Video of Huey Lewis and the

News comes on. Huey Lewis walks into a party looking confused. Huey Lewis reminds me of Sean. Huey Lewis also reminds me of my ninth-grade gym teacher. Sean doesn't remind me of my ninth-grade gym teacher. Richard opens the door, still in the tuxedo he was wearing at dinner and he sits down on one of the beds and all he says is, "Lost my sunglasses."

I keep watching Huey Lewis, who can't find his way out of the party. He's holding hands with some blond bubblehead and they can't find their way out. They keep opening doors and none of them contain an exit. One contains a train hurtling at them, another has a vampire hidden behind it, but none offer a way out. How symbolic.

"Do you have any coke?" Richard asks:

A surge of irritation makes me grip the Heineken bottle tighter. I don't say anything.

"There's a lot of coke at Sarah Lawrence," he says.

The video ends and another one comes on, but it's not a video, it's a commercial for soap and I look over at him.

"What's going on?" he asks.

"I don't know," I say. "What's going on?"

"With me?" he asks.

"I guess," I say. "Who else, idiot?"

"I don't know," Richard says. "I went out."

"You went out," I repeat.

"To a bar," he sighs.

"Get lucky?" I ask.

"Would I be here with you if I had?" he says.

His crude attempt at the cutdown, if it was a cutdown, irritates me more than if he had come up with a real . . . what? scorcher?

"Are you drunk?" I ask, vaguely hoping that he is.

"I wish," he moans.

"Do you?" I ask.

"Yes. I do," he moans again, laying back on the bed.

"Quite a little scene you made at dinner," I mention.

We watch another video or maybe it's another commercial, I can't tell, and then he says, "Fuck off. I don't care." After a moment's thoughtful silence, he then asks, "Are they both asleep?" looking over at the wall that separates the rooms from each other.

"Yes." I nod.

"I went to a movie," he admits.

"I don't care," I say.

"It sucked," he says.

He gets up and walks over to the cassette player and puts a tape in; hard punk music blasts out of the box and I jump up, completely startled and he makes a face and turns the volume down, then he starts to giggle mischievously and sits in the chair next to mine.

"What are you watching?" he asks. He's holding the bottle of J.D. which somehow has magically reappeared and offers it to me as he unscrews the top. I shake my head and push it away. "Videos," I say.

He looks at me, then gets up and stares out the window; he's got that restless pre-fucking state about him; expectant nervous energy. "I came back because it started to rain." I can hear him lighting a cigarette, start to smell the smoke. I close my eyes and lean against the chair, and remember a rainy afternoon sitting in Commons with Sean, both of us hungover, sharing a plate of French fries we got at the snack bar since we missed lunch. We were always missing lunch. It was always raining.

"Do you remember those weekends at Saugatuck and Mackinac Island?" he asks.

"No, I don't. I only remember hellish weekends at Lake Winnebago. In fact I've never been to Mackinaw Island," I say calmly.

"Mackinac," he says.

"Naw," I say.

"You're being difficult, Paul," he says sweetly.

"Shoot me."

"Well, anyway, do you remember the Thomases would always come too?" he asks. "Remember Brad Thomas? Good-looking but a mega geek?"

"Mega geek?" I ask. "Brad? Brad from Latin?"

"No, Brad from Fenwick," he says.

"I don't remember Brad Thomas," I say, even though I went to Fenwick with Brad and Richard. I had a crush on Brad in fact. Or was that Bill?

"Remember that Fourth of July when my father got you and Kirk and me so drunk on the boat and my mother had a fit? We were listening to the Top 100 countdown on the radio and someone fell off, right?" he says. "Remember that?"

"Fourth of July? On a boat?" I ask. I suddenly wonder where my father is tonight, and I'm mildly surprised that it doesn't depress me because I sort of do remember my father's boat, and I remember wanting badly to see Brad naked, but I can't remember if anyone fell off a boat, and I'm too tired to even make a move toward Richard so I slump back in the chair and tell him, "I do remember. Get on with it. What's the point?"

"I miss those days," Richard says simply.

"You're a jerk," I say.

"What happened?" he asks, turning away from the window.

Well, let's see, your father left your mother for another woman and Mr. Thomas if I remember correctly died of a heart attack playing polo and you became a drug addict and went to college and I became one too for a little while and went to Camden where I wasn't a drug addict anymore in comparison and I mean what do you want to hear, Richard? Since I have to say something I just say, "You're a jerk," again, instead.

"I guess we grew up," he says sadly.

"Grew up," I say. "Profound."

He sits back next to me in the other chair. "I hate college."

"Isn't it a little too late to complain?" I ask.

He ignores me. "I hate it."

"Well, the first couple of years are bad," I say.

"How about the rest?" He looks over at me, seriously awaiting my answer.

"You get used to it," I say, after a while.

We stare at the TV. More commercials that look like videos. More videos.

"I want to fuck Billy Idol," he says absently.

"Yeah?" I yawn.

"I want to fuck you too," he says in the same absent voice.

"Guess I'm in good company." His comments make me want to take a swig from the bottle of Jack Daniel's. I do. It tastes good. I hand him back the bottle.

"Stop flirting," he says, laughing. "You're a bad flirt."

"No, I'm not," I say, offended that he thinks I'm coming on to him.

He grabs my wrist playfully and says "You always were."

"Richard, I don't know what you're talking about," I say, pulling my wrist away from his hold, looking at him quizzically, then turning back to the TV.

Another video changes into a commercial and then a loud clap of thunder quiets us.

"It's really raining hard," he says.

"Yes, it's raining hard," I say.

"Are you seeing anyone there?" he asks. "I mean, at school."

"Some Sophomore from the South who rides a motorcycle. I can't explain it," I say and then realize that it's a pretty accurate description of Sean and it makes him look a lot less glamorous than he once seemed. Because, what else is there to say about him? There's a minute here where I cannot remember his name, can't even picture features, a face, any sort of shape. "What about you?" I choke, dreading the answer.

"What about me?" he asks. What a finely honed sense of humor.

"Have you 'met' anyone?" I rephrase the question.

" 'Met' anyone?" he asks coyly.

"Who are you fucking? Is that better? I mean, I don't really want to know. I'm just making conversation."

"Oh God," he sighs. "Some guy from Brown. He studies Semiotics. I think it's the study of laundry or something. Anyway, he's on the crew team. I see him weekends, you know."

"Who else?" I ask. "How about at school?"

"Oh this guy from California, from Encino, named Jaime. Transfer from U.C.L.A. Blond, Jewish. He's on the crew team also."

"That is such a *lie*," I have to blurt out.

"What?" He gets embarrassed, looks shocked. "What do you mean?"

"You always say you're seeing someone on the 'crew' team. And you never are. What is a 'crew' team?" I ask and I notice that we have been whispering the entire conversation. "There's not a crew team at Sarah Lawrence, you nitwit. You think you're going to get away with lying to me?"

"Oh shut up, you're completely crazy," he says, disgusted with me, waving me away.

We watch some more TV and listen to the music coming from the cassette player at the same time and finish off the J.D. After we've smoked all the cigarettes in the room, he finally asks, "How is yours going?"

I say, "It's not."

He leans over and looks out the window. Richard has a really nice body.

I pick up the bottle and cough as I swallow the last drops. Richard says, "You know it's bad when you can see the rain at night."

We're quiet for a minute and he looks at me and I start to laugh at him.

"What's so funny?" he asks, smiling.

" 'You know it's bad when you can see the rain at night?' What is that? A fucking Bonnie Tyler song?"

The liquor has made me feel good and he leans up close, laughing also, and I can smell the warm scotch on his breath and he kisses me too hard at first and I push him back a little and I can feel the line where stubble and lip meet and I think I hear a door open and close somewhere and I don't care whether it's Mrs. Jared or my mother, drunk, in lieu of divorce, asleep by Seconal, in a nightgown from Marshall Fields, and though I don't want to, we undress each other and I go to bed with Richard. Afterwards, early in the morning, pre-dawn, without saying goodbye to anyone, I pack quietly and walk to the bus station in the rain and take the first bus back to Camden.

I'm lying, in warm water, in a bathtub, in Sawtell. I'm doing this because I know I'll never have Him. I drag the razor firmly across the hot skin underwater and the flesh peels back quickly, blood jetting out, literally jetting out, from the bottom of my arm. I drag it cross the other wrist jaggedly, up and down, and the water turns pink. When I lift my arm up, above water, blood gushes powerfully high and I have to place my wrist back under so I'm not splattered with it. I sit up, only slash at one ankle because the weakness drenches me and I lay back, the water turning impossibly red and then I start to dream, and I keep dreaming and it's then that I'm not sure if this is really the thing to do. I can hear music coming from another house someplace and maybe I try to sing along with it, but, as usual, I find myself trying to get to the ending before it actually happens. Maybe I should have tried another route. The one that little man at the gas station in Phoenix advised, or shall I say, urged me on to or oww— Guess what? No time. God jesus christ our my nothing savior

LAUREN   And it's quiet now, and over. I'm standing by Sean's window. It's almost morning, but still dark. It's weird and maybe it's my imagination but I'm positive I can hear the aria from *La Wally* coming from somewhere, not across the lawn since the party is over, but it might be somewhere in this house perhaps. I have my toga wrapped around me and occasionally I'll look over and watch him sleep in the glow of his blue digital alarm clock light. I'm not tired anymore. I smoke a cigarette. A silhouette moves in another window, in another house across from this one. Somewhere a bottle breaks. The aria continues, building, followed by shouts and a window shattering, faintly. Then it's quiet again. But it's soon broken by laughter next door, friends of Sean's doing drugs. I'm surprisingly calm, peaceful in the strange limbo between sobriety and sheer blottoness. There's a mist covering the campus tonight lit by a high, full moon. The silhouette is still standing by the window. Another one joins in. The first one leaves. Then I see Paul's room, that is, if he's still living in Leigh. The room is dark and I wonder who he's with tonight. I touch my breast, then ashamed, burning, move my hand away. Won-

174

der what went wrong with that one. What happened the last time we were together? I can't even remember. Last term, sometime. But no . . . that night in September. Beginning of this term. Last term you knew it was over though. He left for three days with Mitchell to Mitchell's parents' place on Cape Cod, but he told you it was to see his parents in New York—but then, who told you that? It was Roxanne, because hadn't she been seeing Mitchell? Maybe it was someone else's lie. But I was still dying with longing for his happy return; what an asshole he was. Maybe I'm wrong. Maybe he was tender, maybe you were greedy. I put the cigarette out on the edge of the window-sill and look back at Sean who has now rolled over, who's dreaming. He's put the covers over his head.

PAUL My lack of trust in him amazes me but I can't help it: *I don't like Sean.* There's no one else on the bus when we pull out of Boston, and not too many people get on at the various stops along the way. Just me and an old couple up front for most of the way there. I idly wonder what Mom will say about this abrupt departure. Will she pop a Seconal? Will she cry? Stay? Flirt with bellhops? Richard will probably be relieved, though he'll still look for a date on Saturday night, and Mrs. Jared won't care—why do I even care what she thinks? I try to sleep as the bus lumbers on some nameless route (7? 9? 89? 119?) toward Camden. And it stops raining somewhere near Lawrence, and the sun comes up, full and rising, at Bellows.

I can't sleep.

I will rush straight to Sean's room and what will I find? Him in bed with a girl I have never noticed or talked to but who I will instantly recognize, or maybe he'll be tired but wake up smiling and we'll look and touch and shake hands and while shaking hands he'll pull me down onto his bed and after that we'll drive to that French cafe on the edge of town—no way, Sean would never eat there. He's probably never been to a nice restaurant; just a life of Quarter Pounders, Tastee Freezes, Friendlys. Do they even have Friendlys in the South? No Walkman, no cigarettes, no magazines on a bus can be unbearable. I'm going crazy, still horny from the okay sex from last night, and I try to masturbate in the bus bathroom but when I realize what I'm doing, the sloshing of the refuse below me as I sit on the toilet, hand wrapped around my dick, and start laughing, it's high-pitched, maniacal, scary.

Some people get on at Newport. Some people get off at Wolcott, and some more get on at Winchester. Hungry, exhausted, my breath repulsive, I finally get off at the station in Camden and take a cab back to campus and by the time I get there, it's almost twelve. I must be dreaming this.

ROXANNE I found the girl when I woke up the next morning . . .

I had spent the night with Tim, Rupert had gone to the Booth orgy . . . I spent the night with Norris. I was still drunk and trippy from the XTC and when I went to the bathroom . . .

. . . I wanted to take a shower so I . . .

When I opened the stall door I had to pull back the . . .

The girl was (it's hard to describe) very blue . . .

No water should ever look that red because it was so dark . . .

. . . Of course I started to freak out and started screaming and pulling . . .

I don't remember pulling the fire alarms off in some of the houses though I guess . . .

Tim told me that's how Security got there after . . .

. . . I started running around.

I didn't stop freaking out until Rupert gave me more Xanax. . . .

. . . Norris slept through the entire thing . . .

PAUL Then I find myself wandering down College Drive, approaching Wooley House, where The Dressed To Get Screwed party was. The campus is dead, unawake, even though it's almost noon, which means they will have all missed brunch, and I smile with satisfaction at the knowledge of this luxury withheld from them. Almost all the windows have been smashed at Wooley, ripped sheets lay rolled up in balls all over the green lawn outside the broken French windows of the living room, or hang from trees like big deflated ghost balloons. Flies buzz around three sticky trashcans that are lying on their sides in the cool autumn sun, drying. There are three people asleep, or dead, two of them sitting up, in the living room, one of them naked, face-down. Vomit, beer, wine, cigarette smoke, punch, marijuana, even the smell of sex, semen, sweat, women, permeate the room, hang in the air like haze. I don't even know what I'm doing here since Sean's room, the house he lives in, is directly across Commons lawn (scared, aren't you?) from Wooley. I'm still carrying my bag, careful not to drop it on the floor, which makes cracking noises every time I take a step. Beer and punch, or maybe it's vomit, is everywhere, in pools, thrown in streaks on the walls from which big chunks of plaster are missing. A broken film projector, half of it crushed, is in the corner, unwound reels surrounding it. Cigarette butts cover the floor like big flattened white bugs. In the hallway are two people, dead, sleeping, on top of each other. The house itself is incredibly silent, even for a Saturday morning.

But then the screaming starts, a girl's screaming, and the fire alarms in Stokes and Windham go off, and I move outside, stepping over the couple stuck together, feet crunching broken glass, walking over numerous plastic cups, the girl's screams coming closer. It's that bitchy lesbian who lives off-campus with Rupert Guest (who, I hate to admit, is really cute) and she's out of her mind, yelling "oh fuck" over and over. People start to stick their heads out of open windows that look onto Commons lawn, awakened by her screams. She disappears into another house, and then the fire alarm in Booth goes off. I look over at the house, at the crazy screaming girl, half-tripping, half-running out of the house, her destination unsure, really just running in circles. In the top corner of the house, Sean's window opens and staring out his window, the window she's pulled open, a flash of breast showing—it's none other than Lauren. Then Sean's head peeks out. He looks around, shading his eyes with his hand, shirtless. He spots me and waves, yells out, "Hi, Dent!" and I stand there too dazed to laugh, to not wave.

So I head back to my room, various fire alarms still blaring, past couples who fucked each other last night standing in hungover amazement at the gibbering girl screaming and pulling at her face, only dressed in blue boy's boxers and a Pee Wee Herman T-shirt. And it's back to my room—a note on my door saying my mother called, another flyer from the Young Republicans Committee. I sit there staring at my bed, wondering was it I who made it before I left? I'm a little amazed, but not nearly as shocked as I should be, or probably should be. Lauren. So.

SEAN On Saturday we hung out, went to Manchester. Me, Lauren, Judy, and some guy Judy was sleeping with named Frank, whose Saab we drove to Manchester in. We hit the record store, walked around, bought ice cream for the girls, talked about purchasing some Ecstasy since some guy who was visiting that weekend from Canada had brought some to campus. We stopped at a liquor store and bought a couple six-packs of beer and a bottle of wine to drink later in case we didn't find a party to go to or missed the movies. We ate dinner at this Italian place that was pretty good and Frank paid with his American Express card. Frank seemed cool and I was warming up to him, even if after I asked him what he wanted to do, he told me with total sincerity, "Rock critic." Had she slept with him? I had heard rumors, meaningless gossip that she had, but you can't believe half the bullshit you hear anyway so I forgot about it. When I thought that maybe she had slept with him, those were the times I thought less of the guy, and stuff he said, like wanting to go on the Paris Program next term since he couldn't "handle America," made him seem like a geek, like someone she could never like, let alone sleep with.

We were in the Italian restaurant when Frank said that, and Lauren stifled a giggle and drank from her glass of red wine quickly. I reached beneath the table and squeezed her thigh, that beautiful, long, smooth leg, that fleshy yet tight (I want to say silky but not really) thigh. Looking at her, I was so crazy about this girl and so relieved I had a decent-looking perhaps permanent girlfriend that it hit me, in that Italian restaurant in Manchester, and on the ride back to Camden—getting a hard-on just from thinking about the way she kissed me last night—that I had something like four papers due from last term that I wasn't ever going to start, and it wouldn't matter since I was with Lauren. It didn't even bother me too much that she was a Poetry major since girls who are Poetry majors are usually impossible to deal with. She asked me what my major was and I said "Computers" (which might end up being true) just to impress her, and I guess it did because she smiled, raised those deep blue long-lashed eyes up, and said, "Really?" that secret yet noticeable dirty smile curling her lips.

Since we couldn't find any parties in Manchester we drove back to campus and hung out in her room. I had my pipe with me and some good pot and we got high. I was going to bring out some coke I had scored earlier but was afraid they'd all get pissed-off and think that maybe I was really a Pre-med major. We laid half-on, half-off the big double mattress that took up a great deal of floor space in her room in Canfield, talking about people we didn't like, classes we didn't go to, how lame the Freshmen were, why the flag was half-mast. Lauren said some girl offed herself last night. Frank and I laughed and said it was probably because she didn't get screwed. Judy and Lauren got pissed off (but not really, the pot had calmed us down, had buried any tension there might have been) and said it was probably because she had. The radio played Talking Heads, REM, New Order, old Iggy Pop. I moved closer to her. She began lighting candles.

I knew she loved me, and not only because of the notes, which I refused to bring up (why embarrass her?), but because when she looked at me, I could see, for the first time, just sense, that she was the only person I'd ever met who wasn't looking through me. She was really the first person who looked and stopped. It was a hard thing to explain to myself, to deal with, but it didn't matter. It wasn't the most important aspect. Her beauty was. It was an all-American beauty, the sort of beauty that can only be found in American girls, with the blond hair, and the breasts that only American girls have. That beautifully proportioned body, thin but not anorexic, her skin, WASP creamy, and delicately pure, in total contrast to her expressions, which always seemed slightly dirty as if she was a bad girl, and this excited me even more. I didn't care about her background which was strictly Upper East Side Park Avenue bullshit, but she wasn't bitchy and paranoid and defensive about it in that way girls from Park Avenue inevitably are, because all I wanted to do was look at her face, which seemed miraculously, perfectly put together, and at her body, which was constructed just as beautifully if not better.

And I told her all this, that night, when the four of us lay on her mattress in the dark, the candles burning out one by one, listening to classic songs on the radio, stoned, Judy and Frank drunk, passed-out, wasted, and I couldn't wait; couldn't wait to go back to my room, and I moved on top of her quickly, quietly and she put her legs around mine and squeezed. She wept gratefully that night, chewing my lips, her hands slipping under my jeans, then moving up my back, pushing me into her deeper, the two of us moving slowly even when we were coming together; still silent she buried her face in my neck; we were panting loudly; I was still hard. I didn't pull out but whispered something to her ear, some of her hair matted against my face, which was hot and sweating. She whispered something back, and it was then that I knew she loved me. That was also when Judy spoke up in the darkness and said, "I hope you two enjoyed that as much as we did," and then I heard Frank laugh, and we cracked up also, too tired to be embarrassed, me still in her not wanting to get out, her arms still draped around my back.

Sunday, after a long lunch at The Brasserie on the edge of town, we spent the rest of the day in bed together.

CLAY   People are afraid to walk across campus after midnight. Someone on acid whispers this to me, in my ear, one Sunday dawn after I have been up on crystal meth most of the week, crying, and I know it is true. This person is in my computer class (which is now my major) and I see him in the weight room and sometimes I see him at the municipal pool on Main Street, in town. A place I spend what some people think is an inordinate amount of time. (They also have a good tanning salon next door.) I keep my Walkman on a lot this term, listening to groups that have broken up: The Eagles, The Doors, The Go-Go's, The Plimsouls, because I do not want to hear about the mutilated girl they found cut up in North Ashton (literally torn in half) by something the townspeople call The Ashton Ripper, or about the girl in Swan House who slit her throat in that house's downstairs bathtub and who bled to death on the night of The Dressed To Get Screwed party, or hear the voices of the town's incest victims wandering dumbly through the Price Chopper, a place I like to hang out in, a place that reminds me of California, a place that reminds me of the frozen food section of Gelson's, a place that reminds me of home.

I go to an Elvis Costello concert in New York but get lost on the way back to Camden. I cannot get cable to hook up MTV in my dorm room so I buy a VCR and get videos in a cheap video rental store in town. I buy a Porsche, second-hand, in New York before the term starts so I have a car to do these things. People are also afraid to eat sushi in New Hampshire.

Other things: Someone writes Sensory Deprivation Tank on the door that leads to The Pub. Rip actually calls me from L.A. a couple of times. Someone writes his name in red magic marker on my door. I am unsure if it's really him since in a tape Blair sent me she was positive that he had been murdered. She also told me that she had seen Jim Morrison at the Häagen Dazs in Westwood. I see this girl, Vanden, for a while, who paints my futon frame black and who stopped seeing me because she said she saw "a spider the size of Norman Mailer" in my bathroom. I didn't ask her who Norman Mailer was, and I didn't ask her to come back. Then I hang out with this Brazilian guy but mainly just to acquire Ecstasy. Then it was this Dance major from Connecticut who thought she was a witch. We held a séance around a beer keg and tried to summon the spirit of a Senior who had transferred to Bard. Then the Ouija board was pulled out and we asked it if we could find any cocaine. It answered OWTQ. We spent an hour figuring out what it meant. She left me for a Lit major named Justin. I sleep with some rich boys, with some richer girls, a couple from Northern California, a French teacher, a girl from Vassar who knows one of my sisters, some girl who wouldn't stop drinking Nyquil . . .

And I cannot keep my shade open because I have heard the story of why Indians could not settle on the land the campus was built on because the four winds met there on Commons lawn, and some of the Indians went totally insane and had to be killed, their bodies offered to the gods and then buried on Commons. And some say on warm fall nights after midnight, they rise, their faces twisted, bloody, peering in windows, scowling, looking for new offerings, their tomahawks poised.

And in a bathroom, written above the toilet, someone has written "Ronald McGlinn has a small penis and no testicles" over and over. Someone from L.A. sent me a videotape, unmarked, and I am afraid to play it but probably will. I have lost my I.D. three times this term. I tell the person I see in psychological counseling that I feel the apocalypse is near. She asks me how my flute tutorial is progressing. I do not tell her I dropped it and started taking an advanced video course instead.

Someone asks me: "What's going on?"

"I don't know," I say. "What *is* going on?"

Sensory Deprivation Tank.

Rest in Peace.

People are afraid to merge on campus after midnight.

Indians in a video, flashing on, off, on.

Ronald McGlinn has a small penis . . .

And no testicles. Dude.

"What's going on?"

" . . . *I'd be safe and warm if I was back in L.A.* . . ."

I miss the beach.

PAUL   "It's over, isn't it?" I ask this, sitting in someone's car Sean borrowed in the parking lot of McDonald's.

It's too cold to come on the bike, he said when I came over to his room. (His room was a mess. The bed was unmade, bracelets lay scattered on the table, the mirror had been taken down from the wall and placed on a chair, folded papers scattered on top of it, thin veneer of white dust covering it.) He said, and I was listening carefully, You can't use the bathroom.

But I don't want to use the bathroom.

Vomit all over, he said.

I don't want to use the bathroom, I said calmly.

He shrugged. He said no to dinner.

I said, You don't like me. You're seeing someone else.

And he said, That's not true.

And I said, Swear it.

And he said, I do.

I said, I don't believe you.

He said, You can't use the bathroom.

Finally, I talked him into McDonald's and sitting here in the car, he spits out the window, finishes part of his Big Mac, throws the rest out and lights up a Parliament. He tries to start the car but it's freezing even though it's only October and the borrowed car (whose? is it Jerry's?) won't start.

"Well?" I ask. I can't eat. I can't even light a cigarette.

"Yeah," he says. "Goddamnit," he shouts, hitting the steering wheel. "Why won't this fucker start?"

"I guess it's not your fault you don't feel the same way I do," I tell him.

"Yeah. Not my fault," he says, still trying to start the car.

"But it's not going to change the way I feel," I tell him.

"It should." He mutters this, staring out the windshield. Cars drive by, drivers sticking their heads out of rolled-down windows, shouting orders, picking them up, moving on, replaced by more cars, more orders. I touch his leg and say, "But it doesn't."

"Well, it's hard for me too," he says, pushing my hand away.

"I know," I say. How could I fall for such a moron? I thought, looking over his body, then his face, trying to avert my eyes from his crotch.

"Whose fault is this?" he shouts. Nervously he tries to start the car again. "It's yours. You ruined our friendship with sex," he says, disgusted.

He gets out of the car, slams the door and walks around it a couple of times. The smell of the food I ordered, in my lap, getting cold, uneaten, makes me slightly sick, but I can't move, can't throw it out. Now I'm standing in the parking lot. It gets suddenly very cold. Neither of us can stay still very long. He reaches up and turns the collar of his leather jacket up. I reach out and touch his cheek, brushing something off. He pulls his face away and doesn't smile. I look away, puzzled. A car honks somewhere.

"I don't like this arrangement," I say.

Back in the car he says, without looking at me, "Then leave."

Moral of the story?

SEAN   I would smell the pillows after she'd leave. She didn't like to sleep in my bed; she said it was too small and that sleeping together didn't really matter in the end. I agreed. When she was gone and after smelling the pillows, then my arms, my hands, my fingers, I'd think about us fucking, and I'd jerk off, coming once more, thinking about us, fantasizing and reshaping the sex, making it seem more intense and wild than it might have actually been. And in bed with her I could barely contain myself. I would fuck her quickly the first time so I could get off, then spend hours eating her, licking, constantly sucking her cunt; my tongue would ache, become swollen from rubbing my mouth, digging my chin into her, my mouth getting so dry I couldn't even swallow, and I'd lift my head up and actually gasp for breath.

It would take very little, just about nothing, to get turned on by her. I'd see her bending over in just her panties, picking up something that she had dropped off the floor, or watch her get dressed, pulling on a T-shirt or sweater, leaning out my window, smoking. Even the small act, the motion of lighting a cigarette and I'd have to fight the urge to grab her, to tear those panties off, to lick and smell and tongue her. Sometimes the desire would be so strong, that all I could do was lay in bed, unmoving, thinking about her body, thinking about a certain look she gave me and I'd get hard instantly.

She spoke rarely to me, and never mentioned anything about the sex—probably because she was so satisfied, and I didn't say much back. So there were few drawbacks to our relationship, fewer disagreements. For instance I didn't have to tell her what I thought about her poetry, which sucked even though a couple of her poems had been chosen for publication in the school's literary rag and for a poetry journal her teacher edited. If it ever did come up I would simply tell her I liked it and comment on the imagery. But what was poetry, or anything else for that matter, when compared to those breasts, and that ass, that insatiable center between those long legs wrapped around my hips, that beautiful face crying out with pleasure?

LAUREN   Still no mail from Victor. Not a postcard. Not a phone call. Not a letter. No message. The bastard can rot in hell for all I care.

"The school is really going downhill," Judy tells me, explaining that I should be grateful to be a Senior so I won't have to come back next year. And I guess I have to agree with her. The Freshman band is called The Parents—that's enough to send out some message to people's feelers that something wrong is going down. October seems to last forever because of Judy's assessment. Graduation seems impossibly far off.

Gina *did* win the prize for changing the school sign and with the prize money we bought some XTC, which I had never done before, not even with Victor, and it was pretty incredible. I don't think Sean liked it though. He just got very sweaty and kept grinding his teeth, swaying back and forth, and later that night he was even hornier than usual, which was no fun at all. I start drinking a lot of beer because that and play video games is essentially all the boy wants to do. But he gets better-looking as time goes on and though the sex is only okay and even if he's not so great in bed, at least he's imaginative. Yet he doesn't turn me on. No real orgasms. (Well, maybe a couple.) Just because he's so damned insistent. (Contrary to popular belief, being eaten out for two hours straight is not my idea of a good time.) He also seems suspicious. I have the feeling that he's the mastermind of the Young Conservatives Party that had that big dance in Greenwall last Saturday. Other than being on Rec Committee I have no idea what he does here, and in the end, like Judy says, I really don't want to know. Just want December to arrive, just want to get out of this place. Because I don't know how much longer I can keep drinking beer and watching him get the high score on Pole Position which he is superb at.

I asked him about this one night and he just grumbled some monosyllabic answer. But what else is one to do at college except drink beer or slash your wrists? I thought to myself as he got up, stalked over to the video machine, slipped in another quarter. I stopped complaining.

Girl who killed herself got the flyer the rest of us all got in her box, telling her that she was indeed dead and that there would be a memorial service for her in Tishman. I mentioned this one night when Sean and I were at The Pub having pre-party beers, and he looked at me and snorted, "Irony. Oh boy," but he might as well have just snorted, "So?"

The poetry comes along. I haven't stopped smoking. Judy tells me that Roxanne told her that Sean deals drugs. I tell her, "At least he doesn't breakdance."

SEAN   I trudge and Lauren walks up the hill toward Vittorio's house. It's not too cold even if it's late October, but I told her to wear a sweater just in case it got cold when we walked home. I was wearing a T-shirt and jeans when I told her this and she asked me, when we were in her room getting dressed, why she had to wear a sweater if I got to wear a short-sleeve shirt and therefore be more comfortable. I couldn't tell her the truth: that I didn't like the idea of Vittorio staring at her tits. So I went back to my room and put on an old black jacket and changed my tennis shoes to penny loafers, as an added touch to please her.

The jacket is wrapped around my waist now, the sleeves knocking against my thighs as we make our way to the top of the hill. I start walking slower, hoping that maybe I can talk her out of Vittorio's party, hoping that she'll change her mind and walk back to campus with me. The only reason I'm doing this is because I know it means a lot to her (though I cannot understand why) and that this is Vittorio's last get-together before he leaves for Italy on Sunday, before he's replaced by some drunk who was fired from the Lit staff at Harvard (I found this out from Norris who knows all the teacher gossip). I step in front of the gate that leads up to the door of Vittorio's house. She keeps walking, then stops, sighs, doesn't turn around.

"Are you sure you want to do this?" I ask.

"We already talked about this," she says.

"I think I've changed my mind."

"We're here. We're going in. I'm going in."

I follow her to the door. "If he makes one move towards you I'll beat the shit out of him." I unwrap the jacket from my waist and put it on.

"You'll what?" she asks, ringing the bell.

"I don't know." I smooth the jacket out. I brought coke in case I can't deal with it, but I haven't told her this. I wonder if any girls will be here.

"You're jealous of my poetry teacher," she says. "I can't believe it."

"I can't believe he practically rapes you at these god-damned things," I whisper loudly at her. "And you love it," I add.

"My God, Sean, he's almost seventy," she says. "Besides you've never been to one of these things so how in the hell would you know?"

"So what? I don't care how old he is, he still does it. You've told me." I can hear footsteps, Vittorio's, shuffling toward the door.

"He's taught me a lot and I owe it to him to come." She looks at my watch, lifting then dropping my wrist. "We're late. Anyway he's leaving and you won't have to put up with this anymore."

This is the end of the relationship. I knew it was coming to an end. She was starting to bore me already. And maybe this party is a good excuse to end it, to lay blame somewhere. I don't care. Rock'n'roll. I look at her one last time, in the seconds before the door opens, and desperately try to remember why we even got together in the first place.

The door opens and Vittorio, wearing baggy cords and an old L.L. Bean sweater, his thin gray hair longish, unbrushed, raises his arms up in greeting and says, "Lauren, Lauren . . . oh what a lovely, lovely surprise. . . ." His soft voice now high and emotional. This is Vittorio? The guy who makes the passes at Lauren? I'm thinking. He hugs her as she walks in and she looks over at me and rolls her eyes up over Vittorio's aged, stooped shoulder. I register it but it doesn't make a difference. Why doesn't she just fuck him? I'm thinking.

". . . lovely, lovely surprise. . . ."

"I thought we were invited," I say, annoyed.

"Oh you were, you were," Vittorio says, looking at Lauren as if she had spoken. "But it's such a lovely . . . lovely surprise. . . ."

"Vittorio, you remember Sean," she says. "You were in one of Vittorio's classes, weren't you?" she asks me.

I have never met the guy in my life, only heard about his lecherous activities from Lauren who spoke about them plainly and easily, as if it were a joke. When she spoke to me about his behavior it was hard to tell whether she was bragging or trying purposefully to turn me off. Whatever.

"Yeah," I say. "Hi."

"Yes, yes . . . Sean," he says, still gazing at Lauren.

"Well . . ." I say.

He's breathing hard and I can smell the alcohol on the geezer's breath.

"Yes," he says, absent-mindedly as he ushers Lauren into the living room, forgetting to close the front door behind him. I close the door. I follow.

There are only six other people at the so-called party. (I don't understand why Lauren doesn't realize that six people do not constitute a "party," but more like a fucking "gathering.") And they're all sitting around a table in the living room. Some young pale guy with a shaved head wearing John Lennon glasses and a Mobil gas station uniform, smoking Export A's, sitting in an armchair, eyes us contemptuously as we walk in. This couple from San Francisco, Trav and his hot wife Mona, who are living near the college while Trav finishes his novel, and Mona takes a poetry tutorial with Vittorio, are sitting on two chairs next to the couch, where two creepy female editors from the literary magazine Vittorio edits, along with Marie, a plump, silent woman in her mid-forties, who has the Italian widow look and who, I guess takes care of Vittorio's needs, sit.

Lauren knows one of the editors, who has just published a poem of hers in that magazine's last issue. I had thought the same of that poem as I had of all the rest. None of them made any sense to me. All this stuff about depressed girls sitting around in empty rooms, thinking of past boyfriends, or masturbating, or smoking cigarettes on foam-drenched sheets, complaining about menstrual cramps. It seemed to me that Lauren was just writing one endless poem and I told her honestly one night after we'd had sex in her room, that none—no, not none; hadn't said that—that a lot of it didn't make sense to me. She had only said, "Doesn't make sense," and laid back on the pillow we were sharing and when I tried to kiss her, later that night, her mouth and embrace seemed cold, indifferent, frigid.

"This is quite a promising young poet . . . um, yes . . ." Vittorio says of Lauren, resting his meaty, hairy paw on her shoulder.

Vittorio then turns to the bald guy in the armchair and says of the pretentious geek, "And this is Stump, another . . . yes, very promising poet. . . ."

"We know each other," Lauren smiles flirtatiously. "You did your thesis with Glickman last term, right? On . . ." She's forgotten. Must have made a big impression.

"Yeah," Stump says. "Hunter S. Thompson."

"Right," she says. "This is Sean Bateman."

"Hi, Stump?" I offer my hand.

"Yeah. Used to be Carcass but changed it." He salutes instead of taking my hand.

"You . . . look familiar," I say, taking a seat.

"Wine? Uh, vodka? Gin?" Vittorio asks, sitting in the chair next to Lauren's, gesturing at the table we're all "gathered" around. "You like gin, don't you . . . Lauren."

How the fuck does he know?

"Yeah, gin," Lauren says. "Do you have any tonic?"

"Oh, of course, of course . . . I'll make it," Vittorio says in his soft, almost faggoty voice, reaching over Lauren's knees to get to the ice bucket.

"I'll just have one of those beers," I say, but when Vittorio makes no move to get one I reach over and take one of the Beck's.

It's quiet. Everyone waits for Vittorio to make Lauren's drink. I sit there, looking at Vittorio's shaking hands, alarmed at how much gin he's pouring into Lauren's glass. When he turns around to hand the glass to her, he seems shocked, taken aback, and as she takes the drink from him he says, "Oh look . . . look at the sunlight, the sunlight . . . through your golden . . . golden hair. . . ." His voice is trembling now. "The sunlight . . ." he murmurs. "Look how it glows . . . glows in the sunlight . . ."

Jesus Christ, this is really making me sick. *She* is making me sick. I grip the beer firmly, tear at the damp label. Then I look at Lauren.

The sun is still up and streaming through the large stained glass window and it *does* make Lauren's hair glow and she looks very beautiful to me right now. Everyone's giggling and Vittorio leans over and starts smelling her hair. "Ah, sweet as nectar . . . nectar," he says.

I am going to scream. I am going to scream. No I'm not.

"Sweet as nectar . . ." Vittorio mumbles again, and then pulls away, letting strands of her hair fall back into place.

"Oh, Vittorio," Lauren says. "Please, stop."

She loves it, I'm thinking. She fucking loves it.

"Nectar . . ." Vittorio says once more.

One of the editors, after a long silence, speaks up and says, "Mona was just telling us about some of the projects she was working on."

Mona is wearing a white see-through blouse and tight faded jeans and cowboy boots, looking pretty sexy, curly blond hair piled up on her head, and a deeply tan face. Rumor has it that she hangs around Dewey offering Sophomore guys pot then screwing them. I try to make eye contact. She takes a big sip of her white wine spritzer before she says anything. "Well, basically, I'm freelancing now. Just finished an interview with two of the V.J.s from MTV."

"Hah!" Stump exclaims. "MTV! V.J.s! How completely scintillating!"

"Actually it was quite . . ." Mona tilts her head. "Refreshing."

"Refreshing," Trav nods.

"In what way?" Stump wants to know.

"In the way that she really captured the sense of this monolithic corporate superstructure that's bludgeoning and infecting the quote-unquote innocents of America by mind-fucking them with these . . . these essentially sexist, fascistic, blatantly bourgeois video films. Video killed the radio star, that type of stuff," Trav says.

No one says anything for a long time until Mona speaks again.

"Actually, it's not that . . . aggressive." She takes a sip of her drink and tilts her head, looking over at Trav. "That's more of what your book is about, Trav."

"Oh yes, Travis," one of the editors says, adjusting her glasses. "Tell us about the book."

"He's been working on it for a long time," Mona chirps.

"Did you quit the job at Rizzoli's?" the other editor asks.

"Uh-huh. Yep," Trav nods. "Gotta get this book done. We left L.A., what?" He turns to Mona, who I think is flirting with me. "Nine months ago? We were in New York for two and now we're here. But I gotta get this book done."

"We know someone at St. Martin's who's really interested," Mona says. "But Trav has got to finish it."

"Yeah babe," Trav says. "I do."

"How long have you been working on it?" Stump asks.

"Not that long," Trav says.

"Thirteen years?" Mona asks. "Not that long?"

"Well, time is subjective," Trav says.

"What *is* time?" one of the editors asks. "I mean, really?"

I'm looking at Vittorio who's sipping a glass of red wine and staring at Lauren. Lauren takes a pack of Camels from her purse and Vittorio lights the cigarette for her. I finish the Beck's quickly and keep staring at Lauren. When she looks over at me, I look away.

Trav's saying, "But don't you think rock'n'roll killed off poetry?"

Lauren and Stump and Mona all laugh and I look over at Lauren and she rolls her eyes up. She looks at me and smiles, and I'm pitifully relieved. But I don't, can't, smile back with her sitting next to Vittorio, so I watch her inhale deeply on the cigarette Vittorio lit.

"Of course," Stump practically shouts. "I learned more from Black Flag than I ever did from Stevens or cummings or Yeats or even Lowell, but my God, holy shit, Black Flag *is* poetry man."

"Black Flag . . . Black Flag . . . who is this Black Flag?" Vittorio asks, eyes half-closed.

"I'll tell you later, Vittorio," Stump says, amused.

Trav takes in what Stump said and nods as he lights a cigarette.

Stump offers me an Export A. I shake my head and tell him, "I don't smoke."

Stump says, "Neither do I," and lights one.

"Stump is . . . um, working on a very interesting . . .

series of poems about . . ." Vittorio stops. "Oh, how can . . . how can I say this . . . um, oh my. . . ."

"Bestiality?" Stump suggests.

I pull out a pack of Parliaments and light one.

"Well my . . . my, yes . . . I, suppose, that is it. . . ." Vittorio mumbles, embarrassed.

"Yeah, I've been working on this concept that when Man fucks animals, He's fucking Nature, since He's become so computerized and all." Stump stops and takes a swallow from a silver flask he brings out of his pocket and says, "I'm working on the dog section now where this guy ties a dog up and is having intercourse with it because He thinks dog is God. D-O-G . . . G-O-D. God spelled backwards. Get it? See?"

Everyone is nodding but me. I search the table for another beer. I grab a Beck's and open it quickly, taking a long, deep swallow. I look at Marie, who, like me, has been silent for the duration of this nightmarish event.

"That's weird that you mention that," Lauren says. "I saw two dogs making love in front of my dorm this morning. It was really strange, but it was, admittedly, poetic in terms of erotic imagery."

I finally have to say something. "Lauren, dogs don't make love," I tell her. "They fuck."

"Well they certainly have no qualms about oral sex," Mona laughs.

"Dogs don't make love?" Stump asks me, incredulous. "I'd think about that if I were you."

"Um, no . . . no . . . I do believe that dogs make love . . . um, yes they make love in the . . . in the sunlight," Vittorio says wistfully. "In the golden, golden . . . sunlight, they make love."

I excuse myself and get up, go through the kitchen, thinking it leads to the bathroom, then up the stairs and through Vittorio's room to his bathroom. I wash my hands and look at my reflection in the mirror and tell myself that I'll go back and tell Lauren that I don't feel well and that we'd better go back to campus. What will she say? She'll probably tell me that we'd only gotten here and that if I want to leave I can, and she'll meet me back on campus. Did I actually say something about dogs fucking? Forget the coke, I decide, and open Vittorio's medicine cabinet, more out of boredom than curiosity. Sea Breeze, Vitalis, Topol toothpolish, Ben-Gay, Pepto Bismol, tube of Preparation H, prescription of Librium. How hip. I take the bottle out of the cabinet and open it, pouring the green and black capsules into my hand and then popping one to calm myself, washing it down with a handful of water from the sink. Then I wipe my mouth and hands on a towel hanging over the shower stall and go back down to the living room, already cursing myself for leaving Lauren unattended with Vittorio for so long.

They are all talking about a book I haven't read. I sit back down on the chair next to Lauren and hear one of the editors say, "Seminal . . . seminal," and another one say, "Yes, a landmark." I open another beer and look back at Lauren who gives me this questioning, pleading look. I tip the bottle back and look over at Mona and her see-through blouse.

"The way she represented like the total earth mother figure was amazing, not to say audacious," Mona says, nodding her head vigorously.

"But it wasn't just the way she represented her," Stump says. "It was the Joycean implications that blew me away."

"So Joyce, so Joyce," Mona agrees.

"Should I read this book?" I ask Lauren, hoping she'll turn and face me; turn away from Vittorio.

"You wouldn't like it," she says, not looking at me.

"Why not?" I ask.

"It 'doesn't make sense.' " She sips her drink.

"Not only Joyce, but it reminded me a bit of Acker's work," Trav is saying. "Has anyone read by the way, Crad Kilodney's *Lightning Struck My Dick?* It's amazing, amazing." He shakes his head.

"What does that mean?" I ask her.

"Figure it out," she whispers.

I sit back, stifle a yawn, drink more of the beer.

Trav turns to Vittorio. "But Vittorio, let me ask you, don't you think that the admittedly Bohemian punk outlaw scribblings of these wasted post-Vietnam, post-Watergate, post- . . . hell, post-everything minstrels, is the product of a literary establishment bombasting a lost generation with worthless propaganda exploiting greed, blasé sexual attitudes and mind-corrupting, numbing jejunosity and that's why works like *Just Another Asshole*, a searing, searing collection of quote-unquote underground writing, become potent fixtures on the minds of this clan of maladjusted, nihilistic, malcontent, self-serving . . . well, hell, miscarriages, or do you think it's all . . ." And now Trav stops, searches for the right word. ". . . bogus?"

"Oh Tra-av," Mona says.

"Um . . . bogus?" Vittorio mumbles. "What is this bogus . . . you speak of? I have . . . not read the book . . . um . . ." He turns to Lauren. "Bogus? . . . mmm, did you like the book?"

"Oh yeah," Lauren nods. "It was really good."

"I . . . I have not read this . . . this book," Vittorio says shyly, looking down at his drink.

I look over at Vittorio and suddenly sympathize with the man. I want to tell him that I haven't read the book either, and I can see that Lauren feels the same way too, because she turns to him and says, "Oh Vittorio, I wish you would stay."

Vittorio blushes and says, "I have to, go back . . . to my family."

"What about Marie?" she asks, tender, hand on his wrist.

I look over at Marie, who is talking to Trav about the book.

"Oh," Vittorio says, looking over at her, then abruptly looking back at Lauren, "I will miss her very much . . . very much."

I want to say the same thing to Lauren, but yawn instead and drink more of the Beck's feeling drowsy, and a little high. It's over, definitely. I'm about to tell her but Stump jumps up and puts on a Circle Jerks tape which no one can listen to, and Mona and Trav want to listen to Los Lobos, so everyone compromises and we listen to Yaz. Stump starts to dance in the now darkened room with Mona and Trav and the two editors try to dance to the music also. Stump even urges Marie to come join them but she just smiles and says that she is very tired.

Vittorio's laughing about the music and making everyone fresh drinks. Marie lights candles. Vittorio leans over and whispers something in Lauren's ear. Lauren keeps looking over at me. I'm now drinking whiskey from Stump's flask and on the verge of falling asleep. I can't hear what the two of them are talking about and I'm grateful. I keep washing the taste of the cheap whiskey from my mouth with the rest of a warm Beck's. Later everyone makes a toast, wishing Vittorio good luck on his trip, even Marie, who looks sad as she raises her glass and mouths, *"Mi amore,"* to Vittorio, married, father, Vittorio. This is the last thing I remember clearly.

I pass out.

I wake up and find myself sweating on Vittorio's bed, I get up and look at my watch and see that it's close to midnight. I stand up carefully, then stagger down the stairs and into the living room. Everyone's gone except for Lauren and Vittorio who have now moved to the couch talking, candles on the table in front of them still burning. How many beers had I drunk? How much whiskey? Soft Italian Muzak comes from the stereo now. Had I actually tried to dance? Had I actually finished the whiskey from Stump's flask? I can't remember.

"Just get up?" she asks.

"What's going on?" I say, steadying myself as I sit down.

"Drinking," she says, holding up a glass of—what in the hell is it? *Port?* "Want one?"

I can tell that she's drunk because of the rigid way she's sitting on the couch, trying to maintain what's left of her composure. She sloppily lights a cigarette, and Vittorio pours himself what little red wine is left in the bottle. How long have they been sitting on the couch like that? I look at my watch.

"No," I say. I pour myself a glass of tonic water with shaking hands and sip it. "How did I get in Vittorio's room?"

"You were really drunk," she says. "Feeling better?"

"No. I don't." I rub my forehead. "I was really drunk?"

"Yeah. We decided to let you rest awhile before we left."

We? What does "We" mean? Who's "We"? I look around the room and then back at her and notice that her shoes are off. "What are your shoes doing off?"

"What?" she asks. Who me? Little Miss Innocent.

"Your shoes. Why—are—they—off," I ask, spacing each word out.

"I was dancing," she says.

"Great." An image of her slow dancing with Vittorio, his stubby fingers caressing her back, her ass, Lauren sighing, "Oh please," in that soft way Lauren always sighs. "Oh please Vittorio." This all flashes through my mind and my headache worsens. I look at her. I don't know her. She's nothing.

"You . . . you have wonderful . . . wonderful feet," Vittorio murmurs drunkenly, leaning over her.

"Vittorio," she says, warning.

"No . . . no, let me look." He lifts one of her legs up.

"Vittorio," she says, what seems to me coyly.

Vittorio leans down and kisses her foot.

I stand up. "Okay. We're going."

"You want to?" She looks up while Vittorio begins to fondle her ankle, his hand moving up her goddamn knee.

"Yes. Now," I demand.

"Vittorio, we've got to go," she says, trying to stand up.

"Oh no, no, no . . . no, no, no . . . don't, don't go," Vittorio says, alarmed.

"We have to, Vittorio," she says, finishing her drink.

"No! No!" Vittorio cries out, trying to reach for her hand.

"Jesus, Lauren, come on!" I tell her.

"I'm coming, I'm coming," she says, shrugging helplessly. She walks over to the chair I was sitting in and starts to put on her shoes.

"I don't want you to . . . to go," Vittorio calls, from the couch, eyes closed.

"Vittorio, we have to. It's late," she says soothingly.

"Put them on outside," I tell her. "Let's go."

"Oh Sean," she says. "Shut up."

"Where's Marie?" I ask. "Don't tell me to shut up."

"She drove Mona and Trav back to their place." She reaches for her purse on the table.

Vittorio starts to get up from the couch but he can't balance himself and he falls over against the table, crashing onto the floor, starting to moan.

"Oh my God," Lauren says, rushing over to him.

"I don't want to go to Italy," he bellows. She kneels beside him and tries to push him up against the couch. "I don't want to go," he says again.

"Lauren, let's get the hell out of here," I yell.

"Don't you have any compassion?" she yells back.

"Lauren, the man is a drunk," I shout. "Let's get out of here."

"Don't go Lauren . . . don't go," Vittorio groans, eyes shut.

"I'm here Vittorio, I'm here," she says. "Sean, get a wash-cloth."

"Absolutely not," I shout at her.

"Lauren," Vittorio repeats, still moaning, crouched up like a small child. "Where's Lauren? Lauren?"

"Lauren," I say, standing there, above them, completely offended by the scene.

"I'm here," she says, "I'm here Vittorio. Don't worry." She runs her hand along his brow, then looks at me. "If you won't get a washcloth and if you're not going to help me, you can leave now and wait outside if you want to. I'm staying."

It's over. I tell her that I'm leaving, but it doesn't matter.

I walk to the front door and wait to see if she'll come. I stand there for three minutes and only hear whispering from the living room. Then I walk outside, down the path and out the gate. It's cold now, and I put the jacket I had taken off back on. I sit on the curb across the street from the house. The lights in Vittorio's room go on, then after a minute, go off. I wait on the curb, not knowing what to do, staring at the house, for a long time.

I go back to campus, find Judy in The Pub, and we smoke some pot and then go back to my room, where there's a threatening note on my door from Rupert ("UOWEME"). I crumple it up, and hand it to Judy. Judy asks me who it's from. I tell her Frank. She gets sad and starts crying and tells me that Franklin's over with, that she never liked him, that they should have never gotten together. After she feels better, she starts coming on to me.

"What am I going to tell Lauren?" I ask, watching her undress after we've made out.

"I don't know," she says.

"That I fucked you?" I suggest.

"No. No," she says, though I bet she likes the idea.

LAUREN   Lying naked in my bed. Late. Twelve-thirty. Room next door someone is playing the new Talking Heads record. Finish the cigarette I'm smoking and light another one. Look at Sean. He looks away guiltily. Leans his head against the wall. Sara's cat, Seymour, walks up to the bed and jumps into my lap, meowing hungrily. Stroke the cat's head and look back at Sean. He looks back at me, then to the space on the wall he's been staring at. He knows I want him to leave. He has that distinct understanding etched across his face; get dressed, go, I'm thinking. I yawn. In the next room the record skips, begins again. I don't want him to see me naked so I pull the sheet around me.

"Say something," I say, petting the cat.

"Like what?"

The cat looks at him and mews.

"Like why are we always in my room?" I ask.

"Because I have this awful French roommate, that's why," he says.

"Is he awful because he's French?"

"Yes," he nods.

"God." Look at the cigarette I'm holding; the gold bracelet on wrist dangling. He's looking at me. He knows I'm smoking the cigarette just to irritate him, blowing smoke his way.

"You know what he did?" he asks me.

Smell my wrist, then fingers. "What?"

"Since it's Halloween tomorrow he carved a pumpkin he bought in town and put one of those French hats on it, a chapeau, you know, one of those berets and he put it on the fucking pumpkin, and wrote on the back of it, 'Paris Is Forever.' "

This is the most I have ever heard him say and I'm impressed, but don't say anything. Why is it that Victor's seeing Jaime? I like him more than she likes him. That's crazy. I concentrate on Seymour, who's purring, content.

"What's worse than a Parisian for a roommate?" he asks me.

"What?" Barely muster the interest.

"A Parisian for a roommate who has his own phone."

"I'll have to think about that one."

"What's worse than a Parisian for a roommate who has his own phone?"

"What?" Exasperated. "Sean?"

"A Parisian for a roommate who has his own phone and who wears an ascot," he says.

In the next room someone starts replaying side one again. I get out of bed. "If I hear this song one more time I'll scream." Put on my robe, sit in chair by window and wish he would leave. "Let's go to Price Chopper," I suggest.

He sits up now. He knows for a fact that I want him to leave. He knows that I want it badly, as soon as possible. "Why?" he asks, watching as Seymour climbs into his lap and mews.

"Because I need tampons," I lie. "And toothpaste, cat food, Tab, Evian water, Peanut Butter Cups." I reach for my purse and oh shit, "But I don't think I have any money."

"Charge it," he says.

"God," I mutter. "I hate it when you're sarcastic."

He pushes the cat off the bed and starts to dress. He reaches for his underwear, tangled in the bedsheets and puts it on and I ask him, "Why did you push the cat off the bed?"

He asks back, "Because I felt like it?"

"Come here kitty, come here Seymour," I call. I hate the cat too but pretend to be concerned just to bug him. The cat meows again and hops onto my lap. Pet it. Watch Sean get dressed. Tense silence. He puts on jeans. Then sits on the side of the bed again, away from me, shirtless. He looks like he's getting the awful feeling that I know something and am pissed off about it. Poor baby. Puts his head in his hands, rubs his face. And now I ask him, "What's that thing on your neck?"

Tenses up so noticeably I almost laugh. "What thing?"

"Looks like a hickey." I'm casual.

He walks over to the mirror, makes a big deal out of touching his neck, inspecting the mark. His jaw twitches slightly. Watch as he stares at himself in the mirror; at his dull beauty.

"It's a birthmark," he says.

Right, lame-o. "You're so narcissistic."

Then it comes: "Why are you being such a bitch to-night?" He asks this while his back is to me, while he's slipping on his T-shirt.

Stroke Seymour's head. "I'm not being a bitch."

He walks back to the mirror and looks at the small purple and yellow bruise. Wouldn't even have noticed it if I hadn't heard the news. And now he's saying, "I don't know what you're talking about. This is not a hickey. It's a birthmark."

And now I come out and say it, getting none of the expected pleasure I thought I'd receive. "You fucked Judy. That's all." I say this quickly, really fast and offhand, and it throws him off balance. He's trying hard not to flinch, or do a doubletake.

He turns away from the mirror. "What?"

"You heard me, Sean." I'm squeezing Seymour too tightly. He's not purring anymore.

"You're sick," he says.

"Oh am I?" I ask. "I heard you bit the inside of her thighs." The cat screeches and jumps off my lap; pads across the floor to the door.

He laughs. He tries to ignore me. He sits on the bed tying his shoes. He continues to laugh, shaking his head. "Oh my my. Who told you this one? Susan? Roxanne? Come on, who?" he asks, innocent smile.

Dramatic pause. Look at Seymour, also innocent, sitting near the doorway, licking its paws. It looks up at me too, waiting for my answer.

"Judy," I say.

Now he stops laughing. He stops shaking his head. His face falls. He puts the other shoe on. He mutters, "I have not bitten the inside of anyone's thighs. I haven't bitten yours, have I?"

"What do you want me to do?" I ask, mystified. "Tell her to spread her legs and let me check?" What are we talking about? I don't even care that much. It seems to be so minor that I don't understand why I'm harassing him like this. Probably because I want this thing to be over with, and Judy's a convenient marker.

"Oh Christ," he's saying and he looks disappointed. "I don't believe this. Are you serious or like having your period?"

"You're right," I say. "I'm having my period. It didn't happen."

The moron actually looks relieved, and says, "I thought so."

Trying to look crushed and heartbroken, I say simply, "Why did you do it, Sean?"

"I'm leaving," he says, unlocking the door. Steps into the hallway. People are in the bathroom cutting their hair, making noise. He looks freaked. I light a cigarette.

"Are you really serious?" he asks, standing there. "Do you really believe her?"

I start laughing.

He asks, "What's so funny?"

I look at him, think about it, stop laughing. "Nothing."

He closes the door, still shaking his head, still muttering, "I don't believe this."

I push the chair away from myself, put the cigarette out, then lay on the bed. In the next room someone takes the needle off the record and starts to play side one again. There is Ben & Jerry's ice cream in the hall freezer that I plan to steal and eat, but I can hear him standing outside the door, listening. I sit still, barely breathing. The cat meows. The record skips. His footsteps sound up the hallway, clump down the stairs; downstairs door slams. I move to the window and watch him head towards his house. Halfway across Commons he changes direction and moves toward Wooley, where Judy lives.

PAUL While in town one afternoon early in November I happened to pass by the pizza place on Main Street and, through the flurries of snow and the pane of glass and the red neon pizza sign, saw Mitchell sitting by himself in a booth, a half-finished pizza (plain cheese; that was how Mitchell always ordered them; bland) on the table in front of him. I went in. He was tearing open packets of Sweet'n'-Low, pouring them out and dividing the powder into long lines that resembled cocaine. I assumed he was alone.

"Are you lost or something?" he asked and lit a cigarette.

"Can I have one?" I asked.

He gave me one but didn't light it.

"How was the party last night?" he asked.

I stood there. How was the party? House crammed with drunk sweaty horny bodies dancing to old songs aimlessly wandering around blindly fucking each other? Who cares? I was entrusted by Hanna to watch her seventeen-year-old brother, who was visiting from Bensonhurst to see if he wanted to go to Camden. I was attracted to the guy but he was so straight (he would inquire about certain ugly girls, all of whom I told him had herpes) that I pushed whatever kinky thoughts I had out of my mind. He talked about the basketball team he was on and chewed tobacco and had no idea that his sister was Queen Lesbian of Mc-Cullough. We went back to my room to have a final beer. I went into the bathroom and washed my face, and when I came back he had taken off his sweatshirt, had poured what was left of my Absolut out and was using the empty bottle as a spittoon, asking if I had any Twisted Sister records. Needless to say, he had a great body and he drunkenly initiated a rather hectic bout of fucking. In between moaning "Fuck me, fuck me," he'd alternately whisper, "Don't tell my sister, don't tell my sister." I obliged on both accounts. How was the party? "Okay."

Mitchell had taken his American Express card out and slapped it on the table next to the two lines of Sweet'n'Low and he looked at me with such vehemence that I felt like a blip, a fart, in the course of his life. He tells me that this lawyer who he'd been seeing last summer in New York (before me, before us), a real jerk who liked to light everyone's cigarettes and who winked all the time, just got back from Nicaragua and told him it was "dynamite" so Mitchell might be heading down there for Christmas. He said this to irritate me, but I didn't wince. He knew that was a real conversation stopper.

I didn't wince even when Katrina, that blond Freshman girl who told everyone I couldn't get it up, sat down in the booth, slipping in next to him.

"You know each other?" Mitchell asked.

"No," she said smiling, introducing herself.

SEAN   I'm in the middle of having lame nightmares when the phone rings on the other side of the room behind the green and black striped parachute Bertrand hung up earlier this term and wakes me. I open my eyes hoping it'll pass, wonder if Bertrand's answering machine is on. But the phone keeps ringing. I get out of bed, naked with a hard-on from the nightmare, walk through the slit in the parachute and lean down to answer it. "Hello?"

It's a long distance call and there's a lot of static. "Allo?" a female voice calls out.

"Hello?" I say again.

"Allo? Bertrand?" More static.

"Bertrand's not in." I glance over at the pumpkin with the beret on it. Jesus.

"Is it Jean-Jacques?" the voice calls out. "Allo? Ça va?"

"Jesus," I mutter.

"Ça va? Ça va?"

I hang the phone up, walk back through the slit in the parachute and lie down. Then it hits me: I remember last night. I moan and cover my head with the pillow but it smells like her and I have to take it off my face. Why in the hell did Judy tell Lauren? What in the hell was going through that girl's mind when she told Lauren? I tried to talk to the bitch last night but there was no answer when I stopped by her room at Wooley. I moan again and throw the pillow against the wall, depressed and tense and horny. Move my hand over my hard-on, try and jerk off for a little while, reach beneath my bed and pull out the October issue of *Playboy*, reach a little further and find *Penthouse*.

I open up the *Playboy* to the centerfold. First I check out the girl's face, though I'm not sure why since it's her body, tits, cunt, ass, that seem so much more prominent. This girl is okay-looking; contemptibly pretty; her tits are tan and big and smooth; the flesh looks salty; run my hand over the thick, glossy paper, the small triangle of hair between the legs is carefully brushed and fluffy. I don't like the legs too much so I fold part of the centerfold over. This girl thinks she's smart. Her favorite movie is *Das Boot*, which is weird since a lot of these girls' favorite movie has been *Das Boot* lately, but she's obviously retarded, even though she does have nice tits. Spitting on my hand I think she might even look slightly horny, and I move my hand faster, but spit always dries up and I can't find any Vaseline in the mess of my room so I hump the discarded pillow instead and check out her measurements. 35-22-34.

And then I see it: Next to the measurements, next to height and weight (is that information supposed to turn us on? maybe it does) and color of eyes, is her birthdate. My mind does some quick subtraction and I realize that this girl is nineteen and me, Sean, is twenty-one. This girl is *younger* than me, and that does it—instant depression. This woman, this flesh was always older and that was part of the turn-on, but now, coming across this, something I'd never noticed before upsets me more than thinking about the conversation Lauren and Judy must have had. I have to close the *Playboy* and reach for the *Penthouse* and flip it open to the Forum section but it's too late and I can't concentrate on the words and I keep wondering if I really did bite the inside of Judy's thighs and, if so, then why? I can't even remember why it happened or how. Was it a week ago? It was the night of Vittorio's cocktail party. Had there been anyone else since Lauren? Shut my eyes and try to remember.

Throw the *Penthouse* across the room, where it accidentally hits the stereo, somehow turning it on and it's Journey and then "The Monster Mash" coming from a station in Keene and I have to moan again, my erection completely deflated. I drag myself from bed, put on my underwear, walk to the closet, open it, look at myself in the mirror hung there, finger the hickey Judy (or was it Brooke or Susan who I saw last night after stopping by Judy's place?) gave me, scowl at the reflection. I reach for a wire hanger, for the tie draped over it, a brown Ralph Lauren tie that Patrick sent me for a birthday I've forgotten. I tug it, stretching it, toss it away. Pick up another tie I got at Brooks Brothers and it seems stronger. I tug it, testing its strength, then knot it carefully, making a noose. Take the fern that some girl gave me off the large gold hook that some other girl stuck in the ceiling and place the dead plant on the floor, slip the part of the tie with the knot around the edge of the hook. I go to my desk and hurrying, pull the chair from it, stand on the chair, put my head through the pink and gray striped cotton noose and, about to hang myself, have a memory of a Christmas mass, why? "The Monster Mash" still coming from the radio, without any more hesitation, close my eyes and

I kick the chair away. . . .

I hang there for about a second (not even a second) before the tie rips in half and I fall like an idiot to the floor, screaming "Shit." Laying on my back in my jockey shorts I stare up at the piece of ripped tie, swinging from the hook. "The Monster Mash" ends. A cheerful D.J. says, "Happy Halloween New Hampshire!" I get up off the floor and get dressed. I walk across campus to the dining hall. Get this over with.

LAUREN I see the jerk first in the post office where he's throwing away letters without looking at them. Then he comes up to me while I'm sitting at lunch with Roxanne. Reading *Artforum*, wearing sunglasses. Sharing a bottle of beer someone self-dubbed The Party Pig left. Roxanne probably slept with him. Roxanne's wearing T-shirt and pearls, her hair heavily gelled. I'm drinking tea and a glass of Tab, unhungry. Roxanne looks at him suspiciously as he sits down. He takes off his sunglasses. I look him over. I had sex with this person?

"Hi, Roxanne," he says.

"Hi, Sean." She gets up. "I'll talk to you later," she tells me, picks up a book, leaves, comes back for the beer. I nod, turn a page. He takes a sip from my Tab. I light a cigarette.

"I tried to kill myself this morning," he says, offhand.

"Did you? Did you really?" I ask, taking a long satisfying drag from the cigarette.

"Yeah," he says. He's nervous, looking constantly around the room.

"Uh-huh. Right," I skeptically mutter.

"I did. I tried to hang myself."

"My my." Yawn. Turn a page. "Really?"

He looks at me like he wants me to take my sunglasses off but I can't bear to look at him without the bluish tint. He finally says, "No."

"If you did try," I ask him, "Why did you do it? Guilt?"

"I think we should talk," he says.

"There's nothing to say," I warn him and what's sort of surprising is that there really isn't. He's still looking nervously around the big open room, probably on the lookout for Judy, who after breaking down and telling me left for New York with Franklin for the Halloween party at Area. He looks sad, like there *is* something on his mind, and I cannot understand why he doesn't comprehend that I want him to leave me alone, that I don't care about him. How can he still think I really like him? That I ever liked him?

"We've got to talk," he says.

"But I'm telling you there's nothing to say," I smile and sip the tea. "What do you want to talk about?"

"What's going on?" he asks.

"Listen. You fucked Judy. That's what."

He doesn't say anything.

"Did you or didn't you?" I ask, bored silly.

"I don't remember," he says after a while.

"You don't remember?"

"Listen, you're making too much out of this. I realize you're hurt and upset but you've got to know that it didn't mean anything. You want me to admit I feel shitty about doing it?" he asks.

"No," I say. "I don't."

"Fine. I admit it. I feel shitty."

"I feel humiliated," I say, half-sarcastic, but he's too dumb to catch on.

"Humiliated? Why?" he asks.

"You went to bed with my best friend," I say, trying to

act angry, clutching at my teacup, spilling a little, trying to elicit some feeling.

He finally says, "She's not your *best* friend."

"Yes, she is. Sean."

"Well," he says. "I didn't know that."

"It doesn't matter," I say loudly.

"What doesn't?" he asks.

"Nothing." I stand up. He grabs my wrist as I reach for the magazine.

"Why did you still sleep with me if you knew?" he asks.

"Because I didn't care," I say.

"I know you do, Lauren," he says.

"You're pathetic and confused," I tell him.

"Wait a minute," he says. "Why should it matter how many I fucked? Or who I fucked? Since, like, when does having sex with someone else mean, like, I'm not faithful to you?"

I think about that one until he lets go of my wrist and I start laughing. I look around the dining hall for another table to sit at. Maybe I'll go to class. What day is it?

"You're right, I guess," I say, trying to make some kind of exit.

Before I walk away from him wondering about Victor still (not wondering anything in particular, just vague nothing wondering) he asks, "Why don't you love me, Lauren?"

"Just get out of here," I tell him.

SEAN   The rest of my day.

Me and Norris are in Norris's red Saab driving into town. Norris is tired and hungover (too much MDA, too much sex with various Freshmen). He's driving too fast and I don't say anything about it; only stare out the window at the gray clouds forming above red and green and orange hills, "Monster Mash" blaring on the radio bringing this morning back.

"Lauren found out about Judy," I tell him.

"How?" he asks, opening the window. "Is my pipe in the glove compartment?"

I check. "No. Judy told her."

"Cunt," he says. "Are you kidding? Why?"

"Can you believe it? I don't know," I say, shaking my head.

"Christ. Is she pissed?"

We pass a sexy townie girl selling tapestries and pumpkins near the high school. Norris slows down.

"Is who pissed?"

"Anyone," Norris says. "I could've sworn my pipe was in there. Check again."

"Yes. She's pissed," I say. "Wouldn't you be pissed if the girl you loved fucked your best friend?"

"I guess. Heavy."

"Yeah. I've got to talk to her."

"Sure. Sure," Norris says. "But she went to New York this weekend."

"What? Who? Lauren?"

"No. Judy."

That's not who I was talking about but I'm relieved anyway. "Really?"

"Yeah. She's got a boyfriend there."

"Terrific."

"He's a lawyer. Twenty-nine. Central Park West. Name's Jeb," Norris says.

"What about Frank?" I ask, then "*Jeb?*"

"The guy knows Franklin," Norris says.

Maybe it isn't over with Lauren, I'm thinking. Maybe she will come back. Norris parks the Saab behind the bank on Main Street and looks for the pipe himself.

At the drug store. While Norris picks up a prescription for Ritalin, I browse through the porno magazine rack that's placed next to the Oral Hygiene section. Open an issue of *Hustler*—typical—exclusive nude photos of Prince Andrew, Brooke Shields, Michael Jackson, all of them grainy, all of them in black and white. The magazine promises nude pictures of Pat Boone and Boy George next month. No. Put it back on the rack, open the October issue of *Chic*. The centerfold is of a woman dressed as a witch, her cape flung open, masturbating with a broomstick. She's better looking than Lauren but in a sleazy way and it doesn't excite me. Somehow the centerfold comes loose and slips to the floor, open, next to the feet of a blue-haired granny, who's reading, not looking, not glancing, but fucking *reading* the back of a bottle of Lavoris. She looks down at the centerfold and her mouth falls open and she quickly moves away to another aisle. I leave it there and walk back over to Norris who's at the checkout stand with his prescription and tell him, "Let's get out of here." I sigh and look over the racks of candy below the cashier's station. I pick up a pack of Peanut Butter Cups, finger it guiltily and remember last night, but only vaguely. What was it we fought about? Was there any real emotion there? Any raised voices? Or was it just a general feeling of contempt and betrayal and incredulity? I ask Norris to buy the candy for me and a tube of Fun Blood. Norris pays and asks the shy, acne-scarred cashier if she knows who wrote *Notes from the Underground*. The girl, who's so homely you couldn't sleep with her for money, not for anything, smiles and says no, and that he can look in the bestseller paperbacks if he'd like. We leave the store and Norris sneers a little too meanly, "Townies are so ignorant."

Then it's The Record Rack. Norris pops some Ritalin. I stare at the cover of the new Talking Heads. Wasn't that playing last night somewhere, during our talk? It doesn't depress me, just makes me feel weird. I put it down and decide to buy her a record. I try to remember who her favorite groups are but we never talked about things like that. In vain I pick up an old Police record but Sting is too good-looking and I start looking for albums by groups with no good-looking guys in them. But then maybe the Peanut Butter Cups are enough, and I walk back to Norris who winks at me, purchasing some old Motown collection and he hands it over to the fat blond girl behind the counter who's wearing a green ski-jacket and a .38 Special T-shirt. As she rings up Norris's stuff, he asks her if she knows who wrote *Notes from the Underground*. She laughs at him with contempt (a Lauren laugh) and says "Dostoevsky" and gives Norris back the album and no change and the two of us drive back to campus, mildly surprised.

Sitting in class. It's something called Kafka/Kundera: The Hidden Connection. I'm staring at this girl, Deborah, I think, who's sitting across from me at the table. I cannot concentrate on anything and have only shown up in class because I don't have any pot left. She has short blond hair, stylishly shaved in back and up the side, moussed, still has sunglasses on, leather pants, high-heeled police boots, black blouse, heavy silver jewelry (definitely rebellious Darien, Connecticut, material) and she reminds me substantially of Lauren. Lauren at lunch. Lauren not taking the shades off. Lauren's peg pants high, the ankles showing sexy and golden, the low-cut V-neck blue and black sweater. Look at the essay, Xeroxed, in front of me but I can't read it. I'm insatiably horny since I didn't finish jerking off this morning. When's the last time I have? Four days ago. The words I pretend to be interested in *make no sense*. I look back at the girl and start to fantasize about having sex with her, with her and Lauren at the same time, just her and Lauren naked, on top of each other, pressing their cunts together, moaning. I have to shift in the chair, my hard-on actually feeling not good, stretched tight against my jeans. Why does lesbianism turn me on?

The teacher, a large, friendly-looking woman (but not fuckable), asks, "Sean?"

Crossing my legs (no one can see, just a reflex) I sit up, "Yes?"

Teacher asks, "Why don't you tell us what the last paragraph means."

All I can say is "Um." Look at the last paragraph.

Teacher says, "Just encapsulate it for us."

I say, "Encapsulate."

Teacher says, "Yes. Encapsulate."

"Well . . ." and now I get the awful feeling that this girl in the sunglasses is laughing, smirking at me. I glance over at her quickly. She's not. I look down at the essay. What last paragraph? Lauren.

Teacher's losing patience. "What do you think it *means?*"

I skim the last paragraph. What is this? High school for Christ's sake? I will drop out of college. I hope that if I stall long enough she'll ask someone else and so I wait. People stare. Boy with cropped red hair wearing a "You're Insane" button on his ratty black Nehru jacket raises his hand. So does the idiot at the end of the table who looks like he's the lead singer of the Bay City Rollers. Even the blond dude from L.A. whose I.Q. has got to be in the lower forties manages to raise a tan arm. What in the hell is going on here? I will drop out of college. Was I learning anything?

"What is it about, Sean?" the teacher asks.

"It's about his dissatisfaction with the government?" I ask, guessing.

The girl with the sunglasses raises a hand. Do you wear a diaphragm everywhere you go? I want to scream, but stop myself because the idea really excites me.

"Actually, it's about the opposite," the teacher, who has got to be a dyke, says, fingering a long string of beads. "Clay?" the teacher asks.

"Well, like, the dude was totally depressed because, well, the dude turned into a bug and freaked. . . ."

I look down and want to shout out, "Hey, I think it's a fucking masterpiece," but I haven't read it so I can't.

That girl sitting across from me doesn't remind me of Lauren. No one does. She puts a piece of gum in her mouth. I don't feel excited anymore.

And leaving class during the break with the intention of not going back isn't any better since I have to see my advisor, Mr. Masur, whose office is in the Barn. Otherwise known as Administration Row. And walking up the small graveled path I wonder what Lauren is doing right now, this second. Is she in her room at Canfield, or over with friends carving pumpkins and getting drunk in Swan? Up at the dance studio? Computer room? With Vittorio? No, Vittorio's gone. With Stump? Maybe she's just hanging around Commons talking to Judy or Stephanie or whoever the hell she knows, reading the *Times*, attempting Friday's crossword. I pull my coat tighter around me. I'm nauseous. I walk faster. The Swedish girl from Bingham who I always thought was sort of good-looking (who's also fucking Mitchell) is coming down the path, toward me. I realize that I am going to have to pass this Swedish girl and say something or smile. It would be too rude to not say anything. But she passes and smiles and says "Hi" and I don't say anything. I've never said anything to the Swedish girl for some reason and I feel guilty and turn around and say "Hi!" loudly. The Swedish girl turns around and smiles, puzzled, and I start jogging toward the Barn, blushing, heavily embarrassed, feverish, walking in through the main entrance, wave to Getch who's setting up some fossil exhibition, take the stairs up two at a time, and then it's Masur's office. I knock, winded.

"Come in, come in," Mr. Masur says.

I enter.

"Ah, Mr. Bateman, it's good to see you, every, what is it now? Month or so?" the sarcastic bastard asks.

I grin and plop myself down in the chair across from Masur's desk.

"Where have you been? We're supposed to meet every week," Masur says, leaning back.

"Well . . ." Duh. "I've been real busy."

"Oh, you have?" Masur asks, grinning. He runs a hand through his long gray hair, sucking in while lighting his pipe, like a true ex-boho.

"I got your note. What is it?" I know it's going to be something bad.

"Yes. Well . . ." He shuffles through papers. "As you know it's mid-term and it's come to my attention that you are not passing three of your courses. Is this true?"

I try to look surprised. Actually I thought I was failing four courses. I try to guess which one I'm passing. "Um yeah well, I'm having trouble in a couple of classes." Pause. "Am I failing Sculpting Workshop?"

"Well, as a matter of fact, you are," Masur says, glancing ominously at a pink sheet of paper he holds up.

"I don't see how," I say innocently.

"It seems that Mr. Winters said that for your mid-term project, it seems to him that all you did was glue three stones you found behind your dorm and painted them blue." Masur looks pained.

I don't say a word.

"Also Mrs. Russell says that you have not been showing up to class regularly," Masur says, eyeing me.

"What am I passing?"

"Well, Mr. Schonbeck says you're doing quite well," Masur says, surprised.

Who's Mr. Schonbeck? I've never been to a class taught by a Schonbeck.

"Well, I've been sick. Sick."

"Sick?" Masur asks, looking even more pained.

"Well, yeah, sick."

"Ahem." This is followed by an uncomfortable silence. The smell of Masur's pipe nauseates me. The urge to leave hits hard. It's also sickening that even though Masur is not from England he speaks with a slight British accent.

"Needless to say Mr. Bateman, um, Sean, your situation here is, shall we say, rather . . . unstable?"

"Unstable, yeah, well, um . . ."

"What are we going to do about it?" he asks.

"I'm going to fix it."

"You are?" he sighs.

"Yes. You bet I am."

"Well. Good, good," Masur looks confused but smiling as he says this.

"Okay?" I stand up.

"Fine with me," Masur says.

"Well, see you later?" I ask.

"Well, fine with me," Masur laughs.

I laugh too, open the door, look back at Masur, who's really cracking up, yet stupefied, and then I shut the door, planning my overdose.

In my room is Beba, Bertrand's girlfriend. She's sitting on the mattress beneath the wall-length blackboard that came with the room, the carved pumpkin in her lap, old issues of *Details* scattered around her. Beba is a sophomore and bulimic and has been reading *Edie* ever since she arrived last September. Bertrand's phone is cradled in her neck, covered by shoulder length platinum blond hair. She lights a cigarette and waves limply at me as I pass through the slit in the parachute. I sit on my bed, my face in my hands, silent in the room except for Beba. "Yes, I was wondering about a cellophane tomorrow, say, around two-thirty?" The ripped tie is still hanging from the hook and I reach up, pull it off and throw it against the wall. I start rummaging through my room. No more Nyquil, no more Librium, no more Xanax. Find a bottle of Actifed, which I pour into my sweaty hands. Twenty of them. I look around the room for something to take them with. I can hear Beba hang up the phone, then Siouxsie and the Banshees start playing.

"Beba, does Bert have anything to drink over there?" I call out.

"Let me see." I hear her turn down the music, tripping over something. Then an arm sticks through the parachute's slit handing me a beer.

"Thanks." I take the beer from the hand.

"Does Alonzo still have any coke?" she asks.

"No. Alonzo went to the city this weekend," I tell her.

"Oh god," I hear her moan.

I wonder if I should leave a note. Some kind of reason for why I'm doing this, why I'm swallowing all my Actifed. The phone rings. Beba answers it. I lay down after taking five. I drink some more of the beer. Grolsch—what an asshole. Beba puts on another tape, The Cure. I take three more pills. Beba says, "Yes, I'll tell him Jean-Jacques called. Right, ça va, yeah, ça va." I start falling asleep, laughing— am I really trying to O.D. on Actifed? I can hear Bertrand open the door, laughing, "I am back." I drift.

But Norris wakes me up sometime after nine. I'm not dead, just sick to my stomach. I'm under the covers but still in my clothes. It's dark in the room.

"You slept through dinner," Norris says.

"I did." I try to sit up.

"You did."

"What did I miss?" I try to unstick my tongue from the roof of a very dry, stale mouth.

"Lesbians in a fistfight. Pumpkin carving contest. Party Pig threw up," Norris shrugs.

"Oh man I am so tired." I try to sit up again. Norris stands in the doorway and flicks on a light. He walks over to the bed.

"There are Actifed scattered around you," Norris points out.

I pick one up, toss it away. "Yes. There are."

"What did you try to do? O.D. on Actifed?" he laughs, bending down.

"Don't tell anyone," I say, getting up. "I need a shower."

"Just between you and me," he says, sitting down.

"Where's everybody?" I ask, taking my clothes off.

"At Windham. Halloween party. Your roommate went as a Quaalude." Norris picks up a copy of *The Face* that for some reason is on my side of the room. He flips through it thoroughly bored. "Either that or a pastry. I can't tell."

"I'm taking a shower," I tell him. I grab my robe.

Norris picks up the Peanut Butter Cups. "Can I have one?"

"No, don't open them." I come out of my stupor. "They're for Lauren."

"Calm down, Bateman."

"They're for Lauren." I stumble toward the door.

"Relax!" he screams.

I head for the bathroom, dizzy, steadying myself as I make my way down the hallway, and into the bathroom. Enter the cubicle, take off the robe, step into shower, lean against the wall before turning the shower on, think about passing out. I shake my head: the feeling subsides, I turn the water on. It hits me weakly and I try to get the pressure up but the water, barely warm, keeps dribbling out of the rusty showerhead.

Sitting down on the floor of the shower I notice Bertrand's Gillette razor lying in the corner next to a tube of Clinique shaving cream. I pick up the razor by its silver handle and stare at it for a long time. I move it down my wrist. I turn my hand over, palm up, and slowly move it up my arm, the blade catching some of the hair that covers the skin. I pull the blade away and wash the hair off it. Then move it back to my arm, this time bringing the handle up to the wrist, pressing it hard, trying to break the skin. But it doesn't. I apply more pressure, but it only leaves red marks. I try the other wrist, pushing with all my strength, almost groaning with exertion, lukewarm water splashing in my eyes. The blade is too dull. I press it down against the wrist, feebly, once more.

Through the sound of the falling water I can hear Norris calling out, "Sean, how long are you gonna be?"

I stand up clumsily, leaning against the wall. "In a couple of minutes." The razor drops to the floor, clattering loudly.

"Listen, I'll be at the party, okay?"

"Yeah. Okay."

"Drop by."

I wonder if Lauren will be there. I imagine walking into

the living room at Windham, our eyes meeting, her face filled with regret and longing, coming towards me. The two of us embracing in the middle of the crowded room while everyone cheers and resumes dancing. The two of us just standing there, holding each other.

"Yeah. Okay, I will." There's steam in the bathroom now, not because of the heat of the water but because of how cold it is in the dorm.

"See you there." Norris leaves.

I stare at my wrists, then finger the disappearing hickey on my neck.

I wash my hair twice, dry off and go back to my room where I throw the ripped tie away, along with the Actifed scattered all over the floor. I get dressed fast, excited, and pick up the Peanut Butter Cups, and, as I'm about to leave, Bertrand's pumpkin that's sitting on the windowsill, lit. I look into the lighted face of the jack-o'-lantern and since I just know that Lauren will get a kick out of it I have to swipe it. I'm so excited at the prospect of reconciling with her that I don't care if the Frog gets pissed.

I leave the room without locking the door and move quickly across campus to her room, carefully walking across the wetness of Commons lawn so the candle in the pumpkin won't go out. Two guys dressed as girls and two girls dressed as guys pass by drunk, yelling "Happy Halloween" and throw small pieces of hard candy at me. I open the back door of Canfield, bound up the darkened stairs to her room. I knock. There's no answer. I wait and knock louder. I stand there, cursing myself, someone brushes past me dressed as a joint and walks into the bathroom. My excitement at seeing her slowly starts to dissipate. She must be at the party, so I walk with the pumpkin, still lit, and the Peanut Butter Cups, squished and melting in my back pocket, across Commons toward Windham.

The living room of Windham is bathed in this eerie dim orange light. An old Stevie Wonder song, "Superstition," plays loudly. I walk up to the windows in front of the house. The living room is crowded with people in costume dancing. All the lightbulbs in the lamps and walls have been replaced by orange ones. Bertrand is there, as a Quaalude but he really looks like a circle. Getch as a pregnant nun. Tony as a hamburger. A couple of Madonna look-alikes. Rupert as Leatherface from *The Texas Chainsaw Massacre*. A couple of Freshmen dorks as Rambo. I spot Lauren almost immediately, dancing in the middle of the floor with Justin Simmons, a tall pale blackhaired Lit major wearing black sunglasses, black jeans, black T-shirt with a skull on the back of it. Her head is thrown back and she's laughing and Justin has both of his hands on her shoulders.

I moan softly stepping away from the window.

I run back to Canfield and hurl Bertrand's pumpkin at the wall beside her door, and smear the Peanut Butter Cups all over the door. Rip the pen that's hanging off her door from the string it's connected to and also a piece of paper and write "Fuck Off and Die" in big black letters. I place it next to the cracked pumpkin and the smashed, melted candy. I stalk away, down the stairs, out into the night.

Halfway across Commons lawn glaring at Windham House, the party now louder than before, seeming to mock me, I stop and decide to take the note off the pumpkin. I walk back to Canfield, up the stairs to her door and lift the note off the jack-o'-lantern and carry it back with me. I reach the front door of Canfield and then redecide to leave the note where it was. I walk back up the stairs and stick the note back on the pumpkin. I stare at it. Fuck off and die. I leave Canfield and walk back to my room.

I lie on my bed in the dark for close to an hour, drinking the last of Bertrand's six-pack of Grolsch and listening to "Funeral for a Friend" and trying to play along with it on my guitar, thinking about Lauren. Something hits me. I walk over to my desk in the dark and pick up the tube of Fun Blood I bought in town earlier. I sit in the chair, drunk, turn the Tensor lamp on and read the instructions. Since I don't have any scissors to cut the cap off with I bite it off instead, tasting a couple drops of the plastic-tasting liquid. I spit it out, wash the taste away with the warm Grolsch.

Then I squeeze the tube, some of it onto my fingers. It looks very real and I hold my wrist out and squeeze a thick red line across it, the cool liquid slowly dripping off my wrist, onto the desk. I squeeze another line across the other wrist. "Funeral for a Friend" turns into "Love Lies Bleeding." I lift my arms up, both dripping Fun Blood, Fun Blood running down to my armpits. I sit back in the chair and squeeze more Fun Blood across my arms. I get up, go to the closet, and look at myself in the mirror. I bend my head back and squeeze a thick line across my neck. I feel relieved. Fun Blood runs down my chest, staining my shirt. I draw a thick line across my forehead. I move away from the mirror and sit on the floor, next to one of the speakers, Fun Blood dripping from my forehead, past my nose down to my lips. I turn the volume up.

The door opens slowly and I can hear over the music, through the parachute, Lauren calling. "I knocked, Sean. Hello?" A hand parts the slit in the parachute.

"Sean?" she calls out. "I got your . . . message. You're right. We have to talk."

She steps through the parachute and looks over at my bed and then at me. I don't move. She gasps. But I can't help it and I start to crack up. I look over at her, slick with Fun Blood, drunk and smiling.

"You are so fucking sick," she screams. "You're so sick! I can't deal with you."

But then she turns around before she slips through the parachute, and comes back into my room. She's changed her mind. She kneels in front of me. The music swelling to a crescendo as she wipes my face off delicately. She kisses me.

LAUREN   Walk into The Pub. Stand near the cigarette machine. Out of order. Talking Heads are blasting out from the jukebox. Sean is standing near the bar wearing a police jacket and black T-shirt. Visiting punks are talking to him. Walk over and ask him, "Are you okay?" End up sitting with him, staring at the pinball machine, Royal Flush, while he sulks.

"I feel my life is going nowhere. I feel incredibly lonely," he says.

"Do you want a Beck's?" I ask him.

"Yeah. Dark," he says.

I cannot deal with this person one more minute. Brush past Franklin, who's leaning against the out-of-order cigarette machine. Smiles wanly. Push my way to the front of the bar and order two beers. Talk to that nice girl from Rockaway and her awful roommate. That weird group of Classics majors stand by, looking like undertakers. Typical night at The Pub. People dressed in underwear, Drama majors still with make-up on. Brazilian guy who can't drink because he lost his I.D. Someone pinches my ass but don't turn around to look.

Bring the beers back to the table. Sean has faint red stains on his face and I'm about to wet a napkin with Beck's to rub them off. But he starts complaining and he looks at me hard when he asks, "Why don't you like me?"

I get up, walk to the bathroom, wait in line, and when I come back he asks me again.

"I don't know," I sigh.

"I mean, what's going on?" he asks.

Shrug and look around the room. He gets up to play pinball. "This wouldn't happen in Europe," someone in a surfer outfit—actually the boy from L.A.—says and of course Victor comes into mind and then oh shit, someone's kneeling next to my chair telling me about the first times they tripped on MDA, showing me the bottle of Cuervos they smuggled into The Pub, and to my disappointment I'm interested. Sean sits back down and I just know we're going to fight.

I sigh and tell him, "I like someone else."

He plays pinball again. I go to the bathroom again hoping someone will take our table. I'm in line with the same people that I was in line with last time. When I come back to the table he's there. "What's going on?"

"I like someone else," I tell him.

Cute Joseph who Alex-nice-girl-from-Rockaway is sleeping with—walks in and hands the Brazilian boy something. Then I notice Paul. He's looking at Joseph, then the Brazilian. Paul has a new flattop which looks okay, sexy in a goofy way and he looks over at me and I raise my eyebrows up and smile. He looks at Sean and then at me and waves tiredly. Then he looks back at Sean.

"I want to know you," Sean whines.

"What?"

"Know you. I want to *know* you." Pleading.

"What does that mean? *Know* me?" I ask him. "*Know* me? No one ever *knows* anyone. Ever. You will never *know* me."

"Listen," he says, touching my hands.

"Will you calm down," I tell him. "Do you want some Motrin?"

A fight starts over near the jukebox. Seniors want to put tapes on and unplug the jukebox. Freshmen don't want to and I try to concentrate on that. The Freshmen end up winning just because they're bigger than the Seniors. Physically bigger. How did that happen? "Boys of Summer" comes on. Think of Victor. Sean gets up to play more pinball with an unhappy Franklin. Royal Flush is the name of the game. There's a King and a Queen and a Jack lit up, all looking straight at the person playing pinball and the crowns on their respective heads blink off and on whenever the player scores. It's amusing for a while.

I look back over at Paul across the crowded Pub. He looks miserable. He's looking at Sean. He's staring at Sean. Sean keeps looking over at me, like he knows Paul is looking at him, and then I'm looking over at Paul and Paul is still staring at Sean. Sean catches this and, blushing, rolls his eyes up and turns back to the pinball machine. I look back at Paul. He crumples his plastic beer cup and looks away, agonized. And I'm starting to catch on to something and then I'm thinking no way, oh no way. Not that. I look back at Sean, semi-realization hitting me but then it leaves because he's not staring back at Paul. And then I get angry, start remembering how awful it was with Paul and Mitchell. Paul denying everything, how pathetic I seemed, wondering how I was supposed to act when there was no real competition. If it had been another girl with Paul that weekend on Cape Cod instead of Mitchell, or another girl here in The Pub right now, mooning over Sean, that would have been fine, great, easy to "deal with." But it was Paul and it was Mitchell and there was nothing I could do. Lower my voice? Casually mention I need to shave, Judy and I suggested, hysterical, one night last term, but in the end it wasn't really funny and we stopped laughing. Now the possibility hits that perhaps Mr. Denton is staring at me and not at Sean. "Boys of Summer" ends, starts again.

Rupert sits down next to me wearing a David Bowie T-shirt and a fedora, still hasn't taken off the horrible mask he's wearing, and offers me some of his coke. I ask him where Roxanne is. He tells me that she went home with Justin. Just smile.

VICTOR New York was a real hassle. I ended up staying with some girl who thought her mail was coming from Jupiter. She had no hips and was a Gitano jeans model from Akron, but still it was a drag. She caught me going out with Philip Glass's daughter anyway, and kicked me out. I stayed at Morgan's for a couple of nights and split without paying the bill. Then I stayed at some Camden grad's place on Park and unplugged all the phones since I didn't want the 'rents to know I was back in town. Tried to get a job at Palladium but some other Camden grad got the only job left: coat check. Got into a rock band, dealt acid, went to a couple of okay parties, went out with a girl who worked at *Interview* and who tried to enroll me into Hunter, went out with another model, one of Malcolm McLaren's assistants, tried to get back to Europe, but decided on a cold partyless night in November to head back to New Hampshire and Camden. Got a ride with Roxanne Forest, who was in town for some movie premiere or the opening of another Cajun restaurant and I stayed with her and Rupert Guest Drug Dealer at their place in North Camden, which was cool since he had unlimited supplies of great Indica pot and Christmas Tree bud. Besides that I also wanted to get in touch with Jaime. When I called Canfield, a girl with an unfamiliar voice answered the phone.

"Hello? Canfield House."

"Hello?" I said.

There was this pause and then the girl recognized my voice and said my name, "Victor?"

"Yeah? Who is this?" I asked, wondering if it was Jaime, pissed off that she hadn't been in Manhattan when I got back.

"Victor," the girl laughed. "It's *me*."

"Oh yeah," I said. "You."

Rupert was on the floor trying to glue a beer bong he'd made back together, but he was wasted and kept cracking up instead. I started cracking up too, watching him and said to the voice on the phone, "Well, how are *you?*"

"Victor, why haven't you called me? Where are you?" she asked. Either that or I was seriously tripping.

"I'm in New York City where the girls are pretty and life is kinda shitty and the birds are itty bitty—" I laughed, then noticed movement on Rupert's part. He jumped up and put Run D.M.C. on the stereo and started rapping along with them, singing into the Kirin bong.

"Give it to me," I said, reaching for the bong.

"I've been . . ." the voice stalled.

"You've been what, honey?" I asked.

"I've missed you badly," she said.

"Hey honey. Well, I've missed you too." This girl was looney-tunes and I started cracking up again, trying to light the bong, but the pot kept falling out.

"It doesn't sound like you're in New York," the voice said.

"Well maybe I'm not," I said.

The voice stopped talking after that and just breathed heavily into the phone. I waited a minute and then handed the phone over to Rupert, who made pig noises into it, then turned on the VCR all the while rapping to "You Talk Too Much." He bent down and said, "You never shut up," into the receiver, then "Sit on my face if you please." I had to put my hand over the receiver to keep this girl from hearing me laugh. I pushed Rupert away.

He mouthed, "Who is it?"

I mouthed back, "I don't know."

I get a hold on myself and then finally asked this girl what I called for in the first place, "Listen, is Jaime Fields in? Room 19, I think." The bong dropped against the table. I picked it up before it rolled off the table and shattered.

"You shithead! Be careful," Rupert screamed, laughing.

The girl on the phone wasn't saying anything.

"Hello? Anyone there?" I tapped the phone against the floor. "I'd like to buy a vowel, please."

The girl finally said my name, really whispered it, and then hung the phone up, disconnecting me.

LAUREN Drunk. Blur. His room. I wake up. Music blasting from upstairs. Stumble into hallway. Susie tried to kill herself earlier. Slit her wrist. Blood all over the door across the hall. Guy she likes. Use the bathroom, wearing his shirt, black space, can't find a light, it's freezing. My face so puffed from sobbing that I can barely open my eyes. Wash face. Try to throw up. Walk back to his room. Crying sound coming from phone booth. Probably Susie back from hospital. Walk by phone. Not Susie, but Sean. Kneeling, crying into the phone "fuck you fuck you fuck you." Go back to his room. Fall back on bed. Later he comes in, wiping his face sniffing loudly. Pretend to sleep while he packs, shoves some shirts into an old leather satchel and grabs his police jacket and leaves the door open. Expect him to come back. He doesn't. French guy who told me he loved me comes into the room drunk. Looks down at me lying on his roommate's bed. He laughs and falls on the bed next to me. "Je savais toujours que tu viendrais," he says and passes out.

SEAN The last time I saw my father had been in March when I met him in New York for a long weekend to celebrate my twenty-first birthday. I remember the entire trip quite clearly which surprises me considering how drunk I was most of the time. I remember the look of the morning at an airport in New Hampshire, playing gin with some guy from Dartmouth, a rude stewardess. There was a meal at The Four Seasons, there was the afternoon we lost the limousine, the hours spent shopping at Barney's, then Gucci. There was my father, already noticeably dying: his face yellowish, his fingers as thin as cigarettes, eyes that were wide and always staring at me, almost in disbelief. I would stare back, finding it impossible to imagine someone that thin. But he acted as if this wasn't happening to him. He still held a certain degree of normalcy about him. He didn't appear scared, and for someone apparently quite ill had enormous amounts of stamina. We still saw a couple of lame musicals on Broadway, and we still had drinks in the bar at The Carlyle, and we still would go to P.J. Clarke's, where I played songs on the jukebox I knew he'd like though I don't remember why exactly this rush of generosity occurred, what brought it on.

It was also a weekend when two women in their mid-twenties tried unsuccessfully to pick up on my father and I. They were both drunk and due to the cold weather I had sobered up from whatever drinking binge I had been on, and my father had stopped drinking completely, and we lied to them. We told them we were oil barons from Texas and that I attended Harvard and came to Manhattan on weekends. They left whatever bar we had been at with us and we piled into the limousine which took us to a party someone my father knew at Trump Tower was having where we lost them. What was strange about that situation was not the pick-up itself, for my father had always been quite adept at casually picking up women. It was that my father, who would normally have flirted with these two, didn't this last March. Not in the bar, not in the limousine, not at the party on Fifth Avenue we lost them at.

My father also couldn't eat. So there were meals left wasted at Le Cirque, and Elaine's and The Russian Tea Room; drinks ordered and left untouched at 21 and the Oak Room Bar; neither of us talking, mutually relieved if the bar or restaurant we were at was particularly noisy. There was a dour lunch at Mortimer's with friends of his from Washington. A somber birthday dinner at Lutece with a girl I'd met at The Blue and Gold, Patrick and his girlfriend, Evelyn, who was a junior executive at American Express, and my father. This was two months after he had mother committed to Sandstone and the thing I most remember about that birthday was the fact that no one mentioned it. No one ever mentioned it except for Patrick, who, in confidence to me, whispered, "It was about time." Patrick gave me a tie that night.

We went back to my father's place at The Carlyle after the gloomy birthday dinner. He went to sleep, giving me a disapproving look as I sat with the girl on the couch in the living room, watching videos. The girl and I had sex later that night on the floor of the living room. I woke up sometime early that morning hearing moans coming from the bedroom. A light was on, there were voices. It started snowing that night, just before dawn. I left the next day.

On the plane heading for New York and later in my father's place at The Carlyle, unpacking, pacing, drinking from a bottle of J.D., the stereo on, I think of the reasons why I came to New York and can only come up with one. I didn't come to see my father die. And I didn't come to argue with my brother. And I didn't come because I wanted to skip classes at school. And I didn't come to visit my mother. I came to New York because I owe Rupert Guest six hundred dollars and I don't want to deal with it.

PAUL Have you been in a worse mood lately?

The Freshman you have a crush on passes by you down the stairs out of the dining halls and when you ask him where he's going he says, "Hibachi." You've forgotten your I.D. so they bother you about that but they let you in anyway. You get some coffee and for some perverse reason a bowl of Jell-O and walk to your table. It seems that Donald and Harry went to Montreal last night to visit the natives and got back this morning. "I haven't masturbated in eleven days," Donald whispers as you sit down. "I envy you," you whisper back.

And then there's Raymond who has brought Steve, nicknamed The Handsome Dunce in some circles, to the table. Steve is an economics major who "dabbles in video." Steve has a BMW. He is from Long Island. Now, Raymond has not slept with this guy (gay Freshmen—it's dawning on you—are an anomaly now) even though he did leave the party with him last night. But Raymond is eager still to let everyone think so. He laughs at every lame conversation attempt made by this idiot Steve and asks him constantly if he wants anything and brings him things (cookies, a disgusting/funny salad, garnishes stolen from the salad bar) even if he has said no. It's so nauseating that you are about to get up and leave, sit somewhere else. What's even more nauseating is that you don't. You stay because Steve *is* hot. And this depresses you, makes you think, will you always be the quintessential faggot? Will you only pant after the blond-tan-good-body-stupid-goons? And will you always ignore the smart, caring, sensitive type, who might be four-foot-three and have acne on his back but who is still, essentially, *bright?* Will you always pant after the blue-eyed palooka who's majoring in Trombone Theory and ignore the loving Drama queer who's doing his thesis on Joe Orton? You want it to stop, but . . .

. . . then the tall blue-eyed Freshman, who doesn't even have a hint of interest in you, will ask for a cigarette and you'll be blown away. But the Freshmen, represented here by Steve, look so stupid, so desperate to please, trying so hard, nothing on their minds but partying, dressed like ads for Esprit sportswear. Fact remains however: they are better-looking than the Seniors.

"How was the party?" Harry asks.

"My brother's bar mitzvah was more fun, *maybe*," Raymond says, glancing over at Steve, whose eyes look permanently half-closed, a dumb grin locked on his face, nodding to no one.

"They were actually playing *Springsteen*," Steve says.

"Jesus, I know," Raymond agrees. "Springsteen, for Christ's sake. Who was D.J.?"

"But you *like* Springsteen, Raymond," you say, ignoring the green Jell-O, lighting a cigarette, your four hundredth of the day.

"No, I don't," Raymond says blushing, looking nervously at Steve.

"You do?" Steve asks him.

"No, I don't," Raymond says. "I don't know where Paul got that idea."

"See, Raymond has this theory that Springsteen likes getting, to put it mildly, *boo-fooed*," you say, leaning in, talking directly to Steve. "Springsteen, for Christ's sake."

"Listen to 'Backstreets.' Gay song definitely," Donald says, nodding.

"I never said that," Raymond laughs uncomfortably. "Paul's got me mixed up with someone."

"What was the adjective you used to describe the cover of the 'Born in the U.S.A.' album?" you ask. "Delicious?"

But Steve's not listening anymore. He's not interested in what passes for conversation at the table. He's talking to the Brazilian boy. He's asking him if he can get him some Ecstasy for tonight. The Brazilian boy says, "Saps your spinal fluid, dude."

"Paul, why don't you just mind your own business," Raymond says with a resentful glare. ". . . And get me some Sprite."

"You had this list, Raymond," you say, causing more trouble. "Who else was on it? It was quite a list: Shakespeare, Sam Shepard, Rob Lowe, Ronald Reagan, his son—"

"Well, his son," Donald says.

"But isn't this the century no one cared?" Harry asks.

"About what?" you all ask back.

"Huh?" Steve asks after the Brazilian leaves.

But you stop listening because we all have lapses of taste; we've all slept with people we shouldn't have slept with. What about that tall, lanky guy with the Asian girlfriend who you thought had herpes but didn't and the two of you made a vow to never tell anyone about your two nights together. He's across the room right now, sitting with that same little Oriental girl. They're fighting. She gets up. He gives her the finger to her back, the wimp. Now Raymond's talking about how great Steve's "dabbles in video" are.

"Your stuff is great. Is that class any good?" he's asking. Now, you know Raymond loathes anything that has to do with videos and that even if this guy did something amazing, which is doubtful, Raymond would still loathe it.

"I learned a lot from that class," Steve says.

"Like what?" you whisper to Donald, "The alphabet?"

Raymond hears and glares.

Steve just says, "Wha?"

Harry asks, "Was there a nuclear war somewhere over the weekend?" You turn away and look out over the room. Then one final look at Steve sitting next to Raymond, both of them now laughing about something. Steve doesn't realize what's happening. Raymond still holds his stare at the three of us, and his hand shakes for a second when he brings his glass to his mouth and gives Steve a quick glance which Steve catches. The quick glance gives it all away. But what could it possibly mean to the blond boy from Long Island? Nothing. It meant only "quick glance" and nothing past that. It meant a shaking hand lighting another cigarette. After Sean left, songs I normally wouldn't have liked started having painful significance to me.

PATRICK   The limousine should have picked him up any time between ten-thirty and ten-forty-five. He should get to the airport in Keene by at least ten to twelve, where the Lear will fly him into Kennedy, where his arrival time should be one-thirty or one-forty-five. He should have been at the hospital thirty minutes ago but, knowing Sean, he probably went to The Carlyle first to get drunk or smoke marijuana or whatever the hell it is he does. But since he's always been so mindless about responsibility and about keeping people waiting I'm really not at all surprised. I wait in the lobby of the hospital checking my watch, making phone calls to Evelyn, who will not come to the hospital, waiting for the limousine to get him here. When it appears that he's decided not to show, I take the elevator back to the fifth floor and wait, pacing, while my father's aides sit by the door of his room conferring with one another, occasionally looking over at me nervously. One, earlier in the evening, congratulated me, with what I took to be heavy sarcasm, on the tan I had acquired last week in the Bahamas with Evelyn. He passes again, heading for the restroom. He smiles. I ignore him completely. I don't like either one of these men and they will both be fired as soon as my father dies.

Sean walks down the darkened corridor towards me. He looks at me with pleasurable dislike and I back away, repelled. He motions silently with his arm if he can go into the room. I shrug and dismiss him.

He comes out of the room moments later and not with the white mask of shock I'd thought he'd be wearing, but with a simple and expressionless look on his face. No smile, no sadness. The eyes, bloodshot and half-closed, still manage to exude hatefulness and a weakness of character that I find abhorrent. But he's my brother, and at first I let it pass. He heads toward the restroom.

I ask him, "Hey, where are you going?"

"The john," he calls back.

The night nurse at her desk looks up from the chart she's been going over, to quiet us, but when she sees me gesture at her, she relents.

"Meet me in the cafeteria," I tell him, before the door to the restroom shuts. What he does in there is so pitifully obvious to me (cocaine? is he into crack?) that I'm ashamed at his lack of concern and at his capacity to tick me off.

He sits across from me in the darkened cafeteria, smoking cigarettes.

"Don't they feed you up there?" I ask.

He doesn't look at me. "Technically, yes."

He plays with a swizzle stick. I drink the rest of my Evian water. He puts the cigarette out and lights another.

"Well . . . are we having fun?" he asks. "What's going on? Why am I here?"

"He's almost dead," I tell him, hoping a shred of reality will break through to that wasted mindless head bobbing in front of me.

"No," he says startled, and I'm unprepared for a millisecond at this show of emotion, but then he says, "What an astute observation," and I'm embarrassed at my surprise.

"Where have you been?" I demand.

"Around," he says. "I've been around."

"Where have you been?" I ask again. "Specifics."

"I came," he says. "Isn't that enough?"

"Where have you been?"

"Have you visited Mom lately?" he asks.

"That's not what we're talking about," I say, not letting that one throw me off.

"Stop asking me questions," he says, laughing.

"Stop deliberately misunderstanding me," I say, not laughing.

"Deal with it," he says.

"No, Sean." I point at him, serious, no joke. "*You* deal with it."

One of my father's aides walks into the empty cafeteria and whispers something into my ear. I nod, still staring at Sean. The aide leaves.

"Who was that?" he asks. "C.I.A.?"

"What are you on now?" I ask. "Coke? Ludes?"

He looks up again with the same mocking contempt and laughs, "Coke? Ludes?"

"I put seven thou in your account. Where is it?" I ask.

A nurse passes by and he eyes her before answering. "It's there. It's still there."

Nothing is said for three minutes. I keep looking at my watch, wondering what Evelyn is doing right now. She said sleeping, but I could hear faint music in the background. I called Robert. There was no answer. When I called Evelyn back her machine was on. Sean's face looks the same. I try to remember when he started hating me, when I reciprocated the feeling. He plays with the swizzle stick some more. My stomach growls. He has nothing to say to me and I, in the end, have really nothing to talk about with him.

"What are you going to do?" I ask.

"What do you mean?" He almost looks surprised.

"I mean, are you going to get a job?"

"Not at Dad's place," he says.

"Well, where then?" I ask him. It's a fair question.

"What do you think?" he asks. "Suggestions?"

"I'm asking you," I tell him.

"Because? . . ." He lifts his hands up, leaves them suspended there for a moment.

"Because you're not going to last another term at that place," I let him know.

"Well, what do you want? A lawyer? A priest? A neurosurgeon?" he asks. "What *you* do?"

"How about the son your father wanted?" I ask.

"You think that thing in there even cares?" he asks back, laughing, pointing a thumb back at the corridor, sniffing hard.

"He would be pleased to know that you're taking, let's call it, a 'leave of absence' from that place," I say. I consider other options, harsher tactics. "You know he was always upset about all the football scholarships you threw away," I say.

He stares at me sternly, unforgiving. "Right."

"What are you going to do?" I ask.

"I don't know," he says.

"Where are you going to go?" I ask.

"I don't know."

"Where?"

"I don't know. Utah," he shouts. "I'm going to Utah! Utah or Europe." He stands up, pushes himself away from the table. "I'm not answering any more of your frigging questions."

"Sit down, Sean," I say.

"You make me sick," he says.

"You're not getting out of this," I tell him. "Now sit down."

He ignores me and walks down the corridor, past his father's room, past other rooms.

"I'm taking the limo back to Dad's place," he says, jabbing at the button for the elevator. There's a sudden ping and the doors slide open. He steps in without looking back.

I pick up the swizzle stick he was bending. I get up from the cafeteria and walk down the hallway, past the aides who don't even bother to look up at me. At the pay phone in the hall I call Evelyn. She tells me to call her back later, mentions that it's the middle of the night. She hangs up and I stay there holding the phone, afraid to hang it up. The two men sitting by the door now interested, now watching.

PAUL   At The Carousel I've started a conversation with a townie who, for a townie, is actually pretty good-looking. He works for Holmes Moving Storage in town and thinks that Fassbinder is a beer from France. In other words, he's perfect. But Victor Johnson, who I've never much liked and who's back in town for some reason, in the same condition—alcoholic—as he left, and he keeps pestering me about where everyone is, and I have to keep pushing him away. He eventually stands by the video machines in back with that obnoxious poet who used to be cute before he shaved his head, making faces at me. I ask the townie what he's going to do after he quits Holmes ("labor problems," he confides).

"Go to L.A.," he says.

"Really?" I light his cigarette and order another Seabreeze. "Double," I mouth to the bartender. I also buy the townie another shot of J.D. and a Rolling Rock. He actually calls me "Sir" as in "Thank you, sir."

Lizzie, some awful girl from the Drama Division, comes over right when I'm telling the townie how great L.A. is (I've never been) and says, "Hi, Paul."

"Hi, Elizabeth," I say, noticing how the dumb townie looks Liz over; relieved when he turns back to his drink. Liz has been trying to get me into bed for a long time. If it happens it's not going to be tonight. She directed the Shepard play this term and she's not exactly ugly; in fact she's fairly pretty for the fag-hag she is but still no thank you. Besides I've made it my prerogative to never sleep with Drama majors.

"You want to meet my friend Gerald?" she asks.

"What does that mean?" I say.

"We have some Ecstasy," she says.

"Is that supposed to entice me?" I look back at the townie and then tell Liz, "Later."

"Okay," she squeals and skips off.

I look back at the townie, at his expression—there isn't one—at the greasy T-shirt, and the ripped jeans, the long uncombed hair and the beautiful face, the strong tight body and the roman nose, unsure. Then I turn away and put on my sunglasses, scope the room; it's late and snowing out, and there's no one else available. When I look back at the townie he gives me what I think is a shrug. But am I imagining something, did I make the shrug up? Was I taking each drunken gesture and molding it into what I wanted? Just because the guy is wearing an Ohio T-shirt doesn't necessarily mean that he's from Ohio State.

Yet, I make the decision to go home with the townie. I excuse myself and go to the restroom first. Someone's written "Pink Floyd Rules" on the wall and I write underneath it. "Oh come on, grow up." When I come out, waiting in line are Lizzie and Gerald, an actor who I've met a couple of times before. We were in a Strindberg play together two terms ago. Gerald: okay-looking, blond curly hair, a little too thin, nice suit.

"I see you've got a devastating townie over there," Gerald says. "Wanna share him with us?"

"Gerald," I say, looking him over; he waits expectantly. "No."

"Do you know him?" he asks.

"Yeah, well, I don't know," I mumble, craning my neck to make sure the townie's still where I left him. "Do you?"

"No," Gerald says, "I know his girlfriend though," and now he smiles.

There's a long silence. Someone cuts in front of us and closes the door of the bathroom. New song on the jukebox. A toilet flushes. I stare at Gerald and then back at the townie. I lean up against the wall and mutter "Shit." A girl townie has already taken my stool at the bar. So I join Gerald and the delightful Lizzie for drinks at their booth. Gerald winks at me when the townie leaves with the girl who sat next to him.

"What's going on?" I ask.

"Gerald wants to go to the weight room," Lizzie says. "But just to watch, of course."

"Of course," I say.

"What's 'racecar' backward, Paul?" Gerald asks.

I stare at the floor as I try to figure it out. "Rakacar? Raka—I don't know. I give up."

"It's 'racecar,' " Lizzie squeals, excited.

"How clever," I murmur.

Gerald winks at me again.

SEAN After dinner at Jams, me and Robert go to Trader Vic's. I'm wearing a paisley smoking jacket and a bowtie I found in my father's closet at The Carlyle. Robert, who has just gotten back from Monte Carlo, is wearing a blue Fifties sports jacket and a green cummerbund given to him by his near-perfect girlfriend, Holly. He's also wearing a bowtie he bought today when we went shopping but I don't remember where it was he bought it. It could have been Paul Stewart or Brooks Brothers or Barney's or Charivari or Armani—somewhere. Holly's not back in town yet and we're both horny and on the prowl. I fucked Holly once, while she was seeing Robert. I don't think he knows. That, and both of us fucking Cornelia, are really the only things Robert and I have in common.

I went by the house in Larchmont late last night. It was for sale. Harold still lives in back. My MG was still mercifully kept in one of the garages, but my room upstairs was empty, and most of the furniture from the house had been removed and taken someplace I forgot to ask about. The house itself was locked up and I had to break in through one of the French windows in back. The house still seems enormous, even larger to me now than when I was growing up in it. But there hadn't been much time spent in the house. School was at Andover, holidays were usually spent elsewhere. The house brought back few, almost no memories to me, the ones I had weirdly enough included Patrick. Playing in the snow with him on the front lawn, which seemed to stretch out for miles. Getting high and playing Ping-Pong with him in the rec room. There was the pool no one was allowed to swim in, and the rules about no noise. That was all I could dredge up, since that place was a transient's home for me. I found the keys to the MG in a panel in one of the garages, and I started the car hoping Harold wouldn't hear me. But he was standing there at the end of the drive, in the middle of a cold, snowy November night, and he opened the gate for me, dutiful to the end. I put a finger to my lips—sshhh—as I drove past him.

Robert and I are sharing a scorpion bowl and smoking Camels. We've been staring at a table in back with four girls sitting at it—all very hot, all very blond.

"Riverdale," I say.

"Nope. Dalton," he says.

"Maybe Choate?" I suggest.

"Definitely Dalton," Robert says.

"I bet you it's Vassar," I say, positive.

Robert's working on Wall Street now and doesn't seem to mind. Robert and I went to boarding school together. He went to Yale, and that's where he met Holly. After I beat him at squash today at The Seaport, while we were drinking beers, he told me he's dumping her, but I got the feeling that Holly dumped him in Monte Carlo and that's why she's not back.

We used to go to the Village, I vaguely remember now, sitting in Trader Vic's, sniffing at the flower at the bottom of the barrel.

"Let's do the coke," Robert suggests.

"I'm okay," I say, still on a rum high, trying to make eye contact with at least one of the girls.

"I'll be in the bathroom," he says, getting up. "Order me a St. Pauli Girl."

He leaves. I smoke another cigarette. The four girls are now looking over at me. I order another one of these scorpion bowls. They suddenly all burst out laughing. The Polynesian bartender gives me a dirty look. I flash him a gold American Express card. He makes the drink.

I cross my legs and the girl I was making eye contact with doesn't come over. But one of her friends does.

"Hi," she says and giggles. "What's your name?"

"Blaine," I say. "Hi."

"What's going on, Blaine?" she asks.

"Not too much," Blaine says.

"Great," she says.

"Where have you been?" Blaine asks.

"Nowhere. Palladium," she says. "How about you and your friend?"

"Just hanging," I say. The bartender places the fresh new drink on the bar. I nod.

"This is going to sound really stupid," she says.

"Go ahead." I bet it is.

"But, is your friend Michael J. Fox?" she asks.

"Uh, no," I say.

"Are you two gay or anything?" she asks, steadying herself.

"No," I say. "Are you and your friends dykes?"

"What do you mean?" she asks.

Blaine thinks: forget this girl, even though he wouldn't mind sleeping with her, but she smokes menthol cigarettes and looks a little overweight.

Michael J. Fox comes back and gives the girl a fuck-off look and he whispers something in my ear and hands me the vial. I tell him to deal with this girl and whisper back to him, "She thinks you're Michael J. Fox." I leave, head for the bathroom. "So, did you see *Back to the Future?*" he asks.

In the men's room I sit in a stall and flush the toilet whenever I do a hit. I come out of the stall feeling better, actually feeling pretty good and I go over to the sink to wash my hands, make sure my nose is clean. I can hear someone throwing up in one of the other stalls as I stare at myself in the mirror carefully, wipe whatever residue there was under my nose off. I go back to the bar.

Michael J. Fox has talked the girls into coming out with us. So we take them to Palladium where we leave them on the dance floor and split for the Mike Todd Room where we hang out and get even more wasted. Somewhere along the line I lose my Concord quartz watch, make a rude comment about Bianca Jagger's breasts to her face, and end up with some bimbo back at my father's place at The Carlyle. Robert's in the next room with some other bimbo, some Camden drop-out named Janey Fields, who I think he had an affair with. It always ends up this way. No Big Surprise.

LAUREN End up with Noel tonight. Cute, long-haired post-punk, neo-hippie whose girlfriend Janet is in New York for the weekend and who's really seeing Mary, this girl from Indiana. I had seen Janet's old boyfriend Neal for a little while before Noel, who was Neal's best friend, started seeing Janet. After driving to a Chinese restaurant in town in the snow in Noel's dark blue Saab, and after ordering food with all MSG removed and after checking out a bad party in Fels we go to Noel's room, where he puts *2001* on the VCR that sits on a milk crate at the foot of his futon. Then we split a hit of Blue Dragon and watch the movie, waiting to trip. All I can think of is the night last term when Victor and I made out in Tishman while they were changing reels for the movie, and how it snowed so hard for April and we were drunk on sake and "The Unforgettable Fire" was playing and he smelled like Chapstick. . . . But Noel gets excited and won't stop leaving me alone, and I want to watch the movie which I can't really concentrate on anyway—it's too long and slow and scenes and shots go on forever. I need something clear and fast, and I'm not even sure if the acid is taking effect. Don't understand what's going on. Noel's kissing my neck and rubbing the inside of my thigh and even though I have this urinary tract infection and have been taking horse pills to get rid of it, I let him do what he wants. When the movie snaps off, and he rolls over to put music on, I say, "But I hate the Beatles."

He looks at me and he takes his Grateful Dead T-shirt off revealing a beautiful body I cannot resist, and pulling off his Reebok tennis shoes, says, "Hey, I hate the Beatles too."

SEAN I drive to New Hampshire and find myself back on campus, looking for Lauren, remember my mouth on her neck, her arms around me. I go to her room but she's not there. Roxanne's in the living room of Canfield and tells me that Rupert wants to talk to me, that he's after my ass. I end up in The Pub but she's not there either. Neither are too many other people, most of them probably at a party somewhere. I order a beer. There are around fifteen people in The Pub tonight, either sitting at tables or standing next to the video games, a couple of girls standing by the juke-box, two Freshmen sitting by themselves in the corner discussing movies. I pay for the beer and sit at an empty table near the video games. I realize with depressing crystal clarity that I have slept with three of the girls in The Pub tonight.

One of them is standing by the jukebox. Susan is standing at the bar. The other one is the girl Freshman sitting on the couch talking with her friend. And I tell myself that I'm going to avoid random one-night stands after Friday night parties, and drunken meaningless fucks on slow Saturday nights and I realize I don't want anyone but Lauren. "Heaven," sad Talking Heads plays from the jukebox. I get depressed. Susan walks over.

"Hi, Sean," she says.

"Hi, Susan," I say, hoping she won't sit down.

"Going to the party?" she asks, smiling, not sitting.

"Yeah. Maybe," I shrug. "After I finish this beer."

She looks around the room. "Yeah. I hear it's pretty good."

"Yeah?"

"Yeah. Where's Lauren?" she asks.

"Probably there. I guess."

"Oh," Susan says. "I heard you two were having some trouble."

"No." I shake my head. "Not at all. Where did you hear that?"

"Oh, around."

"Well no," I say. "Don't worry about it."

"Okay."

"Great." I take a sip of beer and wonder how many people know about this; how many care?

"Well, I'll see you at the party maybe later, okay?" she asks, standing there, dying to sit down, with me.

"Okay, sure," I nod, can't remember how it was with us, smile.

She stands there a while longer.

I look up and smile once more.

She finally walks back to her friend.

I hope Lauren and I never have a conversation like that: slight, depressing, hopeless. And I miss her so badly and want her back that the urge to hold and feel her stabs at me, blinding me momentarily and I finish the beer quickly, feeling better, since I'm sure she feels the same way. One of the guys playing Crystal Castles kicks the machine and growls, "Fuck you, bitch." The song "Heaven" keeps playing.

There are things that I will never do: I will never buy cheese popcorn in The Pub. I will never tell a video game to fuck off. I will never erase graffiti about myself that I happen to catch in bathrooms on campus. I will never sleep with anyone but Lauren. I will never throw a pumpkin at her door. I will never play "Burning Down the House" on the jukebox.

PAUL I pretend to look at old notes from last week's Student Council meeting, which are crumpled and muddied on the floor in the backseat of Lizzie's car. Gerald's sitting next to me, trying to give me a hand-job, both of us crammed in the back. Somehow Sean got dragged into the huge Buick, and he's up front with about five other people, eleven of us piled into the car altogether. Everyone is drunk, no one knows where we're going, vague idea about a road trip. Gerald keeps rubbing my thighs. It's freezing. We are lost.

The last time I saw Sean he had stopped by my room sometime in mid-November. I was sitting at my desk doing nothing and I heard a knock on the door. "Come in," I said. There was a silence followed by another knock, this one louder. "Come in," I stood up. The door opened. He walked in. I sat back down. I sat there looking at him and then I got up very slowly.

"Hi, Sean," I said.

"Hi, Dent," he said.

Dent? Had he ever called me that? I wondered about this as we drove into town, had dinner, came back to campus. He parked in front of Booth. We went upstairs to his room. His room looked bigger and emptier than I remembered it. The narrow bed on the floor, the desk, a chair, a chest of drawers, a broken stereo, no posters, no photos, a lot of records leaning against a wall in the corner. And I woke up the next morning laying on the small mattress. He was already up, sitting in his armchair, staring out the window at the morning's snowfall. He needed a shave, his hair was sticking up. I dressed quietly. It was hot in the room. He wasn't saying anything. He just sat in the chair and smoked Parliaments. I went up behind the chair to tell him I was leaving. I stood so close that I could have touched the side of his face, his neck, but I didn't do this. I just left. Then I stood in the hallway and heard him lock the door. . . .

Gerald realizes I'm not interested but keeps trying. I look out the window of the car, at the snow, wondering how I got forced into this. I don't know half the people in the car: heroin addicts, a Freshman, a couple who lives off-campus, someone who works behind the snack bar, Lizzie, Gerald, Sean and me, and this Korean guy.

I have my eye on the Korean boy, some Asian Art major punk I think I made out with last term who only paints self-portraits of his penis. He's sitting on my other side, tripping and he keeps repeating the word "wow." Lizzie keeps driving and circling Main Street, then she's on the highway leaving Camden, looking for a place that's open where we can get beer. A joint is passed around, then another. We get lost again. The Smiths are singing and someone says "Turn that gay angst music off." The Replacements replace them singing "Unsatisfied." No one has I.D. is the consensus so we can't get beer since Camden kids are almost always asked. We almost get stopped by the police. Lizzie almost drives us into a lake. The Korean boy keeps screaming, "Let's call this art," and I keep whispering to him in his calmer moments, "Come to my room." But by the time we get back to campus and I wait in my room for him, Gerald comes by instead and takes his clothes off which means, I guess, for me to take mine off too.

While in bed, later, we hear someone knocking on the door.

Gerald goes, "Sssshhhh."

I get up and pull my jeans on and a sweater. I open the door. It's Sean, not the Korean. He's holding a bottle of Jack Daniel's and a box with The Smiths playing. "Can I come in?" he whispers.

"Wait." It's dark behind me. He can't see anything. "I'll come out," I say.

I close the door and put my boots on, grabbing my coat, any coat, from the darkness of the closet. Gerald asks, "Who in the hell is it?"

"I'll be back in a minute," I tell him.

He says, "You better."

Sean and I end up walking through the woods near campus. It's snowing lightly and not too cold, the moon is high and full and makes the ground glow white. The Smiths are singing "Reel Around the Fountain." He hands me the bottle. I tell him, "I find myself talking to you when you're not around. Just talking. Carrying on conversations." I really don't, but it just seems like the thing to say and he's really so much better-looking than Gerald.

"I wish you wouldn't tell me shit like that," he says. "It's creepy. It weirds me out."

Later, we make love in the snow. Afterwards I tell him I have tickets for the REM concert in Hanover next week. He covers his face with his hands.

"Listen," he says, getting up. "I'm sorry."

"Don't be," I say. "Things like this happen."

"I don't want to go with you."

"I don't want things to turn out this way," I warn him.

"I don't want you to be hurt."

"Yeah? Well, is there . . ." I stop. "Can you do anything about it?"

He pauses, then, "No, I guess I can't. Not anymore."

I tell him, "But I want to know you. I want to know who you are."

He flinches and turns to me and says, raising his voice at first and then letting it drop softer, "No one will ever know anyone. We just have to deal with each other. You're not ever gonna *know* me."

"What in the hell does that mean?" I ask.

"It just means you're not ever gonna *know* me," he says. "Figure it out. Deal with it."

It's quiet, it stops snowing. From where we lay we can see the campus, lit, postcard-perfect, through the trees. The tape clicks off, and then automatically turns itself over. He finishes the Jack Daniel's and walks away. I walk back to my room, alone. Gerald has left, leaving me a long note, describing how much of an asshole I am. But it doesn't matter because there was something fun about tonight, in the snow, drunk, not with the Korean guy.

LAUREN   It happens quite suddenly, while we're at the Winter Carnival in town.

Earlier we had a half-hearted attempt at a snowfight on Commons lawn (actually I threw a snowball at his head; he didn't have enough energy to make one, let alone throw one at me), then we drove in the friend's MG to town and had brunch. After making out on the ferris wheel and smoking pot in the funhouse, I tell him. I tell him while we're waiting for fried dough. I could have told him the truth, or I could have broken it off with him, or I could have gone back to Franklin. But none of those options seemed likely in the end, and there was a good chance none of them would have worked out. I stare at him. He's stoned and holding a Def Leppard cocaine mirror that he won by throwing baseballs at tin milk bottles. He smiles as he pays for the fried dough.

S: What do you want to do when we get back?

Me: I don't know.

S: Should we buy the eighth or rent a movie or what?

Me: I don't know.

S: What is it? What's your problem?

Me: I'm pregnant.

S: Really?

Me: Yes.

S: Is it mine?

Me: Yes.

S: Is it really mine?

Me: Listen, I'm going to . . . "deal with it" so don't worry.

S: No. Don't. You're not.

Me: What? Why not?

S: Listen, I have an idea.

Me: *You* have an idea?

S: Let's get married.

Me: What are you talking about?

S: Marry me. Let's get married.

Me (unsaid): It could be Franklin's and there's always the possibility it could actually be Sean's. But I was very late and had been carrying for a long time and I cannot remember when it was Sean and I met. It could also be Noel's, though that's unlikely and it could also be the Freshman Steve's, but that's even unlikelier. It could also be Paul's. Those are the only people I've been with this term.

S: Well?

Me: Okay.

SEAN Lauren and I decided not to go to brunch today since there were bound to be too many eyes, too many people wandering around trying to figure out who left with who from the party last night, the dining room would be cold and dark in the late morning, people finally realizing who they spent the night with staring at their soggy French toast with regret; there would be too many people we knew. So we went to The Brasserie on the edge of town to have brunch instead.

Roxanne was at The Brasserie but not with Rupert. Susan Greenberg was there with that asshole Justin. Paul Denton was sitting in a corner with that dyke Elizabeth Seelan from the Drama Division and some guy I didn't even think went to Camden. A teacher who I was sure I owed at least four papers to was sitting in back. A townie who I dealt for was by the jukebox. Paranoia fulfilled.

Lauren and I looked at each other after we sat down and

then cracked up. Over bloody Marys, I understood how much I did want to marry her, how much I wanted her to marry me. And after another drink, how much I wanted her to have my son. After a third drink it simply seemed like a fun idea and not a hard promise to keep. She looked really pretty that day. We had smoked pot earlier and we were high and starving. She kept looking at me with these eyes that were wildly in love and couldn't help it and I was feeling good staring back and we ate a lot and I leaned over and kissed her neck but stopped when I noticed someone looking over at our table.

"Let's go somewhere," I told her, as she paid the check. "Let's leave campus. We can go somewhere and do this."

She said, "Okay."

LAUREN   We went to New York to stay with friends of mine who had graduated when I was a Sophomore. They were now married and had a loft apartment on Sixth Avenue in the Village. Sean and I drove down in his friend's MG and they put us up there in an extra room in the back. We stayed at their place since Sean didn't have enough money to stay in a hotel. But it worked out just as well. It was a big space, and there was plenty of privacy and room, and in the end it didn't matter since I was still vaguely excited about the prospect of actually getting married, of actually going through the ceremony, of even becoming a mother. But after two days with Scott and Ann, I became more hesitant and the future seemed more distant and less clear than it had that day at the Winter Carnival. My doubts grew.

Scott worked at an advertising agency and Ann opened restaurants with her father's money. They had adopted a Vietnamese child, a boy of thirteen, the year after they married and named him Scott, Jr., and promptly sent him off to Exeter where Scott had gone to school. I would wander dumbly around their loft while they were both at work, drinking Evian water, watching Sean sleep, touching things in Scott, Jr.'s room, realizing how fast the time was going by, that the term was nearly over. Maybe I had reacted too quickly to Sean's proposal, I would think to myself, while in Ann's luxurious, sunken tub. But I'd push the thought out of my mind and tell myself I was doing the right thing. I didn't tell Ann I was pregnant or that I was going to marry Sean for I was sure she would call up my mother and have this confirmed, and I badly wanted my mother to be surprised. I watched television. They had a cat named Cappuccino.

The four of us went to a restaurant on Columbus the second night we were in New York: Talk centered around John Irving's new book, restaurant critics, the soundtrack from *Amadeus* and a new Thai restaurant that opened uptown. I watched Scott and Ann very closely that night.

"It's called California Cuisine," Ann told Sean, leaning next to him.

"Why don't we take them to Indochine tomorrow?" Scott suggested. He was wearing an oversized Ralph Lauren sweater and expensive, baggy corduroys. He was wearing a Swatch.

"That's a good idea. I like it," Ann said, placing her menu face down. She knew already what she wanted. She was dressed almost exactly like Scott.

A waiter came over and took our drink orders.

"Scotch. Straight," Sean said.

I ordered a champagne on the rocks.

"Oh," Ann said, deliberating. "I'll just have a Diet Coke."

Scott looked up, concerned. "You're not drinking to-night?"

"Oh, I don't know," Ann said, relenting. "I'll be daring and have a rum and Diet Coke."

The waiter left. Ann asked us if we had seen the recent Alex Katz exhibit. We said we hadn't. She asked about Victor.

Scott asked, "Who's Victor?"

Ann told him, "Her boyfriend, right?" She looked at me.

"Well," I said, could not bring myself to say "ex." "I've talked to him a couple of times. He's in Europe."

Sean downed his drink as soon as it came and waved to the waiter for another one.

I kept trying to talk to Ann but felt utterly lost. While she was telling me about the advantages of low-sodium rice cakes and new age music, something flashed in me and pierced. Sean and I in four years. I looked across the table at Sean. He and Scott were talking about Scott's new compact disc player.

"You've got to listen to it," he told Sean. "The sound," he paused, closed his eyes in ecstasy, ". . . is fantastic."

Sean wasn't looking at me but knew I was looking at him. "Yeah?" he nodded.

"Yeah," Scott went on. "Bought the new Phil Collins today."

"You should hear how great 'Sussudio' sounds on it," Ann agreed. The two of them had been big Genesis fans at Camden, and had forced me to listen to "Lamb Lies Down on Broadway" one night when the three of us were on coke my Freshman term. But what can you do?

Sean sat there impassive, his face falling slightly. And though it was at that moment I realized I did not love him and never had, and that I was acting on some bizarre impulse, I was still hoping he was thinking the same thing I was: I don't want to end up like this.

Later that night I dreamed of our new married world. The world Sean and I would live in. Mid-dream Sean was replaced by Victor, but we were still smart and young and drove BMW's and the fact that Sean had been replaced didn't alter the dream's significance to me. Not only did we vote in this dream but we voted for the same person our parents voted for. We drank Evian water and ate kiwi fruit and chomped on bran muffins; I turned into Ann. Sean who had become Victor was now Scott. It was unpleasant but not unbearable and in some indefinable way I felt safe.

The next morning over a breakfast of bran muffins and kiwi and Evian water and wheatgrass juice, Ann mentioned something about buying a BMW and I had to hold back a scream. It was clear that this had not been my best term; it was clear that I was losing it.

At night Sean would lay beside me and I'd be thinking about the baby, something Sean would never mention. He would complain bitterly about how pathetic Ann and Scott were and I would get strange, unexplained urges to call my mother or my sister at R.I.S.D.; to call and explain to them what was going on. But this, like my questioning of my relationship with Sean, vanished.

The last night we were in the loft he turned to me and said, "I can remember the first time we . . ." He stopped and I knew he wanted to say fucked, went to bed, did it, fucked on the floor, but he couldn't bring himself to say it without extreme embarrassment, so he said quietly, ". . . met."

I looked at him sharply, "So do I."

He was sweaty and his hair was sticking to his forehead. I was smoking one of his cigarettes, our faces blue because of the television set. The sheet was pulled down, just enough so that I could see the hair below his waist. I was wearing a T-shirt.

"That night at the party," he said.

His face got sad, or did it? Then the expression left. When he touched me, my whisper was deadly and clear and all I said was, "I'm sorry."

And he asked me, "Why didn't you tell me you were in love with this guy?"

"Who?" I asked. "You mean Victor?"

"Yes."

"Because I was afraid," I said, and maybe at one point somewhere I was.

"Of what?" he asked.

I sighed and didn't want to be there and without looking at him spoke. "I was afraid that you'd leave me."

"You want him to like me?" he asked, confused. "Is that what you said?"

I didn't bother to correct him, or repeat myself, so I said, "Yeah. He likes you."

"He doesn't even know me," he said.

"But he knows of you," I lied.

"Great," he mumbled.

"Yes," I said, thinking of Victor, thinking how can one know yet still hope? I closed my eyes, tried to sleep.

"How do you know it's not . . . his?" he finally asked, nervous, suspicious.

"Because it's not," I told him.

This was probably our last real conversation. He turned the TV off. The room went dark. I lay there holding my stomach, then running my fingers up, then down, over my belly.

"They have the Sex Pistols on C.D.," he said. The statement hung there, accusing me of something.

I fell asleep. We left the next morning.

PAUL   Just another night. December and in Commons watching TV before it's light out on Saturday morning, still slightly drunk and shrooming with Gerald. There had been nothing to do last night. The movie was *The Barefoot Doctors of Rural China* or something and the party seemed hopelessly lame.

Victor Johnson was there and even though I found it disgusting that Rupert Guest and him had given Tim's Secret Santa a vial of semen and a douchebag and were getting a kick out of seeing Gerri Robinson crying in the bathroom after she opened it, I still couldn't help flirt with Victor and we shared a joint and he kept asking me where Jaime Fields was. I had heard from Raymond that Victor had been institutionalized, which meant I had a better than fifty-fifty chance of getting him into bed. When he offered me a bottled beer, I thanked him and asked, "So what's going on with you?"

He said, "Fantastic."

I asked him, "Where have you been?"

"Europe," he said.

"How was it?" I asked.

"Cool," he said and then with less enthusiasm, "Actually it was just okay."

"Do you like being back?" I asked.

"I like America." He winked. "But only from a distance."

Oh please. Gerald had been watching the scene from a corner of the room and before he could come over and ruin it, I traded an REM ticket for a bag of mushrooms.

Now the familiar words—Hanna Barbera—flash on every so often and remind me of a time I used to want to wake up early on Saturday mornings to watch cartoons. The party's still happening at McCullough, and Gerald's talking about old boyfriends, *GQ* models, members of some unnamed crew team, lying shamelessly. I kiss him to shut him up. Then turn my attention back to the TV screen. An especially loud New Order song comes from the open windows at McCullough, "Your Silent Face." Sean liked this song, so did Mitchell in fact. Gerald says, "Jesus, I really hate this song." I kiss him once more. It turns out to be the last song of the party. It fades out, nothing replaces it.

Watching TV nothing makes sense. An Acutrim commercial is followed by a Snickers commercial followed by a Kinks video followed by In The News. My mom likes the new Kinks video. That depresses me even more than Gerald does.

"You bummed?" he asks.

I look at him. "He likes him. He likes her. I think she likes someone else, probably me. That's all. No logic."

"Hmmmmm," Gerald says, checking his pockets. He brings out the napkin he had the mushroom in. There's nothing left, just mushroom crumbs.

"No one ever likes the right person," I say.

"That's not true," he says. "I like you."

That's not exactly what I meant or wanted to hear, but I ask him earnestly, "Do you?".

There's a pause. "Sure. Why not?" he says.

There's nothing worse than being drunk *and* disproven.

LAUREN The next week (or maybe it was a couple of days) seemed like a blur. Motel rooms, driving all night, getting stoned as his friend's MG raced through the snowy roads. Everything seemed speeded up, time moved faster.

There was no conversation, we didn't speak to each other those days on the road. We had reached a point where there was simply *nothing* to talk about. We had passed even the most elementary stages of conversation. There were not even polite "How are you's" in the morning; simple questions like "Can we stop at that gas station?" were discarded. Nothing was said. Neither of us spoke.

Though there were moments that week, even as we sat silently in that car zooming around, when I actually believed something was on his mind. He would slow the car down if we passed anything that even remotely resembled a chapel, or a church, and stare at it, the motor still running. Then he'd speed off again and wouldn't stop until he found a suitable motel somewhere. And it was in these motel rooms where we started doing the cocaine he was carrying, and because of the cocaine the days, short already, seemed even shorter, and he'd drive faster, more recklessly, trying to get to some unknown destination. We would stay up all night in motels, the TV on, inhaling the cocaine, and if we needed something to eat later to keep us going, to fill our stomachs so we could do more coke without getting cramps, he'd leave the motel room and come back with cigarettes, cheeseburgers, and candy which he had bought with someone's American Express card since he carried no cash.

The cocaine, oddly enough, made neither one of us talkative. We would do a few lines and instead of babbling away insincerely, we'd watch the television set and smoke, never confronting each other, just sitting there, or in the MG, or in coffee shops, almost embarrassed. He got thinner, more gaunt, as the amount of cocaine he was carrying dwindled down. More motels, more gas stations, another diner somewhere.

I would only eat candy bars and drink Diet Coke. The radio was always on whether there were stations nearby or not. News would come on but there really wasn't anything to hear. Earthquakes, the weather, politics, mass death. It was all boring. I carried with me a photograph of Victor, and I would take it out and sit in the car, Sean next to me sniffing constantly, his sunglasses kept on, covering glassy eyes, and I'd touch the photograph. It was black and white and Victor was shirtless, smoking a cigarette, half-leering into the lens of the camera, trying to look like an old-young faded movie star, his eyes half-lids, closed in sexy parody. I liked Victor even more because of this photograph and the mystery it contained. But then I didn't, couldn't like him because he stayed with Jaime, and that was unforgivable. The only tape in the car was old Pink Floyd and Sean would only listen to "Us and Them" and nothing else, rewinding it over and over, and the draggy rhythm would put me to sleep, which was probably what Sean wanted, yet then he would turn it up whenever the chorus would blast out *"Haven't you heard, it's a . . ."* and startled I would sit upright, my heart pounding and reach over and turn the volume down once his fingers left the control dial. The song would fade out, then he'd rewind it again. I said nothing.

Sean would light cigarettes, toss the match out the window, take a drag, put the cigarette out.

SEAN All of the trees were dead. There were dead skunks and dogs and even an occasional deer by the sides of the roads, their blood staining the snow. There were mountains full of dead trees. Orange signs announced road-work. The radio was only static, the tape player often broken, though when it wasn't Roxy Music loud and garbled would play. The road seemed endless. Motels. Buying food in malls. Lauren constantly throwing up. She wouldn't speak to me. I would just concentrate on the road or on people in other cars. When we could pick up a station there would only be Creedence Clearwater songs playing which made me sad but I didn't know why. In motel rooms her eyes were dumb and accusing; her body wasted and pathetic. She'd reach out—a plaintive touch and I'd tell her to get away from me. At a gas station in some place called Bethel, across the border and into Maine, I almost left her while she went to the bathroom to throw up. I put close to 2,000 miles on the car that week. I thought of Roxanne a lot for some reason. I thought of where I could go, but couldn't think of anyplace. There was just another motel or gas station. She would sit beside me, listless. She would break glasses in the motel bathrooms. She stopped wearing shoes. I drank a lot. I'd wake up the next morning, if I went to sleep at all, hungover and I'd look at her pitiful body in the bed next to mine and again think about leaving her. Without waking her up, stealing all her stuff, her make-up, which she had stopped wearing anyway, her clothes, everything, and split. She never took her sunglasses off, not even if it was night and snowing hard. The snow was slushy and would fall heavily. It would get dark at four in the afternoon, the snow drifting over the rise and fall of the countryside. . . .

We came back to that gas station in Bethel—somehow we had made a full circle—and while she went to the restroom and was coming back, trudging through the snow, approaching the car, after throwing up, something clicked. The snow on the windshield started to melt. I reached over and turned on the radio but couldn't find anything. The Roxy Music tape was ruined. I eventually found another station that was playing faraway sounding Grateful Dead. I lit a cigarette even though the guy was still filling up the car.

She opened the door and sat down. I offered her one. She shook her head, no. I paid the guy and drove out of the station. It was early morning and snowing hard. Back on the highway, without looking over at her, I said, "I'll pay for it," then cleared my throat.

LAUREN He drops me off, waiting at the Dunkin' Donuts down the street. . . . It had been twelve weeks. I keep thinking it must have been that night with Paul. It had to have been that night with Paul. Forms to fill. They will not accept my American Express, only MasterCharge. Want to know my age, religion. An abortion in New Hampshire: my life reduced. I'm calm but it doesn't last. Tense when I read the words: Hereby Authorize Terminate Pregnancy. Graffiti on the tables in the waiting room: Feminine chaos, End of the term—things only other girls from the college had written. Was Sara here? They give me Valium. Someone explains the operation to me. Laying on my back wondering vaguely if it's a boy or a girl. "Okay, Laurie," the doctor says. An examination of Laurie's uterus. The table rises. I moan. Lift the hips please. Something antiseptic. I can't help it and gasp. The nurse looks at me. She seems nice. Humming noise. My stomach starts heaving. Sucking noises. It's over. I sweat. I go to the recovery room. It doesn't matter. I pass by other girls, some crying, most of them not. Come out onto the street after Sean picks me up, forty-five minutes, an hour later. Two girls from the high school pass by. I'm thinking, I was once that young.

In the car driving back to campus, Sean asks, "Truce?"

And I tell him, "No way."

SEAN At the party I couldn't find the waitress I had picked up earlier at Dunkin' Donuts and who I had invited to the party, but I went crazy anyway, getting drunk and celebrating the end of term by fucking Judy again in her room—just grabbed her arm and we went—and then I made out with the hippie girl on the way back to Windham. Back at the party for a beer, I started feeling really good and still horny, so I made it with Susan and finally around two went home with that Swedish girl. After that I came back to find the party still going and so I sat around with everybody who was waiting for someone to bring more beer, most of the Freshmen pissed off because they wanted Lite beer. I was really drunk and I knew the beer wasn't going to arrive for a long time and The Pub had closed hours ago and I should have gone home, gone somewhere, maybe back to Susan's room, or maybe to visit Lauren, but I didn't want to. I was already worlds away from that shit. And suddenly looking around the living room of Windham,

Roxy Music blasting, a fire roaring, a half-decorated Christmas tree covered with bras and panties tilted to one side in the corner, I hated these people, yet I wanted to stay here with them. Even with the guy who was a shitty guitarist talking to the loudmouth alcoholic; even with the dyke from Welling; even with the waitress from Dunkin' Donuts who had showed up and was hanging on to Tim's arm; even Getch, who was loaded, sitting in the corner, crying, fondling a pony-keg. These were people I would never have spoken to out of this room, but here, at the party, I loathed them more than I thought possible. The music was loud and it was snowing lightly outside, dark in the room except for the fireplace and the lights on the Christmas tree in the corner flickering off and on. This was the moment that counted. This was when it all came together. This was where I wanted to be. Even the ex who was going to fuck Tony. Even her. All that mattered was that we were here. . . .

The feeling sort of clicked off when the beer didn't come and the guys who had been trying to get it were arrested for drunk driving, Getch announced. But I was still in that room and we were still all together: two people I rejected, two people who had rejected me, one girl I had been rude to, but now it didn't matter. Tim left with the waitress from Dunkin' Donuts. I went back to the Swedish girl's room and knocked. But she had locked her door and was probably asleep. I trudged through the snow back to my house and a cold, empty room. My window was open. I had forgotten to close it.

LAUREN

MITCHELL I could sense it wasn't going to go well when I found out I had to drive with Sean Bateman to get a simple dime bag of pot. I didn't really know Bateman that well but I could tell from the way he looked what type of guy he was: probably listened to a lot of George Winston, ate cheese and drank white wine, played the cello. I was pissed off that he had the nerve to come over to my room and tell me we had to go to that scummy idiot Rupert's house, which I really wasn't keen on to begin with, but it was almost end of term and I needed some grass to take with me on the drive back to Chicago. I argued with him for a little while, but Candice was sitting there on my bed trying to finish an overdue paper and she told me to go and I couldn't resist, even though all term I'd been planning to break up with her. I took a Xanax and got in his car and drove off-campus to North Camden where Rupert and Roxanne lived. The roads were slick and he was driving too quickly and a couple of times we came close to spinning out, but we made it there without losing any limbs or causing a major pile-up.

The house was dark and I mentioned maybe no one was home. There was a party going on across the street. I told him I'd wait in the car.

He said, "No, it's okay. Only Roxanne's here."

"What does that mean?" I asked. "I don't want to go in."

"Just come in," he said. "Let's get this over with."

I followed him up the walk to the door and he knocked apprehensively. There was no answer. He knocked again, then tried the door. Someone abruptly yanked it open. And there was Guest, grinning like an idiot. He told us to come in, then laughed ghoulishly.

There were other townies in the darkened living room listening to Led Zeppelin. Someone had lit candles. I was getting suspicious.

Rupert was walking around the kitchen. "So what are you here for, boys?"

The townies giggled from the living room. There were four or five of them. Something glinted against the light of a candle in the darkness.

I yawned nervously, my eyes started watering.

"Came over to pick up some stuff," Bateman said, innocently enough.

"Did you?" Rupert asked, moving in and out of the darkness, circling us.

"Where's Roxanne?" Bateman asked. "You're impossible."

"Where is my money goddamnit, Bateman?" Rupert roared as if he was deaf and hadn't heard Bateman. I couldn't believe this.

"You're crazy," Sean said, perplexed. "Where's Roxanne?"

One of the townies had gotten up. He was mean looking: beer-belly, a crew-cut. He leaned against the kitchen door. I moved back and bumped into a cabinet. I had no idea what the problem was, though it seemed clear to me that it had to do with money. I didn't know if Rupert owed Bateman or if Bateman owed Rupert, but something was clearly fucked. Rupert was coked-up and trying to act tough, but the act was unconvincing and not very threatening. There was little light in the kitchen and where it was coming from I couldn't tell. Something flashed in the darkness and glinted again.

"Where's the money, you asshole?" Rupert demanded.

"I'm waiting in the car," I said. "Excuse me."

"Wait," Bateman said, holding me back.

"Wait for what, you asshole?" Rupert asked.

"Listen," Sean paused. Then he looked at me. "*He's* got it."

"You've got it?" Rupert asked, calming down and seriously interested.

Out of the corner of my eye I saw that one of the townies, big and drunk, was holding a machete. What in the hell was a fucking machete doing in New Hampshire?

"Whoa, now wait a minute," I said, raising my hands up.

"Now, I don't know what the hell's going on. I just came for some bud. I'm leaving."

"Come on Mitchell," Sean said. "Give Rupert the money."

"What in the fuck are you talking about?" I screamed. "I'm waiting in the car."

I started to make my way out but another townie had just gotten up and was blocking the exit. I could see the car sitting there behind him through the window, in the snow, the party behind it. I thought I could see Melissa Hertzburg and Henry Rogers, but I wasn't sure. I could hear Christmas music.

"This is absolute shit," I said.

"Do you really have it?" Rupert was asking me, coming closer.

"Do I have what?" I screamed again. "Now wait, listen, this guy—"

"Does this guy have the money or not?" Rupert asked Bateman.

"Will you fucking tell him" I yelled at Bateman.

It was silent. Everybody was waiting for Sean's answer.

"Okay, he doesn't have it," he admitted.

"What do you have for me?" Rupert asked him.

"I have this." He reached into his pocket and handed Rupert something. Rupert inspected it. It was a vial. Rupert poured something onto a mirror. I assumed it was cocaine. He looked up at Sean, muttering how it better be good. The townies were now silent and interested in what was going on. But of course the stuff wasn't good and a fight broke out. Rupert lunged across the table at Bateman. A townie grabbed at me. There was a scuffle. I was on my way out when I turned around and saw that Bateman had somehow grabbed the machete and was screaming "Back off" and jabbing it at the townies. I turned and ran out to the car, slipping on the driveway and falling hard on my ass. When I got into the car and locked the door I could see that the townies were backing off. Sean kept swinging the sword until he was outside and shut the door to the kitchen, dropped the machete and jumped into the car.

The townies were slow but they made it to their pick-up truck as the MG peeled out of the driveway. Sean raced it down the street, skidded through a stoplight and swerved down the road back towards the college. I could not believe this was happening. I never thought I would die on a Friday. Any other night but a fucking Friday. Bateman was actually smiling and asking me, "Wasn't that fun?"

The townies led by Guest were behind us, but never too dangerously close, though once I thought I heard a gunshot. They caught up to us on College Drive and sped into the other lane trying to push the MG off the road. The MG lurched and then leapt over a snowbank and skidded gently to a stop. The pick-up sped by and then slowed down and with difficulty started to turn around. Bateman waited until they were coming toward us and suddenly reshifted, racing past the townies, and we drove the two miles to the Security gate without much incident. But when I turned around I could see the headlights of the pick-up behind us as it sat there down the road, idling. Sean smiled at the guards and waved as they lifted the gate up. He drove me back to my house. It was then that I noticed his headlights were still off. I looked at him and just said, "Jesus, Bateman, you're an asshole."

He reached into his jacket and pulled out a small, tightly tied dime bag and tossed it through the open window at me. I barely caught it. I didn't bother to ask him what was going on and when he had gotten this. Even if I had it wouldn't have mattered since he had already driven away.

VICTOR I went to the REM concert with Denton in Hanover. Rupert had already kicked me out of his house. He said there was some sort of problem happening and that I had to leave. I didn't have anything else to do so I went with Denton. The auditorium was big but there were no seats. Some lame band opened for them and I hung out in back, drinking beer I'd snuck in with Paul, watching the girls. Once they started playing I left Paul and made my way through the standing crowd up front and sat on one of the speakers with some other guy from Camden named Lars. We sat there staring out at the crowd, at all the young stoned proud sweaty Americans, looking up at the stage. Some were tripping and high, others had their eyes closed, moving their grotesque, well-fed bodies to the beat. This one girl who I had been watching most of the night stood squashed in the middle of the front row, and when she caught me looking at her, I gave her a smile. She made a gagging look and turned back to the band, swaying her head to the beat. And I got really disgusted and started thinking, what was this girl's problem? Why couldn't she have been nice and smiled back? Was she worrying about imminent war? Was she feeling real terror? Or inspiration? Or passion? That girl, like all the others, I had come to believe, was terminally numb. The Talking Heads record was scratched maybe or perhaps Dad hadn't sent the check yet. That was all this girl was worried about. Her boyfriend was standing behind her, a total yuppie with Brylcreamed hair and a very thin tie on. Now what was that guy's problem? Lost I.D., too many anchovies on his pizza, broken cigarette machine? And I kept looking back at that girl—had she forgotten to tape her soap this afternoon? Did she have a urinary tract infection? Why did she have to act so fucking *cool*? And that's what it all came down to: cool. I wasn't being cynical about that bitch and her asshole boyfriend. I really believed that the extent of their pitiful problems didn't exceed too far from what I thought. They didn't have to worry about keeping warm or being fed or bombs or lasers or gunfire. Maybe their lover left them, maybe that copy of "Speaking in Tongues" *was* really scratched—that was this term's model and their problems. But then I came to understand sitting there, the box vibrating beneath me, the band blaring in my head that these problems and the pain they felt were genuine. I mean, this girl probably had a lot of money and so did her dumb-looking boyfriend. Other people might not sympathize with this couple's problems and maybe they didn't really matter in the larger realm of things—but they still mattered to Jeff and Susie; these problems hurt them, these things stung. . . . Now that's what struck me as *really* pathetic. I forgot about her and the other geeks and did some more of the coke Lars was offering me. . . .

Afterwards I wanted to go to The Carousel but Paul told me it had closed down over the weekend; that no one went there much anymore except a couple of Seniors and graduates who never left North Camden. We drove by it anyway. Not that there had been a lot of fun at that place, but it still meant something to me. And it was depressing to see it dark on a Thursday night, the doorway covered with black paint, the path leading to the door covered with thick unshoveled snow.

LAUREN I lose my keys the first time I leave my room in over four days. So I can't lock my door. It doesn't really matter, I've packed all my stuff, there's really nothing to take. I go to the post office to check the board to see about getting a ride tomorrow or the next day. Not a lot of rides. "Lost My Pet Rock," "Ambitious Photography Major Looking for Imaginative Male to Pose in Cellophane," "Madonna Fan Club Starting Soon. Anyone interested? Box 207." I tear that one down but the woman working behind the post office counter sees this and glares until I put it back up. "Skateboarding Club Starting." I want to tear that one down too. "Jack Kerouac Fan Club Starting Next Term." I hate the idea of having that one up since it looks so pathetic next to the others, so I tear it down. She doesn't say anything. Someone's put a copy of *One Hundred Years of Solitude* in my box and I look inside to see if anyone's left a name or message. "Really good book. Hope you like it—P." But it doesn't look like it's been read, and I put it in Sean's box.

Franklin passes by in the mob of people lining up for lunch. He asks me if I want to go to The Brasserie. I've eaten lunch eight times today but I have to get off-campus. So we go into town and it's not bad at all. I buy a couple of tapes, and a frozen yogurt, and then at The Brasserie I have a bloody Mary and take a Xanax. For the past week I have been hoping the job was botched; that maybe the doctor had somehow screwed things up, had left everything incomplete. But of course, he hadn't. They had done a good, thorough job. I have never bled so much before.

I stare out the window, at the snow. Jukebox plays depressing pop. I make a mental list of things I need to get done before I go to New York. Christmas presents.

"I screwed her," Franklin says, sipping his drink and pointing at the waitress in back; some foul-mouthed bitch from campus who I think is hideous, who told her boyfriend that I was a witch and he believed her.

The waitress disappears into the kitchen. A waiter takes her place. He sets something on the table next to ours. In a blinding moment of recognition I realize who the waiter is. He keeps looking at me, but there's no recognition on *his* face. I start laughing, the first time in over a week.

"What's funny?" Franklin says. "No, I really did screw her."

"I screwed him," I tell Franklin. It's the townie I lost my virginity to.

"Hey," Franklin says. "We are the world."

SEAN   Tim helps me pack the next morning. I don't have a lot to take with me, but he has nothing else to do and he carries most of the stuff out to my car. He doesn't ask about Rupert, though he knows that's why I'm leaving. From across the lawn Lauren is on her way to Commons. She waves. I wave back.

"Heard about Lauren," Tim says.

"Already?" I ask, closing the trunk of the MG.

"Yeah." He offers me a cigarette. "Already."

"I don't know," I say.

"What happened? Is she okay?" He laughs, "Do you care?"

I shrug. I try to light the cigarette and to my amazement the match doesn't go out in the wind and light snow. "I liked her a lot."

Tim's silent but then asks, "Then why didn't you pay for it?"

He's not looking at me. I crack up.

"I didn't like her that much," I say as I get into the car.

VICTOR   I was up all night doing coke with some girl I met at The Pub who worked for my father one summer. The next morning we go to some cafe in town (which has terrible food; soggy quiche, canned snails, tame bloody Marys) and I'm strung out and completely not hungry. I look so pasty I keep my shades on. We stand in the doorway of the place and wait for a table, the service is really terrible, and whoever designed this place must have been lobotomized. This girl wanders around and puts a quarter in the jukebox. The waitress keeps checking me out. She looks familiar. The Talking Heads sing "And She Was" then good old Frank starts singing "Young at Heart" and I'm amused at the disparity of her choices. Suddenly this girl I sort of saw a little bit last summer walks up to me crying softly—the last thing I need. She looks at me and says, "You don't know what a drag it is to see you." Then she throws herself on me, hugging tightly. I just say, "Hey, wait a minute." It was just some rich girl from Park and 80th who I kind of screwed around with last term who's kind of pretty, who's good in bed, who has a nice body. She automatically says goodbye to the guy she's with but he's already talking to the familiar-looking waitress. The girl who worked for my father and who has all the coke is already talking to some townie by the jukebox, and I could of used another gram but this girl, Laura, has already taken my arm and is leading me out The Brasserie's door. But it's probably best like this. I need a place to stay anyway and it's going to be a long, cold Christmas.

LAUREN Walking back to my room. The last day. People packing. Collecting addresses. Drinking farewell kegs. Drifting drunk through the snow-covered campus. I bump into Paul as he comes out of Canfield.

"Hi," I say, startled, embarrassed. "How are you, Mr. Denton?"

"Lauren," he says, still shy. "How've you been, Ms. Hynde?"

"Okay," I say.

We stand there awkwardly.

"So . . . What are you now?" I ask. "Still . . . Drama major?"

He groans. "Yeah. Guess so. What are you? Art still?"

"Art. Well, Poetry. Well, actually Art." Stutter.

"What is it?" he laughs. "Make up your mind."

"Interdivisional." I make it easy.

Long pause and I remember with true clarity how dumb Paul looked as a Freshman: a PiL T-shirt beneath a Giorgio Armani sweater. But I also loved him anyway, later on. The night we met? Cannot remember anything except Joan Armatrading playing on the box in his room; two of us smoking cigarettes, talking, nothing exciting, nothing important, but memorable flashes. He breaks the trance: "So, what are you doing?"

I think about what Victor told me after he found me at The Brasserie, before he went to rent a car in town. "Europe, I think. I don't know. Probably Europe." I would not mind ending the conversation now, since it's been good just to be close to Paul and to hear him talk—but that would be rude, and too pithy.

"Europe's a big place," he says; such a Denton thing to say.

"Yep, it shore is."

We stand there a little while longer. It's still snowing. The streetlights suddenly go on even though it's only a little after three. We both laugh at this. For some reason I think of that night in the cafe when he was looking over at me; how his face had clouded over; was he still in love with me? Was he jealous of other people I was with? I feel I have to glue things. I say, "He really likes you."

He looks confused, and then embarrassed, understanding. "Yeah? Great. That's great."

"No," I say. "I mean it."

Pause, then he asks, "Who?"

"You *know*," I laugh.

"Oh . . ." He pretends to understand. "He's got a nice smile," he finally admits.

"Oh yeah. He does," I agree.

This is ludicrous, but I'm in a better mood, and in half an hour Victor will be back and the two of us will be off. I will not tell him about the abortion. There is no need.

"He talks about you a lot," I tell him.

"Well, that's . . ." He's flustered and doesn't know what to say. "That's nice. I don't know. Are you two still—"

"Oh no." I shake my head. "Definitely not."

"I see."

More pausing.

"Well, it's good to see you again," I say.

"I know. It's too bad we didn't get to talk after, whenever," he says, blushes.

"Oh, I know," I say. He means September; drunken sad night in his room. "That was crazy," I say shaking my head. "Yes. Crazy," I say again.

There are people playing Frisbee in the snow. I concentrate on that.

"Listen," he starts. "Did you put notes in his box?" he asks.

"Whose box?" I don't know what he's talking about.

"I thought you were putting notes in his box," he says.

"I didn't put notes in anyone's box," I tell him. "Notes?"

"I took some notes out of his box that I thought were yours," he says, looking pained.

I study his face. "No. It wasn't me. Wrong person."

"Don't tell him," he says. "Oh, tell him. Whatever."

"It wouldn't matter anyway," I say.

"You're right," he quickly agrees without thinking.

"It doesn't matter to people like him," I say, or to people like us, but that's only a momentary thought and it leaves quickly.

"You're right," he says again.

"Do you want to come up?" I ask him. "I'm not really doing anything."

"No," he says. "I've got to get packing."

"Listen, do you have my address?" I ask him.

We exchange addresses, snow running the ink on the back of the magazine he's holding. The pages in my address book get wet. We stare at each other once more before parting, why? Deciding if maybe something was lost? Not quite sure? We promise to keep in touch anyway and call over vacation. We kiss politely and then he goes his way and I go mine, back to my room which is packed and clean and ready and I wait there feeling not that much different than I did in September, or October, or for that matter, November, for Victor with some certainty.

PAUL I started walking but was then running when I caught sight of the motorcycle at the Guard House. I was walking quickly at first, then jogging, then I broke into a full-fledged run, but Sean, who had a helmet on, started driving faster, skidding at first on the wet snowy lane, then regaining speed. I don't know *why* I was running after that motorcycle but I was. I was running fast too, skipping over piles of snow, moving faster than I can ever remember moving. And it wasn't because of Sean. It was too late for that. There had already been a Richard and a Gerald and too many carnal thoughts about others. But I was running and I was running because it felt like the "right" thing to do. It was a chance to show some emotion. I wasn't acting on passion. I was simply acting. Because it seemed the only thing to do. It seemed like something I had been told to do. By who, or by what, was vague. The bike sped up and disappeared around a curve and I never caught up with it.

I stopped and stood there on College Drive panting, bent over. A car pulled up. It was some guy who lived across the hall from me; Sven or Sylvester—something like that. He asked if I needed a ride. I could hear the song playing on the radio, an old childhood tune: "Thank You for Being a Friend." I stopped panting and I started nodding, laughing my head off, feeling unchanged.

"Come on. Get in," he said, reaching over and opening the door.

Still laughing I stumbled into the car thinking oh what the hell. Rock'n'roll, right? Deal with it. Sven's pretty cute, and who knows, maybe he could give me a ride to Chicago. And then, what was it Raymond told you about German guys?

SEAN I started driving faster as I left the college behind. I didn't know where I was going. Someplace unoccupied I hoped. Home was gone. New York sucked. I looked at my watch. It was noon. It seemed weird. But it was a relief driving around without excess baggage and the D.J. was playing great songs: Clapton, Petty and the Heartbreakers, Left Banke singing, ". . . *just walk away Renee*. . . ."

"I loved you," I said to her the last time we were together. I didn't know it was going to be the last time. The two of us were downstairs, back at the party, and I looked at her face, her hair was combed back, her face still slightly flushed from the sex. There are things about her I will never forget. . . .

I stopped at a phone booth near a liquor store. I pulled out a dime and a couple of phone numbers I had collected during the term from my wallet. I left the car running and got out. The sky was darkening even though it was still early afternoon; clouds were purple and black, undecided if they should snow or not. I wondered where to go. I decided against making any phone calls. I got back in my car. I haven't changed.

I saw a townie girl hitchhiking on the edge of town. She looked at me as I passed by. I made it to the end of town, then turned around in the parking lot of the A&P and picked her up. She was a little fat, but still blond and pretty. She was leaning against a lightpost, smoking a cigarette, a backpack at her feet. She lowered her arm as I pulled the car over. She smiled, then got in. I asked her where she was going. She mentioned some town but seemed unsure. She started telling me her life story, which wasn't very interesting, and when Rockpile came on singing "Heart" I had to turn it up, drowning out her voice, but still I turned to her, my eyes interested, a serious smile, nodding, my hand squeezing her knee, and she

Bret Easton Ellis
Less Than Zero £4.99

Less Than Zero is an astonishing first novel by a twenty-year-old writer. Set in affluent Los Angeles, it is a raw and powerful portrayal of a generation of young people who have experienced sex, drugs and disaffection at too early an age. Its narrator, Clay, comes home to Los Angeles for Christmas vacation. His holiday turns into a dizzying spiral of desperation that takes him through the rich suburban homes, the relentless parties, the seedy bars and the glitzy rock clubs. A shocking coming-of-age novel about the casual nihilism that comes with youth and money, *Less Than Zero* marks the stunning debut of the first voice of a new generation.

'*Less Than Zero* takes its title from an old Elvis Costello song. It is a novel of fast flashes, scenes that shift and drift like Southern California freeway traffic, like frames from MTV. It is bleak, morally barren, ethically bereft and tinged with implicit violence' LA TIMES

'Bret Ellis is undoubtedly the new master of youthful American alienation. With his spare, seamless writing, Ellis tells us a tale of collegiate Christmas in LA that makes Jack Kerouac and his Beat Generation seem like pussies. A harrowing yet poignant indictment of our times that is like a long day's journey into the LA night'
EMILY PRAGER, author of *A Visit From the Footbinder*

'Filled with a languid comic terror, *Less Than Zero* is a startling debut for Bret Ellis, a no wave West Coast La Dolce Vita'
RICHARD PRICE, author of *The Wanderers* and *The Breaks*

'This is the novel your mother warned you about. Jim Morrison would be proud'
EVE BABITZ, author of *Slow Days, Fast Company* and *LA Woman*

'An extraordinary accomplished first novel' THE NEW YORKER

FIRST BRITISH PUBLICATION

Tama Janowitz
Slaves of New York £4.99

'If there were a literary equivalent to a new *Talking Heads* album, *Slaves of New York* would be that book' MADEMOISELLE

'Tama Janowitz is a clever writer. She draws trendy New York propartsies to a T. These New Yorkers are slaves to high rents, migratory relationships and, most significantly, their own contagious modishness ... Janowitz's imagination is vivid and she can invent truly memorable situations and details ... (She) can be laugh-out loud funny and wonderfully sharp ... A talented writer' WASHINGTON POST

'So savagely witty, so acerbic, so piercingly accurate ... Tama Janowitz has a merciless eye for absurdity which she trains primarily on Greenwich Village "artistes". She traps them in self-conscious posturing and serves them up as metaphors for her sardonic and quirky view of *au courant* urban life' LOS ANGELES HERALD EXAMINER

'Janowitz is a fearless writer. Her details are quirky, her language is lean, and her sentences sprint along with deceptive ease. The protagonists in her stories share with her a shyness and a sense of always being out of place. Although they try in earnest to fit in, they put on the wrong clothes or say the wrong thing or fail to grasp the subtle messages other people send their way ... With the publication of *Slaves of New York*, Tama Janowitz could become the most talked-about writer of the year' NEW YORK

'With the younger generation of writers already buried under a mound of volcanic hype, it is remarkable that Janowitz, unsmothered by the critical acclaim for her novel *American Dad*, can writer with such freshness' ELLE

'The shrewd observation, the skewed invention ... the gifts of a singular talent'
JAY MCINERNEY, author of *Bright Lights, Big City*, in the
NEW YORK TIMES

FIRST BRITISH PUBLICATION

Kathy Acker
Blood and Guts in High School Plus Two £5.99

A startling introduction to the writing of the *enfant terrible* of the US literary underground. Compared to the writings of Genet and Burroughs, these three fictions combine detailed eroticism with politics and what Acker calls 'pop content'. Her narrative is a montage of conversation, description, conjecture, moments snatched from history and from literature. Her eerie exposition of anti-social values, her attack on religion, education and government, charts the emergence of the new culture. Acker's first person narratives make use of famous characters from life, history and fiction – Pasolini in *My Death, My Life* and Dickens' Pip in *Great Expectations*.

'Sexy and intriguing . . . her experiments produce an authentic voice which is a rare commodity in modern fiction' VILLAGE VOICE

Ian McEwan
The Comfort of Strangers £4.99

'McEwan, that master of the taciturn macabre, so organizes his narrative that, without insisting anything, every turn and glimpse is another tightening of the noose. The evils of power and the power of evil are transmitted with a steely coolness, and in a prose that has a feline grace' ANTHONY THWAITE, OBSERVER

'As always, McEwan manages his idiom with remarkable grace and inventiveness; his characters are at home in their dreams and so is he' FRANK KERMODE, GUARDIAN

All Pan Books are available at your local bookshop or newsagent, or can be ordered direct from the publisher. Indicate the number of copies required and fill in the form below.

Send to: Pan C. S. Dept
              Macmillan Distribution Ltd
              Houndmills Basingstoke RG21 2XS
or phone: 0256 29242, quoting title, author and Credit Card number.

Please enclose a remittance* to the value of the cover price plus £1.00 for the first book plus 50p per copy for each additional book ordered.

* Payment may be made in sterling by UK personal cheque, postal order, sterling draft or international money order, made payable to Pan Books Ltd.

Alternatively by Barclaycard/Access/Amex/Diners

Card No.

Expiry Date

_____
              Signature

Applicable only in the UK and BFPO addresses.

While every effort is made to keep prices low, it is sometimes necessary to increase prices at short notice. Pan Books reserve the right to show on covers and charge new retail prices which may differ from those advertised in the text or elsewhere.

NAME AND ADDRESS IN BLOCK LETTERS PLEASE

....

Name _____

Address_____

_____

_____

_____

3/87